NEVER MINE TO HOLD

JENNIFER SUCEVIC

CHAPTER 1

FALLYN

"I'm sorry?" My knees buckle as I slump to the queen-sized mattress with a soft bounce. "What do you mean the tuition bill hasn't been paid this semester? There has to be a mistake."

Other than the sharp clicking of a computer keyboard, silence fills the line. Each second that ticks by only ratchets up my nerves and the unsteady thumping of my heart until it sounds more like the dull roar of the ocean in my ears.

"I'm afraid there's not." Her voice softens but remains firm. "I've checked your account several times. The entire balance for the second semester is outstanding. It was supposed to be paid by the first of the month, which means it's ten days overdue."

A thick lump settles in my throat as I stare sightlessly at the silver-framed photo of my brother and me propped on my desk. Our arms are wrapped around each other, and we're both grinning at the camera without a care in the world.

A decade later, life couldn't feel more different.

I'd give just about anything to go back to that idyllic moment. If I squeeze my eyes tight, I can still hear the sound of the lake in the distance and feel the bright sunlight shining down, warming my face.

"Ms. DiMarco?" There's a pause. "Are you still there?"

The memories dissolve like wisps of smoke as I blink back to the present. "Yeah, I'm here."

Unfortunately.

"I'm going to make an appointment for you. Tomorrow at one o'clock, all right? Hopefully you and your advisor will be able to figure out a solution."

My shoulders collapse as if there's a thousand-pound weight resting on them. "As soon as I get off the phone, I'll call my parents. I'm sure it was just an oversight on their part." My palm settles on my lower abdomen as if that will settle the nausea that has taken up residence.

"Perhaps." Skepticism creeps into her tone.

As soon as I disconnect the call, I hit Mom's icon on the screen.

She picks up on the third ring. Already her voice is tinged with concern. "Hi, sweetie. We haven't heard from you in a few days. Is everything good?"

I'm way too distraught to bother with pleasantries. "I don't know. The school just called, and my tuition still hasn't been paid."

The statement is met with a deafening silence that only reconfirms this was in no way an oversight before she murmurs, "I should get your father."

The faint prickling at the bottom of my belly turns into full-fledged pterodactyls attempting to wing their way to life. I don't realize that the hand not holding my cell in a death grip has drifted to the middle of my chest to rub my scar.

There's a brief shuffling of the phone before Dad clears his throat. I can already tell that whatever he has to say won't be good. "Hey, Fallyn."

Exhaustion fills his voice. And maybe something else.

Resignation.

Defeat.

Things I never expected to hear from him.

"Hi, Dad. Why wasn't my tuition bill paid this semester?"

A heavy silence follows.

"We've been dealing with some financial issues. I was hoping they could be resolved, but in light of current events, that now seems unlikely."

My face scrunches as I pop to my feet and pace the length of my room. "What kind of issues?"

"That dirty bastard Westerville staged a coup and forced me out of the company," he bites out. Once his anger has been unleashed, there's no putting it neatly back inside a box.

I stutter to a stop as my eyes widen. My heart stalls before slamming into overdrive beneath my breast. "A coup? When?"

"A few days before Christmas," he says with a grunt.

What?

My tongue darts out to moisten parched lips as I swing around and stalk the length of my room. Even though I try to keep my voice level, it continues to escalate. "But that was weeks ago. I was home during the entire break, and you never said a word."

In hindsight, I realize that he was absent most of the time, locked away in his home office. When he wasn't there, he was preoccupied and grumpy. I didn't think much about it because the holidays are always difficult.

Why would this one be any different?

"I spoke with my lawyer, hoping to overturn the decision or force him out on his ass instead, but there's nothing I can do. The sneaky bastard went behind my back and turned everyone against me." His voice rises with each word he spits out until I have to hold the phone away from my ear. "After everything that family has taken from us, he does something like this!"

Now doesn't seem like the appropriate time to mention that he attempted to do the very same thing a few years ago. Their once-close relationship became tenuous after the accident and then downright hostile when Dad tried to force him out.

It was only a matter of time before everything exploded. This development shouldn't come as a surprise.

Guess I was hoping not to be collateral damage in the inevitable fallout.

"I'm sorry, Fallyn." His voice empties of anger, turning weary.

"There's not enough money in the account to pay your tuition this semester. Your mother and I were just discussing the situation, and we've come up with a solution."

Air gets clogged in my lungs.

I'm almost afraid to hear what it is.

"You'll take this semester off, move back home, and get a job. I'm sure one of my acquaintances from the country club will hire you as an assistant. Between that and financial aid, you could start back in the fall." His voice fills with false buoyancy. "Or maybe you could transfer to the local college here and take a class or two this semester. We could probably scrape enough together for that. You could stay at the house. That would be quite a money saver."

Even though he can't see it, I shake my head.

No way.

There's no way I can move back home.

Getting out the first time was difficult enough. It took a lot of coaxing, not to mention a few tantrums that I'm not proud of, for them to relent enough for me to go away to college.

This specific college.

There's no way I can backpedal now.

When I remain silent, he says with forced jovialness, "Wouldn't that be fun? Your mother misses you terribly."

A shiver of dread scampers down my spine before pooling in my belly. It's quickly chased by guilt. I love my parents, but after the accident, their attention was unbearable.

Suffocating.

Smothering.

They were so afraid that something would happen to me.

Just like—

"Fallyn?"

I shove those thoughts away and focus on the conversation at hand. It takes effort to keep my voice level so that he doesn't realize how much I'm freaking out. "I have an appointment to speak with someone in student services tomorrow afternoon. Maybe there's something they can do to help. I'm midway through my junior year. The last thing I want to do is drop out or transfer."

That thought is like a sucker punch to the gut.

"I never said drop out," he cuts in hastily. "At the most, it would be a short break to regroup. That's all."

Right. How many people say exactly that and then never end up going back to school? Life gets in the way, making it impossible. I refuse to become a statistic. No matter what I have to do, I'll find a way to stay at Western.

"I guess we'll talk after your appointment tomorrow and go from there."

As soon as we hang up, I toss the phone on my bed. There's a brief knock on the door before my cousin bursts in.

"Any interest in ordering pizza for dinner?" Viola asks. "I could really go for a pepperoni and extra cheese. Maybe mushrooms."

I shake my head.

My stomach is a tangle of painful knots from the convo with my parents. There's no way I'll be able to keep down a single bite. Even the thought makes me nauseous.

It feels like a trapdoor just opened, and I'm now in freefall.

One look at my face has her brows snapping together in concern. "Hey, is everything all right? You look like you're about to be sick."

I force out a long, steady breath and relay the phone call.

Her mouth forms a shocked little O before she pads closer and drops down beside me. "What are you going to do?"

I jerk my shoulders as my throat closes up. It's like I'm being suffocated from the inside out. "Talk with student services and hope that it's not too late to apply for financial aid." If I'm lucky, they'll give me enough money to cover the entire semester.

Along with rent.

I really *am* going to be sick.

"Have you thought about getting a job? Madden mentioned that Sully was looking for a waitress at Slap Shotz. Apparently, the other girl quit during the middle of a shift last week, and now they're short staffed."

I stare for a second or two before laughter bubbles up from my lips, and my eyes widen as I press a hand to my chest. "Wait a minute…are you saying that *I* should apply for a job there?" There's a pause before I add, "Where all the hockey players hang out? You do realize that I've spent the past couple of years avoiding them, right?"

"Actually, you've spent the past couple of years avoiding one in particular. If not there, then maybe a restaurant or store close to campus."

I force a smile, appreciative that she's trying to generate a list of possibilities. "You're right, a job is definitely a good idea. I'll scour the employment board tonight."

Will I be applying to Slap Shotz?

Hell no.

There has to be somewhere else I can work.

"What about selling some of your stuff? Any high-end labels sitting in your closet or purses you don't want anymore?"

For the second time in the span of twenty minutes, my hand rises to the scar that bisects my chest. "I do have a few bags I don't use, but it's doubtful that would be enough to take care of the entire tuition bill."

She chews her lower lip before murmuring, "I hate to even bring this up…"

Even though her voice trails off, I know exactly what she's going to suggest.

I shake my head. "Forget it."

"Okay," she says lightly, dropping the topic. "It was just an idea."

No matter how desperate I am, Miles' Porsche is one thing I refuse to part with.

There has to be something else I can do.

I just have to figure out what.

CHAPTER 2

WOLF

"Dude, practice this morning sucked major ass," Bridger says with a grunt as we head across campus to the Union for lunch.

"Tell me when a six o'clock practice *doesn't* suck?" Colby shoots back.

I glance at Bridger before jerking my head toward the blond left wing. "He's got you there. Never met an early morning practice that didn't."

Bridger rolls his blue eyes and grumbles under his breath. He's been in a shit mood for the last month or so. Unsavory texts regarding his social life continue to pop up on the university's message system that gets pushed out to both staff and students.

He's been working with a few tech-savvy friends to figure out who's behind it, but so far, they've remained irritatingly anonymous. We'd actually thought maybe the entire thing was over and done with since they were usually sent out every Monday.

Until this morning.

It was a photo taken at a party. His arms had been wrapped around two drunk sorority girls as he grinned at the camera. One of the girls had her hand resting on his junk.

This is a public service announcement to all the women at Western—stay as far as you can get from this manwhore. He's toxic to the female species.

A skull and crossbones emoji had accompanied it.

Most people wouldn't realize that the pic was taken at a party last year and wasn't even recent.

It took less than ten minutes for his father to call and rip him a new one.

Bridger is a good dude, and I feel bad for him.

A lot of our teammates like to take advantage of the puck bunny situation on campus.

He's never been one of those guys.

A few groupies wave and beeline in Colby's direction. Wide grins wreathe their faces as they throw themselves at him.

I almost roll my eyes.

Now this guy, on the other hand, is a major player. Totally shameless where the chicks are concerned. Hell will likely freeze over before he settles down with just one girl.

Although, the way I hear it, his father, Gray McNichols, was the same way before falling for his mother. And the rest, shall we say, is NHL history. Now the guy is a bigshot sportscaster on ESPN. Colby likes to keep that on the downlow.

Well…as much as he can.

It's not like it's some big secret. But he's not one to play up the relationship. Like Maverick, he wants his talent to speak for itself. Other than the blond hair, he's the spitting image of his father.

"Hi, Wolf."

I'm knocked from those thoughts by a soft feminine voice, only to find Larsa Middleton has sidled up to me while I wasn't paying attention.

I give her a chin lift in greeting. "Hey. How's it going?"

"Good. I was just about to grab lunch. What about you?"

"Umm, yeah…" My voice trails off as my attention gets snagged by a girl with long, inky black hair hurrying along a path that snakes in the opposite direction.

Her head is tipped downward as she taps away at her phone. A thick curtain of shiny tresses obscures her face from view. Although, that doesn't matter. I know exactly who it is. Electricity crackles through my veins as my footsteps stall, and I soak in the sight of her. Even though we attend the same school, it's not often our paths cross.

My hungry gaze slides over her, committing every detail to memory.

She's no more than twenty feet away.

Shockingly close for her not to notice.

My heart picks up speed, thrumming a painful beat against my ribcage.

I've spent all these years keeping a firm distance because that's what she wanted.

This is the closest we've been since…

I squash all thoughts of our past.

If she weren't so absorbed in her phone, she'd catch me staring, and then all hell would break loose.

"Wolf?"

When Larsa's slim hand settles on my forearm, I shake it away. It's not a conscious decision on my part.

More of a habit.

"So, about lunch—"

When Fallyn hustles up the wide stone stairs of Vanderberg Hall and slips inside the glass doors, I make a split-second decision.

"Maybe another time? I need to stop at the registrar's office."

Disappointment flashes across her pretty face. "Yeah, sure."

Before she can nail down a different date, I take off.

"Hey, where are you going?" Colby calls out. "I thought we were grabbing something to eat?"

I raise my hand. "I'll catch you later. There's something I need to take care of."

And then I'm slipping through the doors and into the building. A few groups of students loiter in the hallway. I glance up and down the corridor, wondering if I'm too late.

That's all it takes for me to hesitate and wonder what the fuck I'm doing. It's not like I'm actually going to strike up a convo with this girl. As close as we once were, that's not something that will ever happen.

Not after all this time.

Fuck.

We're coming up on five years.

That thought is like a punch to the gut that nearly robs the air from my lungs.

There's never been a single day that's gone by that I don't think about him.

Or her.

Just as I drag a hand through my short strands, people shift, and I catch a glimpse of her dark head turning the corner at the far end of the hall. Without thinking, I'm on the move again. It's as if there's an invisible string binding us together. Whether she's aware of it or not, we're still connected. There will never be a day when that's not true.

I glance at the sign on the wall that points in the same direction.

Student services.

When there was a problem with my tuition bill last year, this is where I met with an advisor to straighten it out.

As I come to another corner, I pause, peeking cautiously around it. Fallyn is standing outside the office as she glances down at her phone. A few people loiter in the vicinity as well.

From here, I watch as she straightens her shoulders before sucking in a deep breath and walking into the office. A look of determination settles over her features. Even though we're no longer in each other's lives, I know her well enough to recognize that she's gearing up for a fight.

My brows draw together.

What could be the issue?

Her parents are loaded.

I give it a minute or two before skulking closer.

I almost snort at the mental image that conjures. I've never been the skulking sort. In fact, most people take one look at me and steer clear.

Which is exactly the way I prefer it.

A couple of guys exit the office before heading in my direction. They glance at me as we pass by one another, their eyes widening before lighting up with recognition.

"Hey, Westerville!" the closest one says before holding out his knuckles for a fist bump.

I shoot a quick glance past him to make sure Fallyn hasn't stepped back out into the corridor. That's the last thing I need when trying to fly under the radar.

"Dude, that game last week was sweet. You were totally on fire!"

"Thanks."

The other guy shakes his head. "How many saves did you have? Wasn't it a career record or something like that?"

"Twenty-five." Not the most I've had, but still impressive.

"Fuck, dude. That's amazing."

"Thanks." My gaze bounces to the office door again. "I gotta get going, but it was good talking to you."

"See ya around, Wolf!"

With a wave, I take off. It's only when I'm close enough to peek inside that I stop and scan the reception area. It doesn't take long to find her. She's in line at the counter, waiting her turn. She stares at her phone, all the while shifting from one foot to another.

Fallyn never did have a lot of patience.

The corner of one lip hitches as a million memories flood my brain. I can't help but drink in the sight of her.

Her beauty is like a gut punch.

Then again, there's nothing new about that.

Even though the smart thing to do would be to get on with my day and pretend I never saw her, there's no way I'm taking off until I figure out what's going on.

CHAPTER 3

FALLYN

Angel

$\mathcal{I}$ glance up from my phone when the girl in front of me snaps, "What am I supposed to do? Sell my virginity to pay my tuition this semester?"

My eyes widen as my mouth tumbles open at her audacity.

The woman sitting behind the counter wears a matching expression.

We're both shocked by the outburst.

I peek at the girl again, taking a better look. Since I've stepped foot inside the student aid office, I've been glued to my phone, scrolling through job postings.

Big surprise—there aren't many. Most students who wanted part-time work filled out apps in August and early September. They didn't wait around until January.

So, it's slim pickings.

Which only adds to my frustration.

At the moment, nothing seems to be going my way.

In fact, it's all gone straight down the tubes.

"I'm pretty sure that ship sailed back in high school," the blonde standing next to her mutters. "Sophomore year, if I'm not mistaken."

The auburn-haired girl in the midst of a meltdown scowls. "You're not helping matters."

Her friend doesn't seem bothered by the snappish tone and shrugs before inspecting her manicure. "Sorry."

The woman seated behind the desk commandeers the convo again. "Look, miss…there's nothing we can do. I would suggest taking out private loans from a bank and getting back to us."

"That's not possible," she grumbles before spinning on her heel and stalking past me. "Thanks for nothing. You've totally earned your paycheck today."

That's when I'm slammed with the realization that I know her.

Chloe something or other.

We lived on the same dorm floor freshman year.

As the two girls swing into the hallway, I make an impulsive decision to follow them. It's altogether possible that she was joking around…

But what if she wasn't?

"Hey, Chloe?"

They stop and turn. Chloe shoots daggers at me before recognition sets in, and her face softens.

Marginally.

"Oh hey, Fallyn." She jerks her chin toward the student aid office. "I suppose you heard all that?"

"Yeah. You got a little heated in there."

With a snort, she rolls her eyes. "That woman couldn't have been more unhelpful if she tried."

I nod as a rush of sympathy fills me. "It seems like we're both in the same boat. My, ah, money fell through for this semester, so I'm scrambling to figure out an alternative solution."

"Same," she says with a sigh. "Sometimes being a broke-ass college student really sucks."

My gaze darts away as I clear my throat. "What you said back there…were you being serious?"

When she stares blankly, I mumble, "About selling your virginity."

Heat floods my face as two sets of eyes sharpen on me. "I guess what I'm asking is if that's really a thing."

Silence falls over the three of us as Chloe takes a step closer. "Yeah, it's definitely a thing. People do it all the time. From what I hear, it's good money."

"Exactly how good?" The question shoots out of my mouth before I can stop it.

Chloe's brows rise across her forehead. "Good enough that I wish I hadn't given mine away for free in my parents' basement sophomore year of high school. Talk about a complete waste. To make matters worse, it was over before I could blink."

I drop my voice. "Enough to pay for tuition and still have some left over?"

"Yeah. There are men who will pay stupid money to fuck a virgin." She shrugs. "It's so archaic." Before I can ask anything further, she fires off a question of her own. "Are you even a virgin? Because they can tell, you know? Some guys even require a medical examination as proof before any money exchanges hands."

Every drop of saliva in my mouth dries at that terrifying thought. "I am."

"Hmmm." It's slowly that she looks me up and down with narrowed eyes. "Well color me surprised."

My face feels as if it's been set on fire as I force myself to ask, "Where would I even find a place to handle that kind of *transaction*?"

It's almost impossible to believe that I'm considering this as a way to pay for school. A month ago, I couldn't have fathomed it.

What am I saying?

A week ago.

Days ago.

And yet, here I am. It just proves how drastically everything can change.

Shift right under your feet like an earthquake, transforming the landscape until it's unrecognizable.

Chloe and her friend, a tall blonde who looks like a model, exchange a long, silent look chock-full of meaning before she finally says, "I know someone who can help." Her voice sharpens. "But you have to be serious about this. I don't want to waste my friend's time."

I force out the truth in a small voice. "I don't have any other options."

"Okay then." She slips her cell from the pocket of her houndstooth jacket. "Give me your number."

I rattle off the digits.

"Got it. Just sent you a text. When I have more information, I'll let you know."

I release a steady breath back into the atmosphere. Only now do I realize that my heart feels like it's on the verge of exploding in my chest. My head spins as I swing around and walk back inside the student aid office.

With any luck, they'll be able to work some financial aid and scholarship magic, and I can text Chloe that her help won't be needed after all.

CHAPTER 4

WOLF

The low hum of female conversation dies away from around the corner as the click of heels grows closer. Just as the girls come into view, I straighten to my full height and lean against the wall with my arms folded across my chest.

Recognition is instantaneous as Chloe and Janine flash toothy smiles my way. Chloe and I had a class together my sophomore year. If I had a dime for every time she offered to suck my dick, I'd be a rich man.

Well, a richer man.

My family has plenty of money.

It's what one would call generational wealth.

"Mmm, Wolf. What a pleasant surprise," she purrs, eyes drifting over me from head to toe. "I wasn't expecting to see you here. Slumming it in financial aid for shits and giggles?"

I smirk. "Exactly."

She closes the distance between us before one palm settles on my chest.

Her warm breath feathers against my lips as she tips her face upward. "It's your lucky day. I have a few hours to kill between classes. Any interest in heading back to my place?" When I remain silent, she tosses a sly look at her friend. "I'm sure Janine wouldn't mind joining us."

As if on cue, the blonde licks her full lips.

My fingers wrap around her slender wrist, removing it from my sweatshirt and holding it between us. "Actually, what I'm interested in is the convo I just overheard."

Her brows slant together in confusion. "What about it?"

"Let's just say I'm an interested buyer."

She blinks before narrowing her eyes. "Really? I wouldn't have pegged you for the I'm-the-only-dick-who's-been-here chest-pounding BS."

I shrug, refusing to explain myself. It's none of Chloe's damn business as to why I'm interested in Fallyn.

The auburn-haired girl sighs before fluttering her thick, mascara-laden lashes. "That must be the reason why you've never taken me up on my offer."

Sure, we'll go with that.

"Just set it up." There's a beat of silence before I add, "And don't you fucking dare shop her around. Her virginity belongs to me. Are we clear?"

"Crystal." There's a pause before she adds in a more business-like tone, "You do realize that I'll be taking a small finder's fee, right?"

I wouldn't expect anything less. "You'd make an excellent pimp."

Not offended in the slightest, she smirks. "A girl has to bring home the Benjamins, doesn't she? And the title I prefer is *madam*, thank you very much."

My grip loosens from around her wrist as I take a quick step in retreat. "Do you still have my number?"

She taps her cell. "Yup. I'll give you a call once I hammer out the finer details."

My chest expands.

Only now am I finally able to breathe again.

Just as I'm about to swing away, I stop and meet Chloe's eyes. "It's important that she not find out who bought her."

There's no way she'll agree to this arrangement if she realizes that

I'm the man behind the money. It doesn't matter how desperate she is because desperation is the only thing that could propel Fallyn to do something like this.

Years ago, I was her everything. I would have been the first person she turned to for help. But those days are long gone. I fucking hate that so much stands between us.

If this is the only way for me to get close to her, I'll take it. Even if it means deceiving her to do it.

"She'll have to wear a blindfold."

"Ohhh…you're so damn kinky," she says with a burst of laughter and a shake of her head. "I love it! Are you sure that you don't want to come back to our place? I can wear a blindfold and pretend to be a blushing virgin. I'll scream and cry all you want."

"Were you ever a blushing virgin?" her friend asks with a chuckle.

"Probably not," she shoots back before her gaze sharpens on me. "But for you, I'll be whatever you want."

I spread my hands and take another step in retreat, more than ready to end this convo. "Sorry, I gotta get to practice."

With that, I take off. I need to put as much distance between myself and Fallyn before she leaves student services and finds me talking to Chloe.

CHAPTER 5

FALLYN

"Has there been any movement on the job front?" Vi asks as we hike across campus for our morning classes with our friend, Britt.

She's someone we've gotten to know during the fall semester. Even though she's older, she's a freshman and just started college. She's spent the past couple of years working instead of attending school.

I don't know much about her past, but from what she's mentioned, it seems like the two of us have our fair share of family issues and baggage. It's probably why we're both psychology majors. We're trying to figure out our own shit.

It's nice to have a friend who understands what that's like and can sympathize.

"No," I mutter. I spent last evening looking at any and every position I could find.

"Well, there's always—"

"Please don't say it. Not this early in the morning when I haven't sucked down at least one cup of coffee." I spent most of the night tossing and turning, unsure what to do. I probably drafted half a dozen texts to Chloe, telling her that I was no longer interested in selling myself to the highest bidder before deleting every single one.

That thought is enough to make me wince.

But what other choice do I have?

I'm stuck.

Before Viola can give me any words of encouragement, muscular arms wrap around her from behind and hoist her off the snow-covered ground. A yelp of surprise escapes from her before Madden smacks a kiss against the side of her face before returning her feet to the frozen earth. He throws a muscular arm around her shoulders and hauls her close.

Vi and Madden were together in high school and then broke up when he went away to college. The pressure of balancing academics and hockey got the best of him, and he crumbled. Even though he tried to reach out and get back together, they spent three years apart. After Madden realized that my cousin had transferred to Western in the fall, he forced her into spending twenty-four hours together. If she still wanted nothing to do with him after that, he'd walk away and leave her in peace.

Whatever happened in the course of that day worked because now they're an item. Even though it's only been a month or so, it's as if they were never apart.

He gives Britt and me a chin lift in greeting. "What's up?"

"Not much," our new friend says.

I shrug.

There's no way in hell I'm going to tell him how my life is crumbling around my ears and the options that are now on the table. I haven't worked up the courage to tell Viola about my conversation outside student services with Chloe.

I can't imagine what her reaction would be.

That's all it takes for embarrassment to rush in and scald my cheeks as we continue walking. This is starting to feel like a nightmare I'm unable to wake from.

"Vi mentioned that you're job hunting. Do you want me to give Sully a call and set up an interview?"

"Sully, the owner of Slap Shotz?" Britt asks.

"Yeah. Do you know him?"

She flashes a smile. "Actually, he's my uncle."

"Oh, wow." Vi snuggles against her boyfriend. "I didn't know that."

"It's one of the reasons I decided to move here for school."

"That's cool," Madden says.

My shoulders wilt beneath my jacket because I don't have any other recourse at this point. If Madden can get me a job working at the bar where all the hockey players congregate, then I should bite the bullet and accept it.

"If you wouldn't mind, that would be great. I really appreciate it."

"I'll put in a good word, too," Britt adds.

I loop my arm through hers as we navigate our way through the crowd. She's turning out to be a really good friend.

Madden drops a kiss on the top of Vi's blonde head. "It's not a problem. Between the two of us, you should be a shoe-in."

I stare at my cousin and her boyfriend. Their affection is so open and easy. Natural. I can't help but envy that. My hand rises to rub the six-inch scar that bisects my chest.

Embarrassment over the jagged line has stopped me from being intimate with anyone in the past. Ever since the first time a guy felt me up during my sophomore year of college and then pulled away to ask about the puckered skin, I've shied away from those types of situations.

It's also the other reason I've considered nixing the idea of selling my virginity. The last thing I need is a stranger staring in disgust and asking a ton of invasive questions. Or worse, walking away. A shiver of dread slides through me as I break out into a cold sweat.

If I actually go through with this disastrous idea, I'm hoping I can leave my shirt on. Or maybe we can do it in the dark.

For all I know, there won't be any interested clients.

I almost stumble.

Is that what they're referred to as?

Clients?

My belly swoops before bottoming out.

I'm knocked from the dangerous whirl of my thoughts when Madden says, "I just want to make sure that you're cool with working at the bar." There's an awkward pause before he adds in a softer tone, "You know Wolf will be there, right?"

Since Madden and Viola were together in high school, he knows all about the accident. He and Wolf didn't know each other back then. I have no idea if they've discussed the situation now that Madden is dating my cousin.

I force a smile. "I appreciate your concern."

He pops a brow when I don't add anything more. "And you're still interested in the job?"

With no other prospects on the horizon?

"I don't really have a choice."

"Okay, I'll shoot him a text and get back to you. At the very least, you'll get an interview."

"We'll make sure of it," Britt tacks on.

"Thanks again. You guys are the best."

"No worries." Madden flashes a grin.

When my cell rings, I slip it from my coat pocket and take a peek. My heart drops to the bottom of my toes when Chloe's name flashes across the screen.

"Who's calling your ass this early in the morning?" Britt asks, craning her neck to get a better look like the nosy bitch she is.

I take a quick step away and point to the snow-covered grass on the side of the cement walkway. "Um, someone from student services. Are we still meeting up for lunch at one?"

"Yup," Viola says with a nod. "Good luck."

"Thanks." My heart jackhammers as I weave my way through the crowd of students hustling their way across campus and off to the side.

Just seeing Chloe's name makes my palms break out into a slick sweat.

There's no way I can go through with this.

I can't do it.

I can't sell my body.

I'll have to figure something else out. The last thing I want to do is drop out for the semester, but maybe my parents are right, and I'll need to return home and regroup.

It's a depressing thought.

On the fourth ring, I release a steady breath and answer the call. "Hello?"

"Hey, Fallyn. It's Chloe."

Only wanting to get this convo over with, I blurt, "I apologize for wasting your time, but I thought about everything last night, and I just can't go through with it."

There's a second or two of silence that has my nerves ratcheting up even further.

"Really? Are you sure?"

Relief spirals through me that she doesn't sound angry.

"Yeah. I don't want my personal info on a website."

"That's too bad. I was calling to let you know that we already have an interested buyer."

Buyer.

I cringe as the word ricochets around in my head.

There's actually a man who wants to buy my *virginity*?

That seems crazy.

My teeth scrape across my lower lip as I stare at the thinning crowd. "You mentioned that someone might want...*proof.*" Nausea stirs in my belly. "Is that a requirement?"

"Actually, he didn't mention it." There's a beat of silence. "That's good news for you."

"Yeah...good news." I'm slammed with another thought. "Is he...old?"

Why am I even asking?

It doesn't matter.

"Sorry," Chloe says primly. "I can't disclose any details regarding clients. The same way I wouldn't give out any pertinent info about you. The important thing is that he has funds and is willing to pay."

I tip my face upward toward the blue, cloudless sky and allow the bright rays of sunshine to beat down on me. With the chill in the air, it's invigorating.

Confusion rushes in.

Can I really treat this like a business transaction and sell my V-card to a complete stranger?

The flipside is that I need to pay for school by the end of the week. Wouldn't I rather do that than move back home?

Even if it's just for six months?

It's a shitty choice.

One I shouldn't be forced to make.

Anger rushes through me as my fingers tighten around the slim device.

As I glance around, watching people laugh and joke, oblivious to my inner turmoil, my attention gets snagged by a tall, muscular guy standing about thirty feet away. The moment our gazes fasten, electricity sizzles through my veins.

In the past, if our gazes happened to collide across a crowded room or on campus, I've always been quick to rip mine away and pretend it didn't occur. It's taken me a long time to blot him out of my life.

I'm unable to do that this time.

"Fallyn?" Chloe says, pulling my distracted attention back to the call. "Are you still there?"

"Yeah," I mutter, eyes narrowed. "Sorry."

Fury flares within me as we continue to lock eyes. He should have the common decency to look away and leave me in peace. I've always been careful to avoid the places he hangs out. Lately, it seems like we've been running into each other with more frequency.

I don't like it.

We're no longer friends and haven't been for a long time.

Not only did he steal the most important person from my life, but his family bankrupted mine, forcing my father to leave the company they started more than twenty years ago.

This is what Wolf Westerville has reduced me to—selling my fucking virginity to a stranger so I can continue my education. Rage like I've never felt engulfs my insides as I glare, willing him to do the right thing and back down.

"Let me think about it."

"Really?" Surprise colors her voice.

"Yeah."

"Okay. That's a start. We didn't get a chance to discuss the price. Do you have a number in mind?"

"Thirty thousand."

That clipped out response is met with deafening silence.

"Umm…that might be a bit too steep." An awkward chuckle follows that comment. "But, then again, I suppose that's what the art of negotiation is for, right?"

"I won't take anything less," I tell her flatly. "If this guy isn't willing to pay my price, then he doesn't want it badly enough."

With that kind of money, I wouldn't have to worry about this semester. Or the next one. And I'd still have enough to pay rent and tuck some away in a savings account in case there's an emergency.

I release the air trapped in my lungs as my brain continues to cartwheel.

I just have to make it through one night.

That's it.

Then I can finish school and get a job. No one ever has to know. As much as I hate the thought of being forced into selling my virginity, this decision makes the most sense. It'll do the impossible and buy me some peace of mind.

"All right. I'll reach back out and tell him that your price is nonnegotiable."

My tone softens when I realize that I'm taking out my anger on the wrong person. "Thanks, I really appreciate it."

"No problem. I'll be in touch soon."

When the line goes dead, I slip the small device back into my pocket. Fury crashes over me as Wolf continues to stare from across the distance that separates us, making no move to turn away.

Before I realize what I'm doing, my feet stomp across the snow-covered lawn. If he's at all surprised that I'm acknowledging his presence for the first time in almost five years, his expression remains impassive. There isn't a tightening of his jaw or a flash of emotion in his eyes. I have no idea what he's thinking.

As soon as I'm within striking distance, my hand whips out, cracking him across the face.

"That's for taking my brother away." When he doesn't give me the reaction I'm searching for, red-hot fury sweeps through me, and I strike him again.

Silence settles around us as his bottle green eyes cling to mine, and he lifts a hand to the bright red skin. He palms the flesh before murmuring, "It's good to see you too, Fallyn."

CHAPTER 6

WOLF

My fingers graze the spot where she slapped me.

Twice.

Even with the sting of my cheek, I can't stop my greedy gaze from sliding over her face, trying to take in all the changes five years have wrought. Sure, I've caught sight of her on campus and twice at Slap Shotz last semester. But with only a couple of feet to separate us, this is the closest we've been since the night of the accident.

It's so damn tempting to reach out and yank her into my arms, but I know exactly how that will end.

With more physical violence.

It's almost comical. When we were kids, I couldn't have imagined Fallyn attacking me. Or anyone, for that matter. She spent her childhood trailing after me and Miles. No matter where we went, she was always with us.

Miles never gave a shit, and neither did I. He loved having his little sister around. They were inseparable.

Miles' death splintered my world apart and took away everything that was good in it.

Even hockey was shaky in the beginning because we'd played

every season together. Stepping onto the ice after the funeral was the second most difficult thing I've ever had to do.

Keeping my distance from Fallyn was the first.

As painful as it was to be at the rink without him by my side, it was the only thing that made me feel like I was still alive.

The chill of the air that seared my lungs.

The smell of the ice flooding my nostrils.

The sound of the fans rising to their feet and cheering when I saved a goal.

I chose to spend all my time at the arena because the alternative was to be at home.

Not that anyone was there to notice my absence. Dad worked long hours, and Mom filled her calendar with charity functions and social engagements.

It's the reason why I spent every waking hour at the DiMarco house while growing up. After Miles' death, that was no longer an option.

I was alone.

Adrift.

Fallyn's blue eyes continue to spit fire. Any moment, they'll singe me alive. Maybe it would be better that way. I wouldn't have to live with the guilt I carry around with me like a thousand-pound stone. If it were possible to go back in time and change the actions and outcome of that one night, I'd do it in a heartbeat.

Careless decisions were made, and we've been forced to live with the consequences. That's the fallacy of youth…

You feel invincible.

Until tragedy strikes and you realize with sickening certainty just how fragile life is.

Even though I know there won't be any hints of softening, I still search her eyes, hoping that enough time has passed for us to start fresh.

I shift from one foot to another and realize that nerves are skittering across my skin. There isn't anyone who makes me feel ill at ease.

Save this girl.

She makes my heart beat erratically in my chest.

My tongue flicks out to wet my parched lips. "I'm so—"

She gives her head a violent little shake as wetness floods her bright blue depths. "Don't say it," she rasps. "Don't you *dare* say it."

"Can we sit down and talk?" I swallow thickly. "Please?"

"There is *nothing* we have to talk about."

One quick step brings her closer as she stabs a finger at my chest. With her head tilted upward, her warm breath drifts over my lips. It's tempting to suck in a big breath of her and take it deep into my lungs. I want to hold it—*her*—captive there forever.

Even with the anger that vibrates off her in heavy, suffocating waves, she's nothing short of intoxicating.

"There once was a time when we were friends, but that's over." Her lips peel back into a snarl. "Stay the fuck out of my way."

Before I can respond, she swings around and stalks away without another glance in my direction.

CHAPTER 7

FALLYN

Angel

’m still shaking from that run-in with Wolf as I slide onto my seat in psychology and yank out my computer. I wish I could say it's just anger swirling within me, threatening to swallow me whole, but that would be a lie.

There's sadness, too.

So much of it.

More than I expected after all this time.

Maybe I shouldn't be so surprised.

Almost five years might have passed, but it's nothing compared to the decade of friendship we shared before that. There was nowhere we went that Wolf wasn't right by our side. Miles and I were always close and got along. But Wolf was the missing piece. I loved him just as much as I loved my brother.

Maybe even more because I'd always assumed—

I shake those thoughts away before they can do permanent damage.

It doesn't matter what I believed years ago.

Miles is gone, and the fault lies with Wolf.

Just as the professor begins class, a text pops up from Vi.

How'd the call with student services go?

A second one quickly follows.

You have an interview with Sully at 4 today!
Yay!

My fingers hover over the miniature keyboard. After my run-in with Wolf, I'm not sure I want to work someplace where he's a regular.

But I need the money.

All I can do is hope he'll heed my warning and stay the fuck away. It would be the best thing for both of us. I just need to make it through this semester, and then Wolf Westerville will graduate. If the gossip I hear swirling around campus is true, he'll move up to the pros. Then I won't have to worry about running into him around every corner.

I can live my life in peace.

Decision made, I fire off a quick response.

I'll be there. Tell Mads thank you!

Viola hearts the comment.

Good luck!

I release a steady breath, knowing I'll need it.

The rest of the hour-long lecture passes slowly. Normally, this is one of my favorite classes, but I can't focus. My brain keeps bouncing back to Wolf and the handful of minutes I spent in his company.

I'm shocked and ashamed of myself for slapping him.

Twice.

I've never hit anyone before.

What makes it even worse is that he'd just stood there and taken the abuse before quietly asking if we could talk.

Talk!

Ha!

Like that would change anything between us.

Or bring Miles back.

That thought is enough to bring a burst of agony to my heart, and my hand unconsciously rises to rub the scar that lies beneath my shirt.

As soon as the professor dismisses us for the day, my phone rings, cutting through the chaos unfolding around me. My heart hitches when an unknown number flashes across the screen. I glance at the students flooding the corridor as I step into the swiftly moving stream and get swept away by the current.

"Hello?"

"Ms. DiMarco?"

"Yes. Who is this?"

There's a slight chuckle from the other end of the line. "Oh, sorry about that. It's Sharon from student services."

"Oh." My belly dips as my feet falter. "Hi."

"When we spoke yesterday, you talked about applying for a private loan at one of the local banks to pay your tuition. I was hoping you could give me an update."

I chew my lower lip. "Actually, I did talk to a few places. They said it would take a couple of weeks to get the funds." And that's if I qualified in the first place. Which is doubtful since I've never held a job.

There's an uncomfortable pause.

"I'm afraid our hands are tied at this end. If you're not able to pay your bill by the cutoff date, we'll have to drop you from your courses."

Icy fingers wrap around my heart, squeezing until it becomes impossible to breathe and I blurt, "I'm, ah, working on another potential solution. Can I call you back later this afternoon?"

"Of course. I hate to say this, but our deadline is strict. There isn't any wiggle room."

"I understand. Just…give me a bit more time to figure something out."

Her voice gentles. "Let's talk tomorrow morning. Hopefully, you'll have some good news to share."

By the time I end the conversation, my knees are weak.

Not more than thirty seconds later, my phone rings for a second time. Everything inside me nosedives when Chloe's name flashes across the screen.

It's tempting to ignore it.

After the money I demanded, I'm pretty sure she's going to tell me the guy is no longer interested.

And I certainly can't blame him for that.

"Hey," I say.

"I just spoke with the client, and he's agreeable to the amount."

My mouth tumbles open as I nearly stumble to a halt until the person walking behind me jostles me back into motion again, grumbling something under his breath. Normally, I'd swing around and give him a quick apology, but all I can think about is the fact that some man agreed to the outrageous amount of money I threw out in a fit of anger.

"He did set a few conditions of his own," she says cautiously.

Unwilling to have this conversation around so many people, I duck into an empty classroom and close the door. "What kind of conditions?"

"You agree to meet three times and get ten grand after each one."

That's all it takes for my heart to spasm under my chest.

I was hoping this would be a one-and-done kind of thing.

"After each visit, the money will be directly deposited into an account of your choosing. And if you want to cut things off at any time, you can do it, no questions asked."

My mouth turns bone dry. Hearing her discuss the transfer of money slams home the reality of my situation, making it feel even more real than before.

"Fallyn? Did you hear what I said?"

Air gets wedged in my lungs as I think about whether I can actually sell my body to a stranger.

But the real question is—how can I not?

Thirty thousand dollars is a shit ton of money.

Way too much to turn down.

"Sorry, just thinking." My mind continues to whirl before I finally blurt, "I'm good with the condition."

"There's one other…tiny little thing…" Her voice trails off.

Every muscle tightens as I smash the cell closer to my face. "What?"

"He, um, wants you to wear a blindfold."

A shiver slides through me.

A blindfold?

"Why?"

"He wants to remain anonymous. And the deal is void if you refuse. Are you agreeable to the terms?"

Maybe it'll be easier that way. I won't have to see him. Or his expressions. I can just lie there and…

I swing around and stare out the window. "Yeah, okay. If that's what he wants."

"Great! I'll let him know and get back to you with a date for the first meeting."

A burst of nerves explodes in my belly, making me feel nauseous. "Okay. Thanks."

We say our goodbyes before disconnecting. It takes a few minutes for my jumbled emotions to level out. Only then do I slip from the empty classroom and into the hallway. By now, the congestion has cleared, and there's a trickle of students heading to their classes.

As I push out through the glass doors and into the chilled morning air, someone pulls up alongside me. I glance over only to find Anthony. He's the guy I went out with last year, and I liked him well enough, but…

I kind of freaked out when he tried going to second base. Ever since then, I've done my best to avoid him.

I force a smile and tuck a stray lock of hair behind my ear. "Hey."

"Hi." He falls in line with me as we hit the concrete path that winds through campus. "I haven't seen you around very much this semester."

"It's been pretty busy," I say, picking up my pace, only wanting to get away from him. His presence brings all my insecurities to the forefront, and I hate that.

"It's a bummer that we don't have any classes together."

More like a relief, but obviously, I need to keep those feelings to myself.

"Yeah, a real bummer." I point toward the library as the large brick building comes into view. "Well, I should probably get going. I have a ton of homework to catch up on."

He clears his throat before plowing a hand through his wind tousled hair. "I was wondering if maybe we could grab a coffee sometime soon."

"Oh." I glance away and mentally grapple for an excuse. "I, um, wish I could. It's just been so busy. I'm kind of buried at the moment."

He closes some of the distance between us. "I had a really good time when we went out, and I was kind of hoping we could do it again."

I take a quick step in retreat, uncomfortable with the proximity. Anthony is a nice guy, but still…

"I'm sorry. I just can't." It takes effort to force the words out and keep my tone light.

His voice drops as he shifts. "I hope you don't think I was bothered—"

That comment is enough to have me stumbling back a few paces. It feels as if I'm being choked from the inside out and can't breathe. My hand unconsciously rises to massage the ache in my chest, even though I know the phantom pain is in my imagination. There's no reason after all this time for it to hurt.

But that doesn't change the fact that it does.

"Sorry, I need to go."

Before he can stop me, I rush away, hurrying toward the library with my shoulders hunched. Blood rushes in my ears. It's so tempting to fold in on myself. Instead, I release a shaky breath and attempt to calm my racing heart as I take the stairs to the second floor and bury myself in the dusty stacks where no one can bother me.

Yanking out the chair, I drop onto it as hot tears prick the backs of my eyes.

At some point, I need to get over the fear eating away at me that the scar on my chest makes me ugly.

That anyone who sees it will be repulsed.

Turned off.

And maybe the best way to do that is to allow this man to see exactly what he's purchased.

CHAPTER 8

WOLF

I draw a sharp breath into my lungs as I reread Chloe's text for the tenth time.

I can't believe that Fallyn is actually going through with this. The thought that I'll be her first is enough to have my cock stiffening right up.

There's no way she'd allow me to touch one damn hair on her head if she did.

But I have to be sure.

I roll my eyes and quickly tap out a response.

This chick is relentless. I'm reminded of why I went out of my way to avoid her in the first place. Although, who knew she had these kinds of connections. Can't say that's not a surprise.

It's a none-of-your-business thing.

A laughing emoji and then a shrugging one immediately pops up on the screen.

Just know there's more where that came from.

It's a one-time deal.

That's too bad.

A second later, another text pops up.

When do you want to meet with her?

My heart slams against my ribcage as I think about my upcoming hockey schedule and type out a response.

Set up the first one for Tuesday.

I'll text Fallyn with the info and get back to you.

Sounds good.

Pleasure doing business with you.

She tacks on an emoji that's blowing a heart.

Instead of responding, I pocket the phone and glance around the Union, where we're camped out for lunch. There was a time in the not-so-distant past when puck bunnies would be buzzing around the table like drunken bees.

Now there are girlfriends.

Juliette, Maverick's sister, is going out with Ryder McAdams. That relationship sprung up out of nowhere and totally caught me off guard. Ford and his ex-stepsister, Carina, are now an item. Although, anyone with eyes could see that one coming from a mile away. It was only a matter of time before the sexual chemistry they always seemed to generate exploded. And then Riggs and Stella. That was another relationship I would have laid odds on. It's only recently that Riggs got fed up with being friend zoned and made his big move.

My gaze lands on Madden and Viola. I knew there'd been a girl in his past, but I had no idea that it was Fallyn's cousin. We haven't talked about it, but it's pretty obvious that he knows about what happened since they were together when the accident occurred. At some point, we'll have to bite the bullet and discuss the situation. But I'm in no hurry to do that. Now that Viola has been coming around more, I give them a wide berth.

And I fucking hate it.

Not only is Madden my roommate, but teammate. And he's a good friend.

One of the best I have.

When our gazes catch, he gives me a chin lift in acknowledgment.

I return the gesture.

I hate that he knows about my past and what happened with Miles. There's never been a day that I haven't thought about the guy who was more like a brother to me.

Or how Fallyn was snatched from my life.

One day she was there, and the next she was gone.

I drag a hand through my short strands and jerk my eyes away. The last thing I need is him sifting through my inner thoughts.

The ones I keep locked up tight.

Even from myself.

There's only a handful of single guys left in our tight knit group.

Colby, Maverick, Bridger, and Hayes.

The girl on Colby's lap twines her arms around his neck as she presses closer. Every time I see the dude, there's a different groupie trying to dry hump him. I don't know where he finds these chicks. They certainly don't care if he's allergic to monogamy.

As soon as my phone dings with an incoming message, I slip it from my pocket and glance at the screen, hoping that it's Chloe. I want the situation with Fallyn locked down tight. I want to know that in four days, I'll finally be able to get my hands on her.

Instead, I find a text from the university.

> Looks like the chancellor's son thinks he can slip underground and avoid detection. That's a negative, ghost rider.

That text is accompanied by a picture of Bridger with a baseball hat pulled low over his eyes. A couple of girls are snuggled up against him. I recognize the shot from the other day. There's a second photograph. This one is from Slap Shotz after the game last Thursday. Again, he's wearing a black ballcap that covers the upper portion of his face.

The caption reads—

> You can run, but you can't hide. We see you!

"Motherfucker," he swears, tacking on a few other expletives.

"Any closer to discovering who's behind these BS messages?" I ask, feeling bad for the guy.

It's got to be some crazy chick he slept with. Who else would do something like this?

He yanks his gaze away from the screen long enough to glare. "No. But I'm going to figure it out or die trying."

"Let's hope it doesn't turn out to be the latter," I mutter.

He grunts in response before staring around the Union with narrowed eyes. A few seconds later, he shoves away from the table and rises to his feet.

"Hey!" he bellows, sharp tone slicing through the babble of voices that fill the large, sun-filled space.

People in the vicinity turn and look.

I scan the area, wondering who the hell he's barking at. It doesn't take long for my gaze to land on a girl with strawberry blonde hair dressed head-to-toe in black. One glance is more than enough to confirm that she's not a groupie.

That thought is only reinforced when she glares at him in response before baring her teeth like a rabid dog.

My attention bounces between them with growing interest.

I have no idea who the girl in question is, but she's scowling right back at him. If looks could kill, he'd be DOA.

I've known Bridger for more than three years, and I've never seen a female react to him quite like this.

Then again, I've never seen my teammate respond to a girl like this, either.

There seems to be a mutual dislike between them.

The situation unfolding before me is almost enough to make me forget my own issues.

Almost.

But not quite.

CHAPTER 9

FALLYN

I burrow into the collar of my jacket and pull my knit hat farther down until it covers the tips of my ears as I turn the corner onto West Elm, which leads downtown, where the bar is located. Slap Shotz is about a mile from my apartment. Even though it's sunny, there's a chilly breeze that cuts through the warmth pouring down from above. I would have asked Viola for a ride, but she has a three o'clock class.

And since I'm short on funds, setting up transportation when I could walk my ass there seemed foolish.

Would it be easier if I had a car?

Sure.

But I'd need a license, and I don't have one of those. I was midway through driver's education when the accident occurred and ended up dropping out a few weeks later. The following year, I finished the classroom instruction, but when it was time to get behind the wheel for the actual driving portion, I freaked out and had a panic attack.

And that was the end of that.

If I need to go somewhere, my parents or Viola are more than happy to drive me. When money wasn't an issue, I'd set up a lift through an app. At twenty, I should probably woman up and get some behind-the-wheel experience, but the thought of actually doing it makes me sick to my stomach. My mind tumbles back to the night of the accident.

The moment of impact.

The screech of the tires against the pavement and the crunch of metal that still echoes in my ears during my nightmares.

What it felt like to be trapped against the seats.

And Miles…

The painful groans and blood.

An icy shiver slides through me before wrapping around my heart and squeezing until sucking air into my lungs becomes agonizing. I quickly shove those memories from my head and focus on my breathing.

One breath at a time.

In through my nose.

Hold for a beat.

Out through my mouth.

I concentrate on that until my chest loosens.

No amount of therapy has been able to help me move past that night. Or the aftermath that followed. The loss of my brother. How my parents went from being happy and chill to being overprotective and suffocating. I couldn't move a muscle without Mom pouncing, wanting to make sure I was all right.

When my therapist asked to meet with both of us so she could help me open up better lines of communication and tell Mom in a safe space how I felt, along with the steps needed to become more independent, my mother yanked me out of therapy, saying that the woman was a quack and had no idea what she was talking about.

It took all of my senior year to convince them to let me go away to Western. Mom wanted me to attend a local university so I could live at home. There was no way I could do that and retain my sanity.

Moving out after graduating from the small, private school they switched me to after the accident had been scary but totally necessary. I've grown so much during the past two and a half years. And now that Viola is here and we're living together, it's even better.

As much as I hate to admit it, getting my license is the next logical step in my quest for independence.

Especially if I get a job. I can't continue to bum rides forever.

I'm halfway to the bar when the loud rumble of an engine catches my attention. From the corner of my eye, an electric blue muscle car rolls up beside me. When it slows to a crawl, a shiver skates down my spine, and I turn my head, glancing at the occupant. That's all it takes for my fight or flight instincts to kick in. Western is as safe a school as anywhere, but that doesn't mean bad stuff doesn't happen. It's still light out. Although, if this interview lasts for more than thirty minutes, the sun will start to sink in the western sky. Maybe I'll have to call Vi after all.

The glass disappears between us, and my gaze collides with bottle green eyes as my feet stumble to a halt. After our disastrous interaction this morning, I was hoping we wouldn't run into each other for a while.

Or ever.

This is twice now in just one day.

I don't like it.

His eyes lock on mine. I hate the way they see straight down to my soul. That only comes from knowing someone on a deep and intimate level.

"Need a lift?"

Laughter tumbles from my lips.

Is he legit crazy?

I could be naked and frostbitten in a snowstorm, and I still wouldn't accept a ride from this guy.

"Nope." I rip my attention away and continue walking.

Hopefully, that's all it'll take for him to get the hint and leave me alone.

The Mustang crawls alongside me. When my strides quicken, he matches my speed, keeping pace.

"Where are you going?"

"None of your damn business," I snap.

"Just know that I have zero problem following you to make sure you arrive safely at your destination."

I grit my teeth. When it becomes apparent that he wasn't joking around, I glance at him from the corner of my eye. "I'm going to Slap Shotz."

"Why?"

"None of your business."

"Tell me why." His voice deepens.

When a vehicle slows behind him, Wolf sticks his hand out the window and waves the car by.

"Why are you heading to the bar?" he asks again.

I grind to a halt for a second time in as many minutes and glare. Not that it does a damn bit of good.

"Because I have an interview."

"You're looking for a job?" His brow furrows as concern fills his expression. "Do you need money?"

As if he doesn't know.

The question is like a slap to my face, and my cheeks flood with heat. "That's also none of your damn business."

"I'm not taking off, Fallyn. So, you can get in the car, or I'll just follow you to the bar. It's your choice."

We stare for a handful of seconds before a growl leaves my lips, and I stomp to the sleek vehicle. For some unknown reason, he refuses to leave me alone. The quickest way to get rid of this guy is to get in the car and endure the five-minute ride downtown.

I jerk the handle before popping open the door and sliding onto the buttery soft leather. Instead of looking at him, I stare straight ahead out the windshield.

He shifts the gear as we pick up speed. "Why are you walking?"

"Because I didn't want to spend money on a ride."

He glances at me as if thrown off by the response. "You don't have your license?"

"No."

He shifts the gear into third. "Why not?"

"Are we really going to play a game of fifty questions?"

He flicks a glance at me and raises his brow. "If that's what it takes to get the information I want, then yes."

A frustrated sigh escapes from me. This isn't a conversation I want to have with him, of all people. "Does it really matter?"

"Yeah, it does." A heavy silence blankets us before he finally ventures, "Is it because of the accident?"

I turn away and press my forehead against the cool glass of the passenger side window. "I don't want to talk about this with you."

The city blocks disappear as his tires eat up the asphalt, and we enter downtown.

"I would hate to be the reason anything else was taken from you," he murmurs.

The soft comment arrows to the heart of me, and even though it pisses me off, hot tears prick the backs of my eyes. It takes effort to blink them away.

"You have no idea just how much was stolen," I snap, barely able to keep the anger from quivering in my tone.

CHAPTER 10

WOLF

"*T*rust me, Fallyn. I know, and I'm so fucking sorry."

Laughter twisted with bitterness escapes from her. The sound of it scrapes something deep inside me. Ten years ago, I could have never imagined her voice brimming with so much resentment.

The worst part is that there's no way to change it or make it better. There's no way to douse the pain that now lives inside her like a living, breathing entity.

I'm powerless.

"My entire existence changed that night," she snaps. "Yours didn't."

My fingers tighten around the steering wheel until the knuckles turn bone white as I swing into the parking lot of Slap Shotz. At this time of the day, the place is empty. The moment I cut the engine, I swivel in her direction, needing to finish this conversation. Crystal-like tears sparkle in her eyes, turning them even brighter. It's so damn tempting to reach out and stroke my hand across her cheek before holding it tenderly in my palm. The same way I want to pull her into my arms and offer comfort.

But there's no way she'll accept it.

Or anything I have to offer.

"You're wrong about that. Everything changed. Miles was like a brother to me."

"He *was* my brother!" Her voice escalates with every syllable that falls from her lips. "Not yours!"

"He was taken from both of us."

"*You* took him." One lone tear rolls down her pale cheek.

Both her words and tone gut me. It's as if a knife is slicing through my very heart. Mincing it into tiny pieces that will never be put back together again.

"It was an accident," I whisper. "I never meant for it to happen. We were young and stupid. We shouldn't have left the house that night." I gulp down the bile that gurgles up in my throat as memories crash over me, threatening to suck me under. For a second or two, that's all I can see. Swirling snow in the darkness. The flash of lights. Losing control of the vehicle. If I closed my eyes, I'd be right back there again.

I force myself to spit out the rest. "If it were possible to change places with him, I'd do it in a heartbeat."

We stare at each other for a painful tick of time.

Then another.

Just when I think my words have finally penetrated the grief she now cloaks herself in, she whispers, "I wish it had been you."

Her venom steals the very air from my lungs as she slams out of the Mustang and stalks to the back entrance of the bar. I can only sit and stare as she vanishes through the metal door.

It takes a few minutes for the sickness in my belly to abate. The pain of it is almost enough to have me doubling over. I plow my fingers through my short strands before slamming my fists into the leather steering wheel. It's so tempting to howl in agony.

I have no idea how to make anything better with her.

Hell, I don't even know if it's possible.

I'd been hoping that after all this time, the worst of her grief and anger would have been laid to rest, but clearly, that's not the case. She hates me now more than ever.

I've spent all these years thinking about her, wondering how she's doing, wanting to reach out and make amends. To see if there's a way to reclaim the fragmented tatters of our friendship.

Even just a little.

Just enough for me to live at the periphery of her universe.

In light of this convo, it's doubtful she'll ever forgive me.

It should give me enough pause to reconsider my decision to buy her virginity, but how can I do that?

How can I allow another man to touch her?

To be the first to claim her?

The simple answer is that I can't.

It's not a question in my head.

Fallyn DiMarco belongs to me.

She's *always* belonged to me.

Whether she understands it or not.

That decision was taken out of my hands the moment I was old enough to understand the gravity of it.

After all these years, I've finally cracked open the lines of communication. It doesn't matter if she hates my fucking guts. There's no way I can retreat or give up now. Even though nothing between us will ever be the same, and she'll never smile at me without a care in the world, I have to push forward.

Decision made, I pop open the door and slip from the vehicle before trailing after her to the red brick building. Slap Shotz is flanked on one side by a restaurant and on the other by a thin alleyway.

I push through the door into the dimness of the room. The place is long and narrow. There's a guy sitting at the bar, nursing a beer, who lifts his chin in silent acknowledgment before his gaze returns to one of half a dozen high-def televisions that are mounted to the wall.

My gaze roams over the empty stools until it lands on Fallyn. Sully stands behind the smooth stretch of wood with his elbows resting against the surface. He's yammering on about something, his voice booming in the quiet that surrounds them. Once my attention locks on the dark-haired girl, looking away becomes impossible. Her expression has softened, and her lips are tipped upward at the corners. She's like the sun, and I just want to soak in her warmth even though none of it is directed my way.

Sully glances at me before straightening to his full height and beaming in my direction. "Yo, Wolf! Good to see you. Is there something I can help you with?"

My gaze slices to Fallyn. Any trace of a smile has disappeared from her expression. The glare is back full force.

I nod toward her. "I drove Fallyn here for her interview."

Sully's gaze flickers back to the girl who has never been far from my thoughts. "You mentioned Madden and Britt, but I didn't realize you knew Wolf as well."

Before she can tell him otherwise, I beat her to the punch. "We grew up together."

The older man crosses his arms over his chest as his smile widens. "Is that so?"

"Yup."

When he glances at Fallyn, she flattens her lips and jerks her head into a tight nod.

"So, I'd imagine you wouldn't have a problem vouching for her?" he presses.

"Yeah. She'll do a good job bartending." I have no idea if she can mix a drink or not. After almost five years of silence, I realize that I don't know Fallyn the way I once did.

"Oh, I'm hiring her as a waitress. Zoey quit last week. She walked out during the middle of her shift and never came back." He shakes his head as the smile fades. "The girl couldn't have picked a worse night to flake. So, I need someone dependable. It can get pretty crazy after the games and on the weekends."

Fallyn nods as she straightens her slender shoulders. "It won't be a problem."

Waitressing?

My brows draw together. I can just imagine her moving through the thick crowd, taking orders from drunk assholes.

No...I don't like the sound of that at all. I'd much rather have her working behind the bar where no one can get their hands on her. It's bad enough that they'll have to converse with her.

Can't say I really want that, either.

Although, one glance at Fallyn tells me that it's not my decision. Which is exactly why my ass will be here every night she has a shift. Otherwise, all I'll do is sit at home and wonder what the hell is going on.

Who's decided to take their life into their own hands by hitting on her.

Or worse...

He reaches up and strokes his jaw as his gaze bounces between the two of us. "I've got about a dozen applications I was going to sort through, but I'll give you the job since my boy here is willing to vouch for you. It'll save me the hassle of setting up interviews. Half the time, these people can't be bothered to show up for that." He shakes his head and mutters under his breath, "Kids these days. It's like they think they're doing you a big favor by waltzing through the door two minutes before the start of their shift."

I'm barely aware of the mini tirade Sully has launched into. My attention is locked on Fallyn and the emotion that flickers across her features. It's obvious that she doesn't want to accept the offer of employment if I'm the reason behind it. But she needs the money and doesn't want to turn it down. Air gets wedged in my lungs as I wait for her decision. This just feels like another way to tie her to me. Even if it's tissue paper thin. I don't give a rat's ass at this point.

I'm a desperate man.

When Sully raises his brows, waiting for an answer, I clear my throat. "So, what's it going to be?"

Her gaze cuts to mine as she smashes her lips together before her attention returns to the owner of the bar. Only then does her expression soften.

Marginally.

"I'll take it. Thank you. I really appreciate you giving me this chance, and I promise—I won't be late. Ever."

"Good. I guess there's only one thing left to say—welcome to the

Slap Shotz family!" With a grin, he jerks his thumb over his shoulder. "Give me a sec and I'll grab a couple of T-shirts. It's the unofficial uniform around here." He cocks his head and takes her in. "You look like a medium."

She nods. "Yup."

"I'll be right back. Or BRB, as the kids like to say." And then he's gone, ambling across the bar and disappearing into the backroom.

We're alone except for the dude engrossed in the hockey game.

She side eyes me before grumbling, "I didn't need your help getting this job."

I shrug and try to keep it casual, even though everything inside me is screaming to swallow up the distance between us and take her into my arms. "Never said you did. I just wanted to make sure you had the best shot at getting it."

Instead of thanking me, which was a stretch to begin with, she gives me a full-on glare. Our gazes stay locked in silent combat as Sully returns with three black and orange shirts.

He holds one up and glances at her. "That looks like it should fit just fine. If it doesn't, just bring 'em back, and we'll find something else. As soon as I get you on the schedule, I'll give you a call. Most shifts will start at seven o'clock until close."

"That works for me."

When he smiles again, the fine lines bracketing his eyes and mouth deepen. As long as I've known the man, Sully has always been easygoing. He used to play hockey for Western back in the day. A decade later, he opened Slap Shotz and dedicated it to all things Western Wildcats hockey. It's nice to hang out at a place that has so much love for the team.

Fallyn stalks past me without so much as a second look.

I glance at Sully. If he thinks her behavior is odd, he doesn't mention it. "Thanks. Really appreciate it."

He claps me on the shoulder. "It wasn't a problem. We're family around here. Once a Wildcat, always a Wildcat. Right?"

I jerk my head into a nod as his words seep into my heart and warm it.

Ever since I was recruited freshman year of high school by our old head coach, that's exactly the way this team has felt—like family. There's nothing I wouldn't do for any of these guys. Over the years, they've become more like brothers. When we're on the ice, we work together, fighting for one common goal.

I glance at Fallyn as she shoves through the back door.

And yet, no matter how close we are, none of them will ever replace Miles.

Or his sister.

CHAPTER 11

FALLYN

I slip into the apartment and huff out a relieved breath that I'm home. Spending time alone with Wolf makes me twitchy. It doesn't matter if I now despise him. All those old feelings lying dormant for years have been roused and are now attempting to fight their way to the surface. It takes every ounce of strength to shove them back down and pretend they don't exist.

Never existed.

It's the dinging of an incoming message that knocks me from the whirl of my chaotic thoughts as I fish my phone from my pocket. My heart skips a beat when Chloe's name pops up on the screen.

> First meeting on Tuesday afternoon. Four o'clock sharp. Wiltshire Hotel downtown. A key will be waiting at the front desk under the name Abby Mitchel.

That's all it takes for nausea to roll around in the pit of my gut. Any moment, I'll be sick.

If my predicament didn't feel real before, it certainly does now.

My hand rises to rub my chest through the thick fabric of my winter jacket. I quickly unzip and toss it over the back of the dining room chair before beelining to my room. On the way, I notice that my cousin's door is closed. Since the place is quiet, I had assumed she was out.

Mental exhaustion takes hold as I sink to the mattress and stare at the text until it swims before my eyes. My mouth turns cottony as I focus on what will happen in less than four days.

Will this guy just take me, and it'll be over with quickly?

I squeeze my eyes tightly closed, praying that's the case. What I don't need is for this to drag out. I don't want to think about him running his hands over my naked flesh, touching me in places no one ever has.

Why do we have to meet three separate times?

The dude can only take my virginity once.

It occurs to me that not only will there be pain, or, at the very least, discomfort, but there could also be blood.

Blood!

A shudder scuttles down my spine. That's all it takes for bile to rise in my throat as another text from Chloe pops up on the screen.

> Make sure you take care of birth control.

For the second time in a matter of minutes, the reality of my situation slams into me with the force of a two-by-four.

I've been on the pill since arriving at Western. Even though I wasn't in a hurry to do anything, it felt important to have that part of the equation taken care of in case something unforeseen happened. Before the accident, my parents had the rule that I wasn't allowed to date until I was sixteen years old. Afterward, they refused to let me out of their sight long enough to do anything or go anywhere. And since then, there's been a few guys here and there, but not many.

I force out a slow breath and try to steady everything that riots painfully inside me.

Maybe this situation is for the best.

I can get my first time over with.

No fuss. No muss.

And it won't be with someone from the university. The guy won't be lurking around every corner of campus or turning up in my classes.

Can you say awkward?

I'm yanked from those thoughts when a soft moan fills the air. My brows slam together as I tilt my head and listen more intently. When it happens for a second time, my eyes widen, and my jaw crashes open. Even though I've never heard that particular sound come from her room before, I'm pretty sure—

The bedframe knocks into the wall as a masculine grunt follows.

Holy crap, Madden and Viola are having sex.

I clap a hand over my mouth before reluctantly glancing toward my cousin's room as the noise continues to pick up. All we need is some cringey seventies music to go along with the porno soundtrack that's intensifying by the second.

It's obvious that Vi doesn't realize I've returned home from the interview.

They're both adults. And since Madden sleeps over most nights, I assumed they were, um, having relations. On more than one occasion, Vi has stumbled out of her room in the morning after Madden takes off for practice, looking bleary eyed, like she's barely gotten a wink of sleep.

Have I teased her mercilessly about it?

Damn right I have.

What kind of cousin would I be if I didn't?

But Vi has kept all the intimate details to herself. She's never been one to kiss and tell. Even when I was trying to live vicariously through her.

With my phone clenched tightly in my hand, I jerk to my feet. I should take off for a while. If I come face to face with either of them after hearing all this, I'll probably self-combust. Waves of heat are already stinging my cheeks.

A sneaky little thought invades my brain that has me grinding to a halt. Since agreeing to this situation, my focus has been on getting it over with. Only now does it occur to me that there's a slight possibility it could feel...*pleasant.*

Viola cries out, her voice growing louder.

What would *that* kind of pleasure feel like?

Before my world was blown to bits, I'd lie awake at night in my bed and think about what it would be like if Wolf kissed me.

Or touched me.

He's the only guy I ever dreamed about.

As soon as that sly memory invades my brain, I shove it away, not wanting to dwell on Wolf or the past. There's already been too much of that this afternoon. Everywhere I go, there he is. It's no longer possible to ignore him.

Although...it's doubtful I'll feel anything like what's happening in the next room.

I mean, what kind of man buys a girl's virginity?

Or can even afford to piss away that kind of money?

I really hope he's not decrepit.

Another shudder slithers down my spine.

Is that why he wants me to wear a blindfold?

For all I know, the dude could be eighty years old. My face scrunches. That thought is like a punch to the gut and is enough to have nausea stirring at the bottom of my belly.

I stare at the phone in my hand as doubt creeps in at the edges. Maybe I should pull the plug on this unorthodox situation. It's not like any money has been exchanged yet.

Just as my fingers hover over the keyboard, ready to fire off a text to Chloe, my phone rings. I nearly jump a foot, my heart getting lodged somewhere in the middle of my throat as I glance toward Viola's bedroom and quickly answer the call.

"Hello?" I squeak, still trying to get my heartbeat under control before quietly padding across the room and closing my bedroom door.

"Hi, sweetie," Mom says. "I just wanted to check in. You never called back to tell us what happened with school."

"Oh, um, sorry about that. I spoke with someone in student services, and we're trying to work it out."

"I know you're really disappointed by what happened, but maybe it's for the best."

"The best?" I echo in confusion. My father being ousted from the company he started and not being able to pay for my education can in no way be considered *for the best*. My life has turned into a veritable nightmare.

Doesn't she understand that?

"Yeah," she continues, enthusiasm brimming in her tone. "I think you moving back home again is the perfect solution. Western feels so far away. We'll help you get a job, and then you can take a few classes. I've already freshened up your room and changed the sheets on your bed. It's all ready for you."

Sweat springs to my palms as an icy hand wraps around my heart before squeezing until sucking in a full breath becomes impossible. Any minute, it'll explode.

"I don't think that'll be necessary," I blurt. "I just got a job this afternoon."

"You did?"

"Yeah, at a restaurant," I lie, gravitating toward the window that overlooks the courtyard. The sky is filled with leaden gray clouds. Any minute, it'll snow. As I continue staring, a few flakes drift from the sky.

There's no way I can tell them about Slap Shotz.

Mom would lose her shit if I mentioned that I was not only working at a bar but at an establishment dedicated to all things hockey where the team likes to congregate. Anytime Wolf or the Westerville family is mentioned, my father foams at the mouth, and my mother gets teary eyed. It's hard to blame them for continuing to grieve, but it's time for them to move on and stop dwelling on what happened.

It was only when I escaped to college and then returned home for Thanksgiving break a couple of months later that I realized just how mired in the past they were. It was difficult to be around without becoming depressed and sad.

By the end of the four-day vacation, it was a relief to flee to school.

And I hate that.

Hate that I now feel this way about them.

I love my parents more than anything, but I have no idea how to help them through the loss of my brother. At every turn, they're trying to suck me back in, and I refuse for that to happen.

It's like the spiel they give you on an airplane. In case of an emergency, put your own oxygen mask on and make sure you're all right before attempting to help others.

That's what I'm trying to do.

Make sure I'm good before offering assistance.

It doesn't take Sigmund Freud to figure out why I was drawn to psychology as a major or am interested in being a therapist.

"Oh." Disappointment laces that one word. "Wouldn't it be easier to come home? Just for a semester?"

Even though she can't see me do it, I shake my head. "No. I don't want to drop out."

"No one is asking you to drop out, Fallyn," she shoots back. "We've scraped together a little money by selling a few antiques from your grandmother. We can help pay for a class or two at the local college."

They've sold off some of our furniture?

That comment only proves how dire the situation is.

I can't believe this is what it's come to.

When I remain silent, she continues in a rush, "I just worry about you, sweetie. Will you be working late at night?"

"Um, not too late. But I'll find a ride home. It's perfectly safe." I have no idea if that's true or not, but if I tell her any differently, she'll get in the car, drive to Western, and drag my ass back home.

"Hey, Fallyn," my father chimes in. Exhaustion creeps into his voice, making him sound even older.

"Hey, Dad."

"Did your mother mention that we're putting the house up for sale?"

Shock crashes over me as I swing away from the window and resettle on the bed. "No, she didn't."

A heavy silence descends. I can just imagine the looks they're exchanging. Tears are probably filling Mom's eyes. She's always loved that house.

We all do.

Even with the ghost that rattles around inside it.

I squeeze my eyes closed and drag a cleansing breath into my lungs before releasing it back into the atmosphere.

"Yeah, it's time. We need something smaller, more manageable," Dad adds.

No one dares to mention all the memories that have kept them from moving on. Even though it's been almost five years since the accident, Mom hasn't touched my brother's room. It looks exactly the same as it did the night we snuck out of the house. As if Miles is away at college and will return any moment.

A soft sob fills the line.

I clear my throat, trying to keep all the thick emotion from invading my tone. "That sounds like a good idea. Something smaller would be nice for you guys."

"We'll make sure it's a three-bedroom house so you always have a place to stay," Mom says tearfully.

"Of course we will," Dad adds with an awkward chuckle.

They've both grown so bitter over the years. Miles would hate that his death did this to them. Our home no longer rings with laughter and happiness the way it once did.

"We've also decided to sell the Porsche."

I blink, jarred from my thoughts. "Wait…what?"

Did I hear him correctly?

"We should have done it years ago." His voice grows soft. "It's just sitting in the garage collecting dust."

"No! You can't do that. You promised I could have it."

"Fallyn," he murmurs. "You don't drive."

"I'll learn," I blurt, a cold sweat breaking out across my forehead as

I leap to my feet and pace the length of the room. "I'll get my license. Now that I'll be working downtown, it'll make getting around easier."

"You've tried to get through the driving segment."

I wince as if slapped before squeezing my eyes tight. "I know, but I'll actually go through with it this time, all right? Just...don't sell the Porsche." I suck in a painful breath. *"Please."*

"Are you sure? Maybe it would be better to get rid of the damn thing and be done with it."

"No, I want it. You promised."

"All right," he says with a sigh. "We'll hang onto it for a little longer, but if you don't get your license by the end of spring semester, we're putting it up for sale."

"Okay." The tension filling my muscles drains away, leaving me to feel limp. "Thank you."

A suffocating silence falls over the line. All I can think about is getting off the phone.

"I need to go. I've got some homework to finish up for tomorrow."

"Let us know what happens with the tuition bill."

"I will."

We say our goodbyes before hanging up. Relief courses through me as I end the call. That emotion is quickly chased away by guilt.

Instead of dwelling on everything my parents just revealed, I focus on my breathing.

Deep breath in.

Slow breath out.

Repeat.

It feels like the walls are closing in on me. I need to get out of here before I totally lose it. Snagging my backpack from the chair next to my desk, I head for the door. As soon as I yank the handle, I find Viola in the cramped hallway and ground to a halt over the threshold. My gaze slices from my cousin to Madden, who hovers over her with his hands wrapped possessively around her shoulders.

They both look mussed up, making the reason they've been locked away in her room even more obvious.

Color stains Vi's cheeks as she mutters, "I suppose you heard all that."

I didn't think there was anything that could make me smile after the depressing conversation with my parents, but I was wrong.

That forced-out comment does the trick.

My lips tremble at the corners as Madden flashes a smug grin from behind her. "Vi will be sure to give you a heads-up next time."

My cousin twists around to glare at her boyfriend before whacking him on the chest. "Keep it up, and there won't be one."

CHAPTER 12

WOLF

The moment Fallyn steps out of her building, she spots my Mustang idling in the parking lot and momentarily falters. Her eyes narrow before she rips them away and continues walking at a brisker pace.

Just as she's about to stalk past, I lean over and pop open the passenger side door. "Get in. I'll give you a ride to work."

"I don't need one," she snaps. "I'm more than capable of walking."

"Come on, Fallyn," I cajole. "It's at least a mile, and your shift starts in twenty minutes. That's barely enough time to get there." Then I add the clincher. "You don't want to be late on your first day, do you?"

She stops and glares, crossing her arms tightly against her chest. "How do you know my schedule?"

"I called and asked Sully."

Her eyes widen. "And he just gave it to you?"

Even though I know it'll piss her off, I can't help the grin that trembles around the corners of my mouth. "Yup. Just one of the perks of knowing the owner."

"He shouldn't be giving out my personal information." Her upper lip curls as her eyes narrow further until they're slits. *"Especially* to you."

"Did you forget that we're old friends? Of course he gave it to me. I'm the reason he hired you on the spot, after all."

"Don't remind me," she grumbles, gaze drifting over the interior of the vehicle before dropping to my right hand. Emotion flickers across her face as she steps closer to get a better look. "Your car is a stick?"

"Sure is," I say with a snort. "What would be the point of driving it if it weren't?"

Her teeth scrape across her lower lip as I carefully study her expression. I have no idea what thoughts are racing through her brain. There used to be a time when it only took a fleeting glance in her direction to know exactly what she was thinking.

That's no longer the case, and I fucking hate it.

Her private thoughts are now inscrutable.

A long silence follows as her brow furrows and her jaw tightens. "I need a favor."

From me?

Every muscle goes on high alert. "What exactly do you have in mind?"

Her gaze flickers from my hand to my face. That's all it takes for electricity to zip through my veins. I'm like a high-strung racehorse straining impatiently against its bit.

"I need you to teach me how to drive a stick shift."

"Get in the car and we'll discuss it."

She steps from one foot to the other, obviously reluctant to get any closer. "Can't you just give me an answer?"

"Nope. Get in."

If this is the only way to spend a little time with her, I'll happily pounce on it. I just want to be close to her. Breathe the same air, if only for five minutes.

"Fine," she growls with an angry huff, sliding in beside me and slamming the door shut with more force than necessary.

She stares straight ahead as I shift into first and then second, pulling out of the parking lot and into traffic, which is always busy near campus no matter the time.

When she remains silent, I ask, "Why the sudden urge to learn how to drive a manual?" As soon as the question flies out of my mouth, I'm slammed with the answer, and my tone instantly softens. "They're giving you the Porsche?"

I glance at her just in time to see her shoulders slump as if the weight of the world rests on those slender bones.

"Yeah. My parents are threatening to sell it since it's just sitting in the garage."

Her words are like a gut punch and leave me wheezing for breath.

Miles loved that car. His father bought it for him right before he turned sixteen. He spent that year working on it, getting it to purr. I can remember sitting in the oversized garage after hockey practice and watching him fiddle with the transmission. They were ordinary moments when we'd shoot the shit, but they're some of my most cherished.

I glance at her. "Why would they do that?"

"You know why," she grounds out.

"No, I don't. It's not like your folks need the money. I assume they no longer want the reminder sitting around, taking up space."

"Nailed it." Her voice is flat, devoid of emotion.

For some reason, her response pricks at me. None of this makes sense. Fallyn selling her virginity. Getting a job at Slap Shotz. This is what someone who's cash strapped and desperate does. Not a girl who comes from a family flush with money. The company our parents co-own has only made them wealthier.

After all these years, it makes sense that Hugo and Eleanor would finally part with the vehicle. But why wouldn't they just give it to Fallyn?

"So, let me get this straight," I say slowly, trying to work it all out in my head. "They agreed to let you have the Porsche if you learned how to drive it?"

"Yeah," she says warily, the bitterness that had flared to life surprisingly absent from her response.

"Okay. Here's the deal—I'll teach you if you let me drive you to and from work until you get your license and have your own mode of transportation."

Her expression transforms into one of disbelief as she swings toward me. "Forget it."

I shrug and watch her from the corner of my eye. "Is there someone else who can teach you?" I hold my breath, hoping like hell there's not. My guess is that she wouldn't have asked me unless she had no other choice.

Including the devil himself.

With gritted teeth, she shifts and stares straight ahead. "No."

Relief escapes from my lungs like a tire with a slow leak. "That's what I want in return. To make sure you're safe. I'll pick you up and drop you off from Slap Shotz each time you work. Take it or leave it, Fallyn. That's my final offer."

I really hope she'll take it. The last thing I want is for her to tell me to fuck off and that she'll find someone else to teach her.

Then I'd have to kill them.

With my bare hands.

I flex my fingers against the wheel in order to release some of the growing tension.

When she remains silent, I add, "You shouldn't be walking home alone at two o'clock in the morning anyway. It's dangerous. You're just asking for trouble. You realize that, right?"

"I really fucking hate you," she whispers, voice cracking with pent-up emotion.

My shoulders collapse at the animosity that bleeds through her tone. I can't even take joy at her capitulation or the fact that I've managed to strong arm her into spending time with me after all these years.

"I know."

As soon as I pull into the parking lot at Slap Shotz, Fallyn jerks the handle and jumps out of the vehicle, stalking to the brick building. My heart twists as I watch her slip inside the door and disappear from sight. Only then do I pull into traffic and head to campus, knowing I'll be back after practice to keep an eye on things.

On her.

CHAPTER 13

FALLYN

"*N*ext time you work, we'll divide the place up into sections. It's pretty easy, don't you think?"

Easy?

Ha!

I've been running my ass off nonstop since I stepped foot through the door. But Erin, one of the waitresses who works here, has been great, helping me out and smoothing over any mistakes I've made when placing an order with a bartender or dropping off a tray full of drinks.

"It's been something but easy, isn't it," I joke.

She flashes a grin. "Trust me, it'll get better. It won't always feel so hectic, even when it's busy. Most of the customers are pretty chill."

"If you say so," I mutter, unsure if I believe her assessment of the situation.

Even though the music is cranked up and there are a ton of students packed into the space, the energy shifts. People crane their necks as the chatter escalates, reaching unprecedented levels. An air of anticipation fills the bar as if something is about to happen, but I'm unsure what.

Erin glances toward the backdoor as she bounces on the tips of her toes, her own excitement growing. "The hockey team just walked in."

I reluctantly search the crowd until my attention lands on the guys. Even though I hate myself for it, I scan each face until it settles on him. Electricity sizzles through my veins when I find his steady gaze locked on mine. Even from across the distance that separates us, I feel the intensity that snaps in his green eyes.

I've never experienced that kind of awareness with anyone else.

It shouldn't surprise me that it would only happen with Wolf.

Even after all these years.

As much as I wish it were possible to dismiss him, I can't.

There's a part of me that doesn't think I'll ever be able to do it. Not completely. No matter how much I wish otherwise. It would be like digging out a vital organ and trying to live without it. There's just too much history between us.

Too much joy.

And too much heartache.

It's all intertwined.

For better or worse, *we're* intertwined.

"Are you ready?"

Erin's question breaks into my scrambled thoughts, severing the strange connection.

"For what?"

"To wait on them, of course." Her coffee-colored eyes sparkle with excitement.

"Oh, no." I shake my head and take a quick step in retreat. "I don't think—"

Before I can force out the rest, her fingers lock around my wrist, and she drags me through the thick crowd to the back of the bar where most of the team has settled. Earlier in the evening, I noticed that no one dared to sit at the long stretch of tables. Only now does it make sense. It might not be officially reserved for the team, but everyone seems to understand the unwritten rule.

Already there are girls buzzing about, looking for available laps to plunk themselves down on. Ryder McAdams is with his girlfriend,

Juliette. I give her and Carina, who's now going out with Ford Hamilton, a little wave. They smile in return.

Even though I don't know them well, I like them. Not long ago, we all got together and hung out at Blue Vibe for a girls' night. Riggs and Stella are also here. His arm is draped across her shoulders, and she's leaning against him. He drops a casual kiss against the top of her head. Those two are so into each other. I get a toothache every time I'm around them.

Madden and Viola are noticeably absent. My cousin mentioned that they were going to stay in and watch a movie. After the other day, I can just imagine what else will be taking place. It was a mentally scarring experience for all involved.

All right. Maybe not Madden. He seemed unfazed by the entire episode.

Britt was also here for a while before she took off for the night. She doesn't seem interested in hanging with the hockey players.

And that, I can appreciate.

Reluctantly my gaze returns to Wolf. He's lounging on a chair with his long legs stretched out in front of him. His eyes are pinned to me even though there are three girls trying to capture his attention. A few of them run their hands over his bulging biceps.

It's enough to make me grit my teeth in irritation. The urge to swat them away like the pesky flies they are thrums through me.

"Wolf Westerville is such a hottie, don't you think?"

My gaze stays fastened to him as she whisper-yells the question over the thumping beat of music.

When I remain silent, she continues. "He's definitely the strong and silent type. And broody. God, but I love a broody man."

My attention slices to her.

She has a thing for Wolf?

I mean, duh…I'm sure she does. Most of these girls do.

And why wouldn't they?

As much as I hate to admit it, he's even more attractive than when he was in high school.

Hot.

And she's right, the man is broody. He gives off a *don't fuck with me* vibe. Which only makes him even more attractive to the fairer sex. It's like waving around a red, pheromone-soaked cape in front of a horny bunch of bulls.

When we were younger, he wasn't quite so sullen. He laughed and smiled all the time. At least he did around us. Only now do I realize that all the times I've caught sight of him on campus, there's been an air of seriousness hanging over him. Almost as if he was mentally removed from the people around him.

Even his friends and teammates.

Much like me, he's no longer the person he once was.

I blink out of those sobering thoughts when a pretty blonde with perky tits strokes her hands over him before pressing closer and whispering something in his ear. That's all it takes for me to tumble back to high school when he and Miles were sophomores. Even back then, he and my brother drew female attention.

And I hated it.

Hated the way girls flirted with Wolf, clinging to him like unwanted barnacles. It made me pea green with jealousy. One particular time has always stuck with me. About a month before the accident, a girl from school was hanging all over him. I grumbled something under my breath while we were walking to class. Wolf stopped in his tracks, forcing me to do the same. His gaze locked on mine, and he told me that I had nothing to worry about. He never explained exactly what he meant, but in that moment, he didn't have to. The look in his bottle green depths said it all. Even though they were doing everything they could to draw his attention, he wasn't giving it to them.

I guess that's why it hurt so much that he never bothered to visit after the accident.

In the blink of an eye, he vanished from my life.

Not only did I lose my brother that night. I lost Wolf as well.

It was devastating.

The memories disintegrate when I'm jostled from behind. I glance at Erin and find her flirting with Maverick McKinnon, Juliette's younger brother.

When all of my emotions have been locked down tight, I allow my gaze to return to the boy who used to be my entire world. Even though the same blonde continues to buzz around him like a drunken bee, his attention stays pinned to me. My breath catches when he wraps his fingers around her wrists and gently pries them away before setting her aside. With a pout, she moves on to greener pastures.

I hate that his easy dismissal of the girl is enough to settle something deep inside me like a much-needed balm. It would be so much easier if I felt nothing where he was concerned.

Wolf Westerville is part of my past.

Just like my brother.

And if I can't have one, I don't want the other.

CHAPTER 14

WOLF

I lean back against the chair before bringing the bottle of beer to my lips and taking a long swallow. My gaze stays fastened to Fallyn as she shadows the other waitress. Even in the darkness of the bar, I can see guys rubber necking when she walks by, checking out her ass. A few have even been ballsy enough to approach, attempting to shoot their shot. The flash of smile that appears across her face is a gut punch. That's all it takes for jealousy to eat away at my insides. It's all I can do not to jump out of my chair and stalk over there. Punching one of these assholes in the face would be so damn satisfying.

I crack my knuckles in an effort to alleviate the growing pressure.

I want to hoard all of her smiles and the girl will barely give me the time of day.

It feels like a lifetime ago when she'd watch me as if I personally hung the moon and stars in the sky just for her.

And I loved it.

Reveled in her adoration.

I remember Miles joking around that I could always marry Fallyn when we were older, and then I'd truly be his brother. I might have rolled my eyes at the time, but the innocuous idea took root and grew from there.

That's when I knew I'd marry Fallyn DiMarco and be part of their family forever.

After that day, she became mine. I watched out for her even more than normal. When she needed something, I made sure that I was the one who took care of it. And I protected her when Miles wasn't around to do it. In every way that mattered, Fallyn belonged to me.

During hockey season, she'd wear her brother's jersey for one game and mine the next. I always played better when she was sitting in the stands with my name and number stamped across her back, cheering me on.

My mind conjures up an image of the first time I saw Fallyn in a bikini at the pool the summer she turned fifteen. I hadn't been able to get out of the water because my dick had been so damn hard. After that, it was impossible to look at her the same way.

I thought about kissing her a hundred times but never dared.

I didn't want to start something when her parents wouldn't allow her to date.

But then, a month before her sixteenth birthday, the crash occurred.

And Miles died.

Fallyn was in the hospital for more than a week. After that, Hugo and Eleanor yanked her from the public school we attended and sent her to a small, private academy on the other side of town.

Life as I knew it was blown apart.

Never to be the same again.

And now, here she is.

After years spent apart, our worlds have once again collided. And I'm not about to let her go.

Not for a second time.

Not ever.

At two o'clock on the dot, the final song of the evening is played, and then the lights are flicked on. Most of the crowd has thinned. All the guys who are wifed up took off earlier. Colby has his arms wrapped around two girls as Hayes attempts to charm a puck bunny who's been flirting with him all night into making him a decision she'll no doubt regret in the morning. Maverick gives me a chin lift before taking off alone.

Sully hefts himself up onto the makeshift stage and says in a booming voice, "It's closing time! You know what that means! You don't have to go home, but you can't stay here."

A few boos go up as the bouncers clear out the place. One of them tips his chin at me as he herds drunk customers toward the exit. Fallyn shoots a glare in my direction as she helps Erin clear glasses from the tables before wiping down the tops. It takes about twenty minutes to clean up and then count out the tips. Fallyn beams when Erin gives her a fat stack of bills before shoving them into her front pocket.

Even though exhaustion creeps across her features, she's no longer scowling. If I had to guess, I'd say she probably forgot I was waiting around to take her home. She says goodnight to everyone before taking a step toward the backdoor. One glance in my direction, and she falters before straightening her shoulders and dragging her attention away.

I wave to the crew before silently trailing after her. If Sully thinks it's odd that she didn't bother to acknowledge my presence, he doesn't comment.

Which is for the best.

It's not like I'm about to explain how messed up our past is to him.

Or anyone, for that matter.

As I push through the metal door into the chilled night air, my gaze searches the nearly empty parking lot. Fallyn waits beside my Mustang GTO with her arms crossed tightly against her chest. Instead of clicking the locks before reaching the vehicle, I beeline to her side. My gaze stays fastened to hers as I brush against her body before popping open the handle.

She lifts her chin and holds my eyes under the silvery moonlight that slants down on us. It's as if we're locked in a silent battle of wills.

"I could have opened it for myself."

"I wanted to do it for you," I murmur.

She presses her lips together before gingerly slipping inside the car. When she doesn't immediately fasten her seatbelt, I lean down and snag the strap before stretching it slowly across her chest. Her pupils dilate as her muscles stiffen beneath my touch. We're so close that I can feel the warmth of her breath ghost across my lips. I can't help but scan her face in the darkness, looking for some kind of softening.

It's so damn tempting to close the distance between us and take her mouth.

Instead of doing what every instinct within is clamoring for, I click the belt into place and rise unsteadily to my feet.

With my hand pressed against the side of the car, I stare down at her dark head. This time, she keeps her attention focused on the windshield. Her hands rest against the front of her legs. The way her fingernails dig into her jean-clad thighs is the only telltale sign that she's as shaken by our proximity as I am.

It's carefully that I close the door before inhaling a shaky breath and walking around the muscle car. After sliding in beside her, I start up the engine and pull out of the parking lot. The ride to her apartment is made in suffocating silence. The entire way there, I rack my brain for something to say, but it remains frustratingly empty.

Halfway to her apartment, it occurs to me that being this close to Fallyn sets me on edge. That's never happened before. No girl has ever made me nervous.

No matter how pretty or popular.

They never bothered me because none of them mattered.

But Fallyn is different.

She's always been different.

As I turn into the parking lot of her building, I realize that I need to say something. The second I cut the engine, this girl will fly out of the car like a bat out of hell.

"When do you want to get together for your first driving lesson?"

Her muscles fill with tension. "I have a big test to study for tomorrow and Monday. So maybe Tuesday afternoon?" As soon as the words leave her lips, she immediately shakes her head. "Actually, that doesn't work." Then she mutters, "I already have plans."

Anticipation explodes inside me before racing across my skin, leaving goosebumps in its wake.

I know *exactly* what she has going on.

And I can't fucking wait.

"Oh, yeah?" It takes effort to keep my voice casual. "Hot date?"

A frown morphs across her features. "No. Just…something I need to take care of."

Guilt pricks at me. If I were a better man, I'd offer her the money with no strings attached. But I also realize there's no damn way she'd accept it from me.

"How about Wednesday then?"

She turns just enough to scrutinize my eyes. Her gaze sifts through them in the darkness that presses in on us, and I find myself holding my breath before she finally jerks her head into a stiff nod.

And then she's gone. Disappearing into the frigid air before hurrying toward the entrance to her apartment building. Her long, dark ponytail waves behind her in the wind like a flag.

It's only when she slips safely inside the lobby that I shift the car into gear and head home. It's doubtful I'll be able to sleep a wink until I get my hands on her.

CHAPTER 15

FALLYN

I force out an uneven breath as I stare at myself in the mirror. My gaze slides over my reflection with a critical eye. There's not a single hair out of place. I've left it long and loose around my shoulders before adding some soft curls with the iron. Then I applied just a bit of eyeshadow, dark liner, and pink lip stain. My hand trembled the entire time. It feels as if I'm being eaten alive by nerves. Earlier this afternoon, I spent two hours in the bathroom.

Everything's been shaved.

Everything.

I've never done that before.

But the guy is paying big money and should have a clean work surface. I mean…I assume that's important. Although, what do I know? It was tempting to text Chloe and ask.

Had I realized it earlier, I would have made an appointment to get everything waxed, but by the time it occurred to me, it was too late. The last thing I want to be is all red and puffy from having the hair follicles ripped from my skin.

No, thank you.

I'm self-conscious enough. No reason to make the situation any more embarrassing than it already is.

It took forever to pick out an outfit which is ridiculous because it's doubtful I'll be spending much time in it. Or that he'll care about my fashion choices. It's not like we're going out on a date.

But still…

I want to look my best. It'll give me the confidence boost I need to go through with this.

My gaze slides over the pink cashmere sweater and brown corduroy skirt that hits mid-thigh. I'm wearing brown suede boots that are soft and stretch over my calves. Beneath is a pink lacy bra and matching panties that I picked up last year while shopping with Viola at an expensive little boutique when money wasn't an issue.

My ears are adorned with little diamond studs that are barely visible through my thick hair. I've never been one to wear a lot of jewelry, but these are important to me.

I wish that weren't the case.

Wolf gave them to me for my fifteenth birthday. I've always worn them on special occasions. And in a weird way, this feels like one.

I'm about to lose my virginity.

As soon as that thought floats through my brain, my belly spasms with a burst of anxiety. My palm settles over my lower abdomen as I draw in another breath, hoping to settle everything that riots dangerously inside.

But it's no use.

I'm a nervous wreck. The only thing getting me through this moment is that a large chunk of my tuition will be taken care of after this is over. I won't have to worry about leaving school.

Or moving home.

In the end, that's all that matters.

With one final look in the mirror, I snag my small black purse from the top of my dresser and head for the door. As I pass through the dining area, I catch sight of Viola in the kitchen. Even though it's almost four o'clock in the afternoon, she has a big bowl of cereal and is just about to shovel a spoonful into her mouth.

Her eyes widen when she sees me, and she drops the utensil back into the container.

"Wow! You look amazing! Where are you going? Hot date?"

Well, shit.

Why didn't I bother to come up with a cover story?

"Um, yeah," I improvise, feeling guilty for lying. "I'm meeting up with someone for coffee."

"Anyone I know?"

I blink, thrown off by the question. "Huh?"

"Who's the guy? Do I know him? Where'd you two meet?"

This is the problem with lies. They have the potential to spin out of control if you're not careful.

"Oh…" I rack my brain and grasp onto the first name that comes to mind. "Anthony."

"Anthony? Didn't you date a guy with the same name last year?"

"Yeah," I say sluggishly, unsurprised she remembers that particular fiasco.

The expression on her face tells me that the cogs in her brain are moving. "I thought you weren't going to see him again," she says, brows drawing together.

Viola and I have always been protective of one another. When Madden hurt her senior year of high school, I threatened to kick his ass. Sure, I would have needed to bum a ride to do it, but that doesn't change the fact that I would have. And when he showed up at the door a month ago, wanting to see Vi, I nearly took his head off.

My cousin is very much the same where I'm concerned.

And I love her for it.

After the date in question, I came home and cried on her shoulder, embarrassed by my reaction, wishing I could be less sensitive about the scar.

"You're right, at the time, I was uncomfortable. But I've decided to give him another chance. He's actually a really nice guy."

That's the only truth sprinkled on top of all the lies. Anthony *is* a nice guy, but I can't get past his reaction. Thinking about it still makes me cringe, which is why I hate running into him on campus.

She studies me carefully before nodding. "I think it's great you're giving him another chance."

Her acceptance of the situation has my chest loosening, making it easier to breathe. "Yeah."

"Are you two meeting up at the Roasted Bean?"

"No. We decided on a coffee shop downtown."

Her brows pinch together. "How are you getting there?"

I inch toward the door, only wanting to make a hasty getaway. "I was going to walk."

The cereal all but forgotten, she scoops up her keys from the breakfast bar that separates the kitchen from the dining area. "Come on, I'll drive you."

I give my head a violent little shake. "No, that's not necessary. I don't mind walking. The cold air will help clear my thoughts."

"Don't be silly," she says with a snort. "I'll drive you, and if he doesn't give you a ride home, just shoot me a text and I'll pick you up. It's not like I've got any plans other than studying my ass off." She adds with a grumble, "The semester just started and already there are a ton of tests."

"Guess that'll teach you to major in engineering," I tease lightly.

"You got that right. I'm not sure what I was thinking."

"That you're a whiz at math and science and wanted to use that big brain of yours for good instead of evil."

She shoots me an easy smile. "And here I was thinking I was just a glutton for punishment."

"That, too."

We slip into our jackets before heading out the door. Less than ten minutes later, she pulls up in front of a fancy coffee shop on the main drag in town. The street is dotted with restaurants, specialty shops, and coffeehouses.

She stares at the pretty storefront from the driver's side of the car. "Is this the right one?"

I nod before flicking a quick look her way. The last thing I want is for her to see the anxiety filling my eyes and offer to come in with me.

"Yup. Thanks again. I really appreciate it."

"I told you—it's not a problem. And I'm serious, call or text if you want me to pick you up."

"I will." My fingers wrap around the handle before popping it open and slipping from the vehicle.

"Have a great time," she says in a raised voice right before I slam the door shut.

Yeah, I can't imagine that happening.

Like, at all.

My plan is to tackle this encounter like I did with my first shift at Slap Shotz…

Paste a pleasant smile on my face and muddle through it the best I can.

With one final wave, I head inside and watch as Viola's white Jeep pulls away from the curb and disappears into traffic. Only then do I slip from the café and rush down the sidewalk. I picked this coffee-house knowing that it was only two blocks from the hotel.

It takes less than five minutes before I'm standing in front of the sprawling stone structure. The place is lavish. At Christmastime, it's decorated with a life-size gingerbread house in the lobby.

It's *that* kind of fancy schmancy place.

I draw in another deep breath before forcing myself to walk through the glass doors and to the counter. The heels of my boots echo off the ocean of glossy marble. With every step, my nerves multiply until it feels like my entire body is a live wire humming with them. If this continues, I'll probably end up having a heart attack. Then I won't have to worry about selling my V-card to some old man.

I'll be dead.

The elegantly dressed woman behind the long stretch of gleaming counter glances at me and reinforces her smile. "Welcome to the Wilt-shire Hotel. Will you be checking in with us today?"

I clear my parched throat. It feels like I haven't had a drop to drink for days. Maybe weeks. I'd give just about anything for a cold glass of water.

"Hello. I'm…" I falter, remembering that I'm supposed to use an alias. Heat floods my cheeks as I mumble, "Um, my name is Abby Mitchel."

She taps a few keys on the computer. "Ah, yes. Here you are, Ms.

Mitchel. It looks like your suite is ready and waiting." She slides a small, rectangular folder my way. "The card is inside, along with the passcode for the internet. The restaurant opens at six o'clock for breakfast." Her smile intensifies. "Please let us know if there's anything else we can do to make your stay more enjoyable."

I don't bother telling her that I'll be long gone by morning.

"Thank you." It's only when I reach out to take the paperwork that I realize my hand is trembling.

If the woman standing on the other side of the counter notices, she doesn't say a word, and for that I'm grateful. Instead, she points toward the lobby. "The elevator is on the other side of the gathering area, and your room is on the fourth floor. Enjoy your stay!"

"Thanks again."

With the folder gripped tightly in my hand, I walk on wooden legs through the lobby to the bank of mirrored elevators. None of the breathing exercises I learned in therapy help to settle my nerves. It's like they're trying to claw their way from the inside out.

I throw a longing glance at the entrance. It's so tempting to break into a run and get the hell out of here. Before I can make the decision to flee, the elevator dings, announcing its arrival and I force myself inside the spacious car. My hands twist together as the elevator rises to the fourth floor. Barely am I given time to suck in a breath when the doors slide open again. Even though my brain is prodding me into movement, my feet remain paralyzed.

Am I seriously going through with this?

My window of opportunity to turn and run is shrinking by the second.

Just as the metal doors are about to shut, a masculine hand reaches inside, and they bounce open. I'm jolted back to the present as the man takes a step toward the car.

Our gazes collide and he hesitates.

He's wearing an expensive gray suit that fits him perfectly. It showcases the breadth of his shoulders and the leanness of his muscular body beneath. There's a light scruff on his jaw, as if he hasn't bothered to shave in a day or so. His eyes are the same blue hue as my own.

With his hand still holding the door, he steps to the side and smiles. "Is this your floor?"

"Yes," I blurt.

Heat licks at my cheeks as we stare for another second or two before I scamper from the elevator, sliding past his bigger body. It's a relief when the metal doors close, and the elevator descends to the lobby. I'm halfway down the hallway when I'm jolted with the realization that the guy who just stepped inside the car could be the man I'm meeting with.

My hand unconsciously rises to rub the scar.

If I had to guess, I'd say he looked to be in his mid-thirties.

It's entirely possible that he wanted to get a look at his purchase.

A shiver slides through me as I force my feet into movement again. The hallway is wide and long, with mini chandeliers that drip from the coffered ceiling. Each door is painted a glossy black and stands out in sharp relief from the ivory walls.

I glance at the number scribbled across the top of the folder and realize that it's the next one down. My feet slow to a gradual halt once I reached the thick wood. Nerves race across my flesh before pooling like liquid in my belly. Any moment, I'm going to be sick.

My arm trembles as I press the plastic key card to the lock. There's a buzz as the light flashes green. With the handle tightly gripped in my fingers, I carefully turn it before peeking inside. My breath gets wedged at the back of my throat as I take one reluctant step and then another inside the entryway. My ears are pricked for the slightest sound, but there's nothing.

The place appears empty.

If I was expecting a simple hotel room, that's not what I find. My gaze flies around the space, absorbing every minute detail. It resembles an elegantly decorated apartment. It's the kind of place we used to stay years ago. My parents always booked three-bedroom suites when we traveled. At the time, I never realized how luxurious they were or how lucky I was.

There's a tiny foyer with an antique credenza and a sparkling crystal bowl. A gold leaf framed mirror hangs above it. I force myself farther into the suite. There's a compact kitchenette to the left and an expansive sitting area with a fireplace and pretty mantle painted in antique white that takes up a good portion of the far wall.

Even though my attention is drawn to the floor-to-ceiling windows that overlook the downtown area, I find myself gravitating to the adjoining room situated across from the fireplace. I peek inside the bedroom. A king-sized bed dominates the space, while two armchairs flank a vintage table in front of an oversized picture window.

I pause over the threshold, afraid to step inside the sumptuous space. It takes a moment to realize that there's a propped-up piece of paper in the middle of the bed. Curious as to what it says, I move close enough to pick up the note and read it.

> *Take off all of your clothes and put on the robe. When you're ready, text the number below. Then, place the blindfold over your eyes and lie on the bed.*

Instructions.

I pour over them for a second and then a third time. Only then does my gaze settle on the fluffy white robe folded next to the notecard.

Air leaks from my lungs.

Okay...I can do this.

I settle on the bed and unzip the suede boots, setting them next to the upholstered armchair near the window. The tall socks follow before I unzip my pink peacoat and drape it carefully over the arm of the chair.

Returning to the bed, I snag the robe on my way to the attached en suite. It's all gray veined marble with a giant soaker tub and an over-sized waterfall shower. Just like in the living area, there's a wall of windows with spectacular views of downtown. If I wasn't so jacked up with nerves, I could probably appreciate it.

I swing away from the window before meeting my gaze in the reflection. Unlike when I looked at myself thirty short minutes ago, my cheeks have been leeched of all color, making the blue of my eyes and the pink lipstick stand out in sharp relief.

My fingers tremble as I grip the hem of my cashmere sweater and slowly drag it up my body and over my head. I fold it neatly on the marble counter before unsnapping the button and lowering the zipper of my skirt. It gets placed on top of the sweater. And then I'm in nothing more than my pink matching underwear set. I suck in another unsteady breath and muster all of my courage before unlatching the snap at the back of the bra. The material springs apart, the silky straps sliding down my arms and baring my breasts to the cool air of the room. My gaze reluctantly settles on the jagged scar that slices down my chest.

I hate that fucking scar.

Unable to stop myself, my fingers trace the puckered skin.

The wound represents two very distinct parts of my life. The first fifteen years that were idyllic with laughter and love. And then the years that came after the accident. The black cloud that descended over our family and continues to hover over us like a specter filled with bitterness and grief.

The happy-go-lucky girl I was growing up could never imagine sleeping with a stranger for money. Those thoughts are too much of a slippery slope and I shake away the darkness before it can swallow me whole.

I just need to get through this.

As I stare at my nearly naked reflection, I realize that all the energy spent picking out an outfit was a total waste of time. The only thing this guy will see me in is the white robe.

That's all he's interested in.

Getting down to business.

That thought has a horde of butterflies winging their way to life in the pit of my belly.

I hook my fingers beneath the thin elastic band of my panties before shoving the fabric down my hips and thighs. I don't want to give myself any more time to think. I'm afraid of what direction my mind will turn if I do.

With another deep breath that does nothing to calm my nerves, I shake out the robe and wrap it protectively around my body. It doesn't escape me that I'm cloaking myself in a false sense of security. I have no idea what will happen when the man who bought my virginity saunters through that door. The only thing I know for certain is that I won't enjoy it. There will be no pleasure to be had. I'll endure it just like I've endured the past five years, and then I'll move on with my life.

Thirty thousand dollars richer.

With the robe tightly fastened around my waist, I head back into the bedroom and pick up the black eye mask, rubbing the silky material between my fingertips. Then I snag my phone from my purse and text the number on the note.

As soon as I hit send, the muscles in my belly spasm, becoming painful. I drop the cell back into my purse and settle in the middle of the bed with the robe tightly cinched around my waist before slipping the mask over my eyes and reclining against the pillows. With my vision obscured, my breath comes out in short sharp pants as nerves careen across my flesh.

Trembles rack my rigid body as my ears stay pricked for the slightest sound. It feels like hours slowly tick by before the door in the entryway opens and then closes, the lock clicking into place. The sound echoes throughout the quietness that presses in on me. Every footfall that brings him closer feels like the heavy step of a giant.

My fingers twist.

Locking and unlocking.

Carefully smoothing the material.

I freeze when he pauses over the threshold.

What does he see when he stares at me?

A virgin sacrifice cloaked in white?

Because that's exactly what I feel like.

My heart thuds painfully beneath my breast. Any second, it'll explode from my chest.

My ears continue to strain, pricked for the slightest sound.

Movement.

An acknowledgment or greeting.

Something that will reassure me that I've made the right decision.

The image of the guy from the elevator pops into my head.

Would I recognize the sound of his voice?

I try to dredge it up but aren't able to. I'm so lost in thought that I startle when the mattress dips beneath his weight as he settles next to me. My lips part as I gulp oxygen into my lungs before releasing it in short bursts back into the atmosphere.

When he inches closer, the air stirs around us before I feel the gentle sweep of his finger across my lower lip. It's slowly that it strums back and forth. Without a word, he traces the curve of my cheek to my jaw before sliding lower along the column of my neck to my collarbone and then back up again.

Just as I become used to his touch, his fingers disappear. I almost miss the tenderness of them.

The realization is jarring.

It's the first sign that this might turn out to be more than what I expected.

A second later, his hands slip into the loose arms of the robe and stroke upward to my elbow. Back and forth he caresses, gently kneading the muscles along the way.

He twists, leaning over me, giving me a sense of his larger form. His woodsy cologne invades my senses, teasing my nostrils. There's something strangely comforting about the scent. The heat of his body permeates mine as he cages me in with his strength. It's an odd sensation to be blindfolded and rely on all of my other senses to piece together a mental picture of this person.

Touch.

Scent.

In the darkness that surrounds me, they feel heightened.

I focus on his hands as they continue to massage my muscles, attempting to loosen the tension that fills them. They're large and strong. Once my arms turn pliant, he shifts, his hands settling on my ankles before gradually sliding to my knees. The thick material gets shoved upward to my thighs.

Air gets clogged at the back of my throat, which is ridiculous. If he made any move to strip off the robe, I'd silently allow him to do it.

He's paid a lot for the honor.

But that's not what happens.

Instead, his hands slide beneath my leg, propping it up until the sole of my foot rests flat against the comforter. Then he works the tight muscles of my calf with an insistent touch. It's slowly that he slides upward to my knee. Only when those muscles have turned pliant does he venture higher up my thigh. When he's thoroughly massaged one leg, he shifts on the bed and gives the same attention to the other. My mind drifts as I sink into the unexpected pleasure. I almost forget why I'm here.

Blindfolded.

Being touched by a stranger.

When he's finished, my muscles feel deliciously malleable. No one has ever handled me like this.

His fingertips drift from my thigh to my ankle before he shifts toward my upper body. That's all it takes for my anxiety to slam back full force. My fingers sink into the plush comforter, clawing the material in order to keep silent.

His thumb settles on my lower lip before ghosting over the plump flesh. Air leaks painfully from my lungs as he strums back and forth. When the tip of his finger slips into my mouth, my tongue darts out, licking at it, tasting the saltiness of his skin. A hiss escapes from him as he jerks away.

My breathing turns jagged, my heart pumping wildly beneath my breast. Even though his finger is no longer there, my tongue slips out to moisten my lips, wanting another taste.

It's almost a surprise when his hands settle on the tie cinched at my waist. For a moment or two, he doesn't move. We hang suspended for what feels like hours. My nerves stretch and lengthen until I want to scream. Until I'm tempted to knock his hands away and rip off the robe myself just to get it over with. The suspense is killing me.

It's almost a relief when he finally loosens the knot. I don't realize that my hands have settled over his larger ones until the warmth of his flesh registers, seeping into my bones. My breath stalls as I wait to see what he'll do. As if by reflex, my fingers tighten around his. Even though I'm blindfolded and can't see my surroundings, I can almost feel the heat of his gaze licking over the lower portion of my face.

Studying it carefully.

A strange kind of disappointment fills me when he slips them free. The warmth of his palm settles over my fingers. He wraps his larger hand around one of mine before carefully prying it away from my waist and placing it at my side. He does the same with the other.

My breathing picks up tempo, turning choppy. It feels like my arms weigh a thousand pounds, and I couldn't lift them even if I tried. I don't understand how they can feel so heavy.

Only then does his hands settle at the knot before slowly loosening the belt, tugging the ends free. His fingers rest along the edges near my lower ribcage. I've never been so hyperaware of anyone's touch the way I am of this unknown man. Without disturbing the robe, his hands slip beneath the thick material. The heat of his palms singes my bare skin.

That's all it takes for my world to shrink down until the only thing it encompasses is the two of us. For a long moment, his hands remain still, the pressure insistent. Seconds and maybe even minutes tick by before I find myself shifting beneath his touch, wordlessly urging him to move.

Explore?

I don't know.

I'm confused.

I didn't expect to feel any kind of pleasure.

It's as if he somehow understands the silent plea. Or was waiting for a signal to continue. Now that he has it, the warmth of his palms slides upward until his thumbs graze the rounded swells of my breasts. My breath catches as anticipation thrums through me. Instead of sliding higher and cupping the softness, they move downward along my ribcage and belly until reaching my hip bones.

My teeth scrape across my lower lip as I wonder if he'll sink to the place that now throbs with awareness. Instead, they do the opposite. Just like earlier, he massages the rigidly held muscles, loosening them, turning them malleable until it feels like I could melt into the mattress.

I don't realize that the edges of the robe have loosened until the cool air of the room ghosts across my nipples, making them pucker and tighten.

Everything within me stills as my breathing turns shallow.

His hands rise to my breasts to palm the softness. He squeezes them in tandem before gently plucking at the hardened tips. A whimper of need escapes from me as my spine arches off the mattress and my lips part.

As much as I hate to admit it, delicious sensation ricochets throughout my being before settling in my core, where it pools like warmed honey. There's no denying that his touch feels good. He's been nothing but gentle the entire time.

When he first walked in, an image of the man from the elevator was firmly in my head. It was so much easier to visualize the person touching me so intimately instead of a faceless stranger. It's disturbing to realize that the figure has morphed into someone else entirely.

Another man.

One with short dark hair and green eyes that see straight through to the heart of me. I imagine that his hands are just as strong and capable of this kind of tenderness.

At least, they used to be.

That thought is jolted from my brain when his fingers slide over the jagged scar in the valley between my breasts. I don't know how I forgot about its existence. For the first time in my life, I wasn't thinking about the mortification that eats away at me at the thought of someone staring at it. Other than the doctors, my parents, and Viola, no one else has seen the ugliness that mars me.

The puckers and ridges of the flesh painstakingly stitched back together again before healing in a jagged line six inches in length. Maybe there was a time when I enjoyed wearing bikinis, but it's been years. When I shop for a swimsuit, I'm careful to buy ones that cover as much of my cleavage as possible. I don't want people staring or asking questions with morbid fascination, wanting a retelling of the accident.

That's not a day I want to mentally relive.

It was hard enough the first time.

"I have a scar," I blurt in a raspy voice.

The thought of him studying me is enough to have my arms rising to shield the old wound from view. Before I'm able to do it, his hands lock around my wrists, halting my movements. Not a sound escapes from either of us as he gently returns my arms to my sides.

He gives me a gentle squeeze before releasing them. Then his fingertips settle at the top of the jagged line before sliding downward, tracing every suture that held my skin together. Fifty of them in total because of the depth of the wound.

I shift, only wanting to dislodge his hand, and choke out, "Please don't."

His fingers stall, pausing over the old wound. With a shift, he looms over my upper torso until I can feel the heat of his breath ghosting across the area. At this point, I'm panting. Any moment I'll hyperventilate as my chest rises and falls in quick succession.

Everything inside stills as he presses his lips to the ruined flesh. His tongue darts out to lave the skin until every millimeter has been touched. He continues to lick and kiss the imperfection as his hands play with my breasts, toying with the nipples. It doesn't take long before they're both erect little points that beg for his attention. He palms the softness until I'm writhing beneath him, seeking out more of his gentle touch.

When he finally pulls away, I almost grieve the loss. His hands drift from my breasts down my ribcage before pausing at my hipbones. I squeeze my thighs tightly together, only now becoming aware that the robe is completely parted.

It's been that way for a while, and I didn't notice.

His fingers ghost over me, sliding to my inner thighs before carefully prying them apart. It's tempting to put up a fight, but this man has been so gentle and giving. I force myself to relax as he presses them wider. On a shaky exhale, I allow them to fall open. For a long, painful moment, there's no movement. My ears strain, attempting to pick up the slightest sound, but there's nothing.

Nothing but the harshness of his own labored breathing.

It almost matches mine, which seems strange.

One hand rises from my inner thigh, and everything in me stops, waiting for him to finally touch me. It's almost a surprise when the backs of his knuckles brush across the top of my mound. Electricity explodes within my core, and I can't help but shift restlessly beneath him.

Am I trying to wiggle away?

Or get closer?

I don't know.

There are so many conflicting thoughts that are racing through my muddled brain.

When he repeats the movement for a second time, a whimper escapes from me and I realize that I've widened my legs, wanting more of his soothing touch. Even though I'm blinded to the world around me, I feel the heat of his stare searing my naked flesh.

No one has ever looked at my body so intensely.

Not even me.

His hands glide across my inner thighs. They're not soft or pampered but calloused. When he squeezes them, the fingertips sink into my flesh. I can't help but wonder if bruises will be left in their wake. He gently forces them further open until the cool air of the room caresses my bare pussy. I've never felt more exposed in my life.

On display.

There's something about having the blindfold partially covering my face that stops me from being eaten alive with embarrassment.

I'm unable to see him.

I have no idea who the man is touching me.

It allows me to feel removed from the situation at hand in a way I didn't expect but is entirely welcome.

A gasp escapes from me when one thick digit slides from my clit to the bottom of my slit before drifting upward again. He retraces the same path until I'm squirming, desperate for more. Only then does one thick finger slide inside me until it's completely buried. My teeth sink into my lower lip as my inner muscles clench around it.

My skin prickles with desire before it pools in my core like liquid heat as a growl reverberates throughout the silent room.

When he drags the finger from my body, a deep sense of loss fills me. As soon as I lift my hips in silence askance, he presses back inside until it's seated completely. He repeats the gesture for a third time before his finger strokes up my bare belly, leaving a wet trail in its wake until he reaches my breast. He circles one tip until the little peak stiffens up as if on command. Then he drags the finger back down to my core and dips back inside. It's slowly that he pumps the thick digit before echoing the movement, circling the other nipple and covering it with my own arousal.

Fire ignites inside my belly as it returns to my center before sliding deep inside. He drags it in and out of my body, finding a rhythmic motion that pushes me closer to the brink until I'm tap dancing on it. My muscles tighten with each deep slide.

I've masturbated before and understand what the sensation blooming to life in my core means.

I don't give a crap if this stranger is playing with my body and watching me teeter on the cusp of falling apart. The only thing I care about is the orgasm that's so close I can practically taste it. I'm so mindless that I can't help but chase after the delicious pleasure just out of reach. My body bows off the mattress as his finger slips free, my inner muscles clenching around nothingness.

A desperate scream builds at the back of my throat as all my inhibitions fall to the wayside. Even though I try to keep it locked deep within, a tortured whimper breaks free, shattering the silence of the room. The deep scrape of his chuckle matches my intensity as his fingers settle back over my clit before rubbing gentle circles.

That's all it takes for me to career over the edge and into oblivion. I moan as he continues to stroke my pussy. This isn't my first orgasm, but it's certainly the hardest one I've ever had. It crashes over me like a tidal wave, threatening to drag me to the very bottom of the ocean. The pleasure rushing through me is so great that I don't care if I ever surface again.

Almost distantly, I realize that all I've been doing in the darkness was fumbling around. The pleasure was nothing more than a paper tiger compared to this. Minutes tick by, or maybe it's hours before I finally float back to earth. My limbs feel heavy as I once again become aware of my surroundings.

He continues to stroke my clit with gentle fingers before he leans over my upper body and presses his lips against my scar. It's so tempting to wrap my arms around him and hold him close. I want to revel in the newfound pleasure he's opened my eyes to. Before I can work up the courage, he pulls away and the moment of intimacy vanishes into thin air.

I lie still as he rises to his feet and wonder if he'll shed his clothing.

Instead, his footsteps fade from the room, growing more distant. The door in the outer area opens before softly clicking back into place. Seconds pass as I lay paralyzed with the robe still gaping open.

Did he really…

Walk out the door and leave me?

After giving me the best orgasm of my life, which granted doesn't mean much, he just left?

I rip away the blindfold and blink, staring around me, looking for some sign of the man who was here.

Who ran his hands over my body.

Who pressed his lips against my scar.

A shiver dances down my spine at the intimate memories.

But there's nothing.

I slip from the bed and tighten the robe around my body before cinching the belt and beelining for my purse to rifle through it. My fingers wrap around my cell as it chimes with an incoming message. A bank notification pops up, announcing that ten grand has been deposited into my account.

I can only stare at the screen in disbelief.

We didn't even have sex.

Did he change his mind?

Was he unable to go through with it?

My heart clenches at the possibility.

Sure, he kissed my scars, but maybe, in the end, they repulsed him. I tuck an errant lock of hair behind my ear as a heavy pit settles at the bottom of my belly. I pull up the number I texted earlier and stare at it.

My thumbs hover over the keyboard.

It's so tempting to reach out.

Is that allowed?

Am I crossing some sort of invisible line?

I chew my lower lip and contemplate it for a minute or two.

I've already been paid for the first visit. No matter what, that'll take care of the majority of my bill.

But I need to know if he's changed his mind. If so, I'll have to figure out another way to come up with the money.

Because there's no way I can go through this again with another man. It was hard enough to work up my courage the first time around.

It's slowly that my thumbs slide over the keys until the question stares back at me. One that makes my heart hammer against my ribcage.

> Was it my scar?

I force myself to hit send, not wanting to chicken out and delete the message.

Before I can suck in a full breath, his response pops up.

> Absolutely not. Why would you think that?

I release the air trapped in my lungs until they're completely empty.

> Because it's ugly.

> There's nothing ugly about you. Every damn inch is beautiful.

I blink in surprise as a hot tear rolls down my cheek. Before it can drop onto the robe, I swipe it away with the back of my hand. Those ten words have all the chaotic emotion swirling within me dissolving into nothingness.

> Thank you.

> Looking forward to our next meeting.

My fingers linger over the miniature keyboard.

> Me, too.

The strangest part of this text interaction is that I actually mean it.

CHAPTER 16

WOLF

$\mathcal{M}$y gaze fastens onto her the moment she slips from the apartment building. When guilt pricks at me for forcing her into this situation, I quash it down. The need I feel for her is almost unbearable. It's been less than twenty-four hours since I laid my hands on her, and already my fingers tighten with the urge to do it again. Being that close, trailing my lips along her silky flesh, stroking every part of her body was even better than I imagined.

And getting her off?

Fuck.

My cock stirs with the memory.

It doesn't matter that I didn't come.

I'm not in a rush.

What I don't want to dwell on is whether these encounters will be enough to satiate me for the rest of my life. Now that I've gotten a small taste, I'm guessing it won't be.

One touch and I'm fucking addicted to the feel of her soft skin beneath my fingertips and lips.

And the taste of her honey...

Because you can damn well bet I licked the finger clean that had been buried deep inside her virgin pussy. My tongue darts out to swipe at my lower lip as if I can still taste her there.

I need to set up our second meeting immediately. As much as I want to draw this out and make it last, that's not possible.

I want her too damn much.

And it's doubtful that will change anytime soon.

Her expression remains shuttered behind a mask of indifference which might not seem like progress, but at least she's no longer scowling at me like I'm the devil himself come to drag her to hell.

It's all about baby steps, right?

She pops open the door and slips onto the seat before fastening the belt. "Hey."

"Hi." I shift the Mustang into first and then second before shooting out of the crowded lot. "You ready to do this?"

She draws in an unsteady breath before releasing it back into the atmosphere. "I think so."

My mind tumbles back to when we were thick as thieves. When I didn't think anything could separate us. "Didn't you take driver's education in high school?"

"Yeah."

As soon as the response leaves her lips, I'm slammed with the reason. It hangs heavy in the air like an impending storm, ready to wreak havoc.

Emotion swells in my throat as I clear it and try to find the right words to frame the question. "You never went back to, um, finish?"

She fidgets in the leather seat next to me. "I completed the classroom portion. It was the behind the wheel instruction that I had a hard time getting through. I just…"

Her voice trails off as she stares straight ahead.

That's all it takes for icy fingers to wrap around my heart and squeeze so tight that sucking in a full breath becomes agonizing.

Before the accident, both Miles and I would let her drive our cars on deserted roads. She never had an issue with it. I'm sure the snowy night and what followed has everything to do with the reason she doesn't have her license.

With nothing left to say, the remainder of the drive to an out-of-the-way church is made in suffocating silence. Once I reach the center of the deserted parking lot, I shift into neutral, allowing the vehicle to idle. I give her a quick refresher on the gears and instruct her on how to shift into first before slowly releasing the clutch while simultaneously stepping on the accelerator.

"Pretty simple, right?" When I glance over to gauge her reaction, I find Fallyn with her lower lip stuck between her teeth.

Her brows are pinched together in concentration as she regurgitates the information back to me.

"Yup, you got it. Ready to slide into the driver's seat and take a little spin?"

"Are you sure you want to do this?" Nerves vibrate in her voice.

I hate that she's riddled with so much anxiety.

And that I'm the cause of it.

"It'll be fine," I soothe. "For tonight, we'll stay in the lot."

"What happens if I break your car?"

One side of my lips hitch. "That's not going to happen. I promise. It's just like riding a bike."

She gives me a bit of side eye. "Are you forgetting about how many parked cars I crashed into while learning how to ride a two-wheeler?"

An unexpected chuckle slips free. Now that she's mentioned it, I do. The summer before first grade, she was a mess of scrapes and bruises from falling off her bike. Miles took off her training wheels and insisted that she learn even though she cried and said she wasn't ready. He wanted her to be able to keep up with us when we were riding around the neighborhood.

By the end of August, she was a pro.

Even though it's tempting to mention Miles and all the memories that flood to the surface, I fight the urge. A tentative peace has settled over us, and I'm loath to disturb it.

"You'll be fine," I repeat. "I'll be beside you the entire time."

"All right." With a jerk of the handle, she steps outside the vehicle, and we meet near the front of the hood.

Our feet stall as our eyes fasten. My fingers slip beneath her chin to tilt it upward until she's forced to hold my gaze.

That's all it takes for the air that surrounds us to shift.

To intensify with pent-up emotion.

"I won't let anything happen to you." There's a beat of silence. "Not again."

She sucks in a lungful of air before taking a step in retreat and slipping around me.

I do the same, settling next to her as the engine continues to idle.

Her hand flutters over the stick before settling on it. As it does, her breathing picks up speed as if her nerves are already jangled. If I weren't so finely attuned to her presence, I probably wouldn't have noticed the slight uptick in respiration.

This is how it's always been between us.

Maybe I don't know everything, but I can still read her.

There's something comforting about the realization.

She squeezes her eyes tightly closed. Her chest rises as she draws in a deep breath and holds it captive before releasing it back into the atmosphere.

I fucking hate that she carries around these mental scars from the accident. That it damaged her not only on the outside but inward as well. There's no way I'll ever be able to forgive myself for putting her through this.

I swivel toward her. "We can wait until you feel more ready. A week. Two weeks. A month. It doesn't have to be tonight."

It's so tempting to reach out and slide my fingers over her cheek.

Instead, I keep my hands to myself.

I'm terrified of pushing for too much, too soon, and scaring her away. I can't go back to a lonely life she's not a part of.

I spent almost five years like that and refuse to do it any longer.

She might not understand that everything changed between us yesterday, but I do. There's no turning back.

Her eyes spring open as she shakes her head. "No. I won't give them a reason to sell the Porsche."

"Then we'll take it nice and slow."

She jerks her chin into a tight nod.

When she remains motionless, I lay my hand over her smaller one on the stick before giving it a comforting squeeze. When she doesn't make a move to dislodge it, I say softly, "I'm going to talk you through it."

Her gaze flickers in my direction for just a second or two. "All right."

A mixture of relief and gratitude seeps into her expression, and it fills me with hope. There are flickers of our past within it.

"The first thing you need to do is familiarize yourself with the clutch, brake and accelerator."

She releases another steady breath before the engine revs.

"See? You found the accelerator. Next time, when you start the engine, you'll press the clutch all the way down."

I scooch closer until I can check out the positioning of her feet. She's wearing well-worn white Chucks.

"We're going to slide the gear into first." With a nod, I guide her hand over the stick. "That's it. Now, you're going to slowly release—"

When she removes her foot from the clutch too quickly, the car stalls. Her fingers tighten around both the steering wheel and the stick until the knuckles turn bone white.

My voice stays gentle, not wanting to make the situation worse. "It's fine, Fallyn. No big deal. Let's try again."

A puff of air escapes from her. "This is more difficult than I remember."

"It's just going to take some time for it to come back to you, but it'll happen. And then you'll get your license and Miles' car will be yours. Just keep the end goal in mind, and don't get frustrated."

"I'll try not to."

I give her a couple of seconds to pull herself together. "Ready to try again?"

With a sigh, she jerks her head into a reluctant nod.

"Start up the engine. With your foot on the clutch, you're going to shift into first gear and then slowly lift your foot as you press down on the accelerator with the other. Once the car begins to move forward, release the clutch."

I keep my hand firmly wrapped around her warm fingers as I guide her into gear.

We get a dozen or so feet before the car stalls, and she groans.

This goes on for about twenty minutes. I can tell that she's getting discouraged by her inability to smoothly shift the car into first and then second without it dying by the way her lips have flattened into a thin line.

"You're doing really well," I tell her, attempting to keep the situation positive.

"Liar," she grumbles. "I'm terrible at this."

"Like everything else, it just takes practice. Do you want to take a break or keep going?"

She glances at me. "Just a little bit longer?"

"Sure. No problem," I say easily.

Fallyn doesn't realize that I'd sit here all damn night if that's what she wanted.

It takes another fifteen minutes, but we finally get to the point where she's able to maneuver the parking lot in circles. She gradually widens them until we reach the outer edges of the pavement. The shift from first to second and then third is a bit choppy before she attempts to downshift.

Then she repeats the process all over again.

Each time gets a little bit smoother.

I'm impressed.

"You're doing really great!"

A tiny smile curls the edges of her lips as her gaze stays trained on the windshield. When another vehicle enters the parking lot, her fingers clench both the wheel and gear. I give her hand a slight squeeze, hoping to calm her nerves.

I glance at the blue mini-van. "There's no need to worry. They're on the other side of the lot. Just keep going."

When she hesitates, panic flashing across her face, I murmur, "You're fine. We're not in any danger of having an accident."

"I know." A fine tremble weaves its way through her voice.

"Okay. Good."

She downshifts before slowly rolling to a stop and then moving the gear into neutral. Once the vehicle comes to a standstill, she releases a steady puff of air.

"I did it." There's so much pride and wonder in those three little words.

"You were amazing. It won't be long before you're on the road."

Her muscles loosen as she collapses on top of the steering wheel, her forehead resting against the middle.

"Fallyn?" Icy cold tendrils of panic rush through my veins.

When her shoulders begin to shake, I realize she's crying.

Oh god.

I really hate female tears. Under normal circumstances, I'd slip away unnoticed, breathing a quick sigh of relief as I make my getaway. There's no way I can do that with Fallyn. Her tears have always had the power to make my heart feel like it's being squeezed in a vise. All I want to do is fix whatever is causing her pain and heartache. That's always been my gut response where she's concerned.

Decades later, nothing has changed.

I go with instinct and slip my arms around her ribcage, hauling her out of the driver's seat and onto my lap before rearranging her so that her breasts are flattened against my chest. It's only when she's situated on my thighs that I come to my senses and realize exactly what I've done and the intimate way I'm holding her. There's no damn way she won't put up a fight. The last thing she wants is for me to offer comfort.

For all intents and purposes, I'm still the enemy.

And what I stole from her was unforgivable.

It's a shock when her warm weight melts into me before she buries her face in the crook of my neck until her tears drip onto my exposed skin. My arms tighten around her, pressing her as close as possible until there's not a whisper of air between us. I squeeze my eyes closed and inhale a giant breath into my lungs.

The rosemary and mint scent of her hair is a straight shot to my dick.

"Please don't cry," I whisper. "I never could stand the sight of your tears."

Her shoulders shake harder as she releases all of the pent-up emotion lying dormant within her soul. It kills me that there's not a damn thing I can do about it. If there were a way to leech it from her body and take it onto myself, I'd do it in a heartbeat.

But that's not possible.

No matter how much I might wish otherwise.

Our history is long and tightly entwined.

Most of it is good.

Wonderful, even.

The worst parts are heartbreaking.

Devastating.

And nothing will ever change that.

There's no way to obliterate our past.

I keep her wrapped up tight in my arms. It's not until she shifts and freezes that I realize my dick is rock hard. For a handful of seconds, neither of us dare to move a muscle.

Barely am I breathing.

If I'm lucky, she'll pretend she doesn't feel the insistent press against the V between her legs. That thought is all it takes for me to remember what her pussy tasted like when I licked her sweetness from my fingers.

If it's possible, I grow even harder.

It wouldn't take much for me to explode in my jeans.

After what happened in the hotel suite, I wasn't even able to make it out of the building without slipping into the bathroom and rubbing one out. Then I got home and did it again.

Fuck.

Those thoughts are in no way helping matters. In fact, they're only making the situation worse.

When she shifts, sliding against my groin, I groan. "Fallyn…"

My voice comes out sounding gravelly, as if it's been roughed up with sandpaper.

Her hands slip between us before she presses the palms against my chest and pushes away just enough for her wide-eyed gaze to lock on mine. Her eyes are shiny from the tears and filled with confusion. Her dark lashes are spiked with wetness, making them look longer and thicker. The fucked-up part is that she's never looked more beautiful.

Even when she was laid out before me, naked, legs spread invitingly.

The mask had obscured her eyes, making it impossible to know what she was thinking.

"You should…I need to move," she murmurs.

It's on the tip of my tongue to argue, but I'm terrified of pushing for too much.

I draw in a deep breath, filling my lungs with fresh air before trying to wrangle all of these out-of-control feelings back into submission.

It doesn't work.

My hands lock around her waist as I maneuver her from my lap. Then I pop open the passenger side door and set her on the seat as I jerk to my feet. Her eyes stay pinned to mine before dropping to my groin and widening.

A strangled gasp escapes from her.

I don't have to glance down to realize what's captured her attention. The thick erection I'm sporting feels as if it'll explode from my jeans.

Or maybe explode in my jeans.

Unsure what to say, I mutter, "Sorry."

Then I turn away and adjust myself. Not that there's any way to rearrange my boner to make it any less noticeable as I slam the car door, shutting her inside the Mustang.

CHAPTER 17

FALLYN

My shocked gaze stays locked on Wolf as he stalks around the hood of the vehicle. Waves of heat radiate from my cheeks until it feels as if I'm moments away from self-combusting.

In light of the circumstances, that might be for the best.

Then I wouldn't have to deal with the aftermath.

Because there is no way to ignore *that*.

Holy crap.

Obviously, I don't have an overabundance of experience where penises are concerned, but my guess is that his is huge. It's almost a shock when arousal pools in my core, and I have to shift, rubbing my inner thighs together in an attempt to stymie the need coursing through me.

Even though he swung away, I know he was adjusting himself. There's no way for me to do the same. Although, I have the feeling there's only one thing that will help with the issue that's popped up…

All right. Bad reference.

With a jolt, I stare straight ahead as he slides in beside me. Energy snaps and crackles in the air that surrounds us. There has never been a time when I haven't been aware of Wolf Westerville but never so much as at this very moment.

I have no idea what to say or do to ease the escalating tension that intensifies with every passing second. My heart thuds against my ribcage as he shifts into first gear and then second before revving the engine and speeding out of the parking lot.

"Do you mind if we stop for something to eat?" He flicks a look my way.

"Oh." Damn. All I can think about is getting away from him before anything else happens. "I, um, was thinking that you could just drop—"

"I came straight from hockey practice. I'm starving. Any moment, my stomach is going to eat itself."

As if to punctuate those comments, his belly lets loose a loud growl.

Guilt suffuses me. "Sure."

I almost wince as the word pops free.

Unable to help myself, I glance at his lap to see if he's still hard.

"Fallyn?"

The sound of his rough voice jerks my attention back to his. The smirk curving the edges of his lips tells me that my perusal didn't go unnoticed.

That's all it takes for heat to scald my cheeks.

Just kill me now.

"What?" I squeak.

"I asked if you wanted to go to Harvey's Eats and Treats. It's a little out of the way on the edge of town, but they've got the best burgers."

"Sure," I mumble, not caring where we go. I just want to get this over with. "Whatever you want."

The remainder of the ride is made in stifling silence, both of us lost in the whirl of our own thoughts. Just when I'm about to tell him that I've changed my mind, he pulls the Mustang into a crowded parking lot.

The place looks like a retro fifties diner.

"You'll like it. The atmosphere is fun, and the food is pretty good."

We exit the car, and Wolf waits for me on the sidewalk before heading toward the entrance. Once we reach the door, he holds it open. My gaze slides over the space. I realize that my first impression wasn't wrong.

It's like stepping back in time.

The floor has black and white checkered tiles, and the ceiling is covered with shiny silver tin. Framed photographs of old Hollywood stars interspersed with Coca-Cola memorabilia decorate the walls. The booths are bright red leather with shiny white linoleum tops. Music from decades ago pours through the speakers.

We slide into a red vinyl booth at the back of the restaurant, away from the crowd. With another glance around the space, I realize that there are a lot of teenagers. They're talking and laughing. Flirting with one another. My mind unconsciously tumbles back to high school when the three of us used to hang out at a place with a similar vibe.

I haven't been back since…

Well, let's just say that it's been a while.

A thick lump of emotion swells in my throat. It takes effort to clear it away as I pick up the oversized plastic menu and stare sightlessly at it.

"How did you find this place?" I ask, trying to distract myself from the memories that push in at the edges of my brain.

It's not close to campus at all.

Wolf watches me carefully before shrugging. Ripping his eyes away, he glances around the bustling space. "It kind of reminds me of—"

"Sinclare's," I finish quietly.

With a nod, his expression sobers. "Yeah. I found it freshman year. It was kind of nice to come here and get away from campus. Anytime I crave a burger, I swing by."

It's almost a relief when a young girl who looks like she's probably still in high school stops by our table. She's wearing a pale pink retro waitress uniform that clings to her curves.

One glance at the guy seated across from me has her upping the wattage of her smile until it's blinding. "Hey, Wolf! Haven't seen you around for a couple of weeks. How's the season going? We've all been rooting for you."

His expression becomes inscrutable as he leans back against the booth. "Thanks, appreciate it."

"Always!" She holds his gaze for another second or two before turning to me. "Hi, what can I get for you?"

I glance down at the menu. "I'll have a burger loaded with the works, minus the onions. Along with an order of cheese fries and a chocolate milkshake." Another wave of nostalgia crashes over me.

The waitress stares at me for a beat longer than necessary before her attention returns to Wolf. "I suppose you'll have your usual?"

The slow smile that spreads across his face, making his eyes crinkle at the corners, is like a punch to the gut and nearly steals my breath away. It seems to have a similar effect on our server.

"You guessed it."

"I'll be back in a minute with two glasses of water." She glances around the brightly lit space before dropping her voice. "Even though it's crowded, I'll put a rush on the order." She gives him a wink before taking off.

"Looks like you have a real fan," I say lightly, not wanting to admit, especially to myself, that a kernel of jealousy is burning a hole at the bottom of my belly.

Wolf is a hot guy with his buzzed hair, green eyes, and chiseled muscles. Even beneath his clothing, the cut of his body is obvious. Add in the colorful tattoos that peek from the collar of his black sweatshirt, and he's catnip for the female species. I haven't even gotten to the part about him being the starting goaltender for the Western Wildcats and no doubt bound for the pros.

As much as I've tried to ignore his larger-than-life presence since arriving on campus freshman year, that would be impossible. He's always been there, lurking in the shadows of my mind.

Even as I sit across from him, I'm hyperaware of the handsome man he's grown into.

I get the feeling that he notices everything.

Every shift of my body.

Every unsteady breath that fills my lungs.

Nothing escapes his attention.

Our proximity is disconcerting.

It's impossible to believe that there was a time when I was drawn to him, couldn't get close enough, wanted to bask in his presence 24/7.

Now the opposite is true.

Or maybe I only wish that were the case.

The lines I'd thought were so clearly drawn now feel blurred. Both my thoughts and feelings are a chaotic, confused mess.

He shrugs.

The gesture is casual, but the way he watches me is anything but. It feels predatory in nature.

Possessive.

I shift and blurt out the first thing that comes to mind, only wanting to break the escalating tension before we choke on it. "Thanks for the lesson."

"It wasn't a problem. I would have taught you years ago if you'd asked."

"I wasn't ready at that point," I admit. I'm not even sure I'm ready now. But what choice is there? I won't allow my parents to sell Miles' Porsche. He loved it way too much.

So, I'll learn.

Even if that means spending time alone with Wolf.

With a nod, his expression softens. It's as if he can read my thoughts as they pop into my brain, and I hate it. Hate that keeping secrets from him is impossible.

We shouldn't be so finely attuned to one another after all these years of separation.

Before he can continue the conversation, the perky blonde waitress arrives with our plates. Another girl trails behind her with milkshakes. She stares at Wolf with a worshipful look in her eyes. Color scorches her cheeks the moment she sets the ice cream drinks down in front of us.

He flashes a charming smile that's capable of melting the panties off a nun. "Thanks."

She sucks in a harsh breath before saying in a rush, "You're welcome, Wolf Westerville."

"Enjoy," the blonde says, cutting off the younger girl before she can word vomit just how much she loves him.

Because it's written all over her adoring face. If I squinted hard enough, I'd find little pink and red hearts dancing above her head.

Instead of rolling my eyes, I focus on my plate. The burger is massive, with all the toppings and fries are piled high next to it. My mouth waters. Only now do I realize how hungry I am. I haven't eaten anything except for a protein bar before running out the door this morning.

I glance at Wolf, wondering what his usual is. A jolt slides through me when I realize we have the exact same thing down to the chocolate milkshakes.

A grin flashes across his face. "Just like old times."

Air leaks painfully from my lungs.

He's not wrong.

After school, the three of us would end up at a diner just like this. My brother would order a basket of chicken fingers and onion rings, while Wolf and I always had cheeseburgers loaded with all the toppings (minus the onions), fries, and chocolate shakes.

When I fail to respond, he mutters, "Sorry. It's hard not to bring up the past. I think about it all the time."

Same.

That's all it takes for my appetite to pull a vanishing act as I stare at the burger with a thick lump wedged in my throat.

I force my gaze to his and blurt out the one question that has been circling around in the back of my head for years. "Why didn't you come to see me in the hospital?"

Color drains from his cheeks as he strains forward, hinging at the waist. Somberness fills his eyes as he searches mine.

Our dinner, which had seemed so tempting seconds ago, is now long forgotten.

"I did, Fallyn. I was there every fucking day, but your parents wouldn't allow me anywhere near you. Or the funeral. They wouldn't even let me say goodbye."

I shake my head as my brows pinch together.

No. That can't be right.

"They told me you didn't want to see me. That you were upset about what happened and thought it best to cut ties so we could all heal."

His upper lip curls as he reaches across the table until his hand can settle on mine, engulfing it. "That's a lie."

My brain somersaults at this new information. "I don't believe you. My parents wouldn't do that. They knew how upset I was. Lost."

His shoulders hunch as he drags a hand through his short strands and glances away. Bitterness creeps into his tone. "We both know that Hugo and Eleanor never liked me. And they certainly didn't think I was good enough to be friends with Miles, let alone you. Immediately following the accident, your number was disconnected, and your social media was wiped. When I showed up at your house, your parents slammed the door in my face. Once you recovered enough to go back to school, they pulled you out and sent you to a small private academy."

He leans closer. It's as if he's getting ready to leap across the table. What he'll do after that, I have no idea.

Or maybe I do.

It's difficult to believe that he could be telling the truth. Or that my parents would go to such great lengths to keep me away from him. I know that they distanced themselves from the Westervilles after the accident. But before that...I don't know. I guess I wasn't aware of the undercurrents between the adults.

Or...maybe Wolf is lying.

Attempting to absolve himself of any responsibility.

The part that unsettles me most is that he's right—my number was changed. My phone was crushed in the accident, and when they gave me a replacement, it was a different one. Their excuse was that the cell company wasn't able to transfer it. At the time, I was so devastated and lost that I didn't give it much thought.

How could I care about a stupid cell number when my brother was dead?

It's also true that my social media was deleted, but only because everyone was posting about the accident and what happened to Miles.

So, I took a long break from it.

Once I felt strong enough to return to school, I transferred to a smaller one. I had so much anxiety and depression to work through. Fewer people hovering around felt safer.

How could I possibly walk the same halls without Miles by my side?

Or Wolf.

By then it had become obvious that he wasn't going to reach out.

Maybe a fresh start isn't what I wanted, but my parents convinced me that it's what I needed.

And I didn't have the energy to fight them.

Not after everything we'd been through as a family.

Not after encouraging Miles to sneak out of the house so I could spend time with Wolf. He might have been the one driving, but I harbor my own guilt about that night.

"I go and see him all the time," he whispers, drawing my attention back to him.

Hot tears prick my eyes. Unwilling to let them fall, I blink them back. "I miss him so much. Even now, there are times when I forget he's gone. Something will happen, and he's the first person I want to share the news with."

It's only when Wolf's strong fingers tighten around mine that I realize he's still holding them. "I feel the same way."

As gut wrenching as this conversation is, there's also relief to be found in it. Even though the specter of Miles hangs heavily over all our lives, my parents refuse to talk about him.

All the good times we had as a family.

Without the reminder, there's just the bad.

The part that came after.

The one filled with heartache and heartbreak.

"Nothing will ever be the same," I whisper.

"No, it won't. But it doesn't have to be like this either. We can find happiness again, Fallyn. You deserve that. You can't live in the shadow of his death forever. What kind of life is that?"

I rip my gaze away and stare out the picture window to the street beyond. Darkness has fallen, and the streetlights now illuminate the shadows.

"It's difficult when my parents refuse to move forward." I pause for a moment before adding, "My father is obsessed with destroying your family."

His normally strong shoulders slump under the heaviness of my words. "I'm sorry. I wish like hell that we'd never gone out that night."

Even though I don't want to, I slip my hand free from his, severing the physical connection before the bond can grow any stronger.

I force myself to say in an icy tone, "Nothing you say or do will change the past."

The misery that floods his expression is like a knife to the heart. "You're right. There's no way to bring him back to us."

CHAPTER 18

FALLYN

It's been a couple of days since my conversation with Wolf. His words continue to buzz around at the back of my brain. And nothing makes it stop. Every time I talk with my parents, it's on the tip of my tongue to bring it up, but I keep biting back the questions.

What I'm most afraid of is that he's telling the truth. I'm terrified that they've been lying to me all these years, and I'm nowhere near ready to go there. Our family has been put through the wringer. It's doubtful we could take much more before splintering apart. I'm not sure there would be a way to repair that kind of damage.

Confirmation of what he said would also change the way I feel about him. And I'm nowhere near ready for that, either.

Somehow, my life has become even more complicated.

When I left for work ten minutes ago, I'd hoped he wouldn't be waiting outside. What I need is space to work through my thoughts and feelings. I can't do that when he's around. He clouds them, turning everything hazy.

It wasn't a surprise to find him waiting at the curb. Now that he's forced himself back into my life, he continues to press in at the edges, refusing to give me the time I need.

On the drive to Slap Shotz, he asked a few questions to break up the silence, and I reluctantly responded.

Relief spirals through me when he swings into the back lot. The moment he shifts into neutral, my fingers wrap around the handle to pop open the door. Just as I'm about to slide from the Mustang, Wolf's palm settles on my thigh. Even though his grip isn't tight, his fingers burn a hole through the denim, scorching the flesh beneath. I glance at it before forcing my gaze to his.

"I'll be back after the game."

I search his eyes, shocked by the intensity that brews like an impending storm within the green depths. It's as if all hell will break loose any second. I'm reluctant to admit that it's been building between us ever since he pulled me onto his lap after our first driving lesson. I get the feeling that he's trying to do the right thing and control himself but it's growing more difficult with the passing of each day.

The need for distance thrums through me as I shove open the door.

His fingers tighten around my thigh, halting my escape. "Aren't you going to wish me luck?"

"You don't need luck," I force myself to say in a voice that doesn't betray how unnerved I am by his presence. "You have talent."

Ever since he was a kid, Wolf's natural ability on the ice stood out and got him noticed by both coaches and scouts.

His gaze continues to burn into mine. That alone is enough to have my breath hitching. When he sucks the corner of his lip into his mouth, my attention drops to the movement, and it's like a punch of desire straight to my core.

"I need to go," I whisper.

With that, I slip from the vehicle. As the frigid air hits my lungs, I inhale a big breath, hoping it'll be enough to clear my thoughts. My brain feels foggy, and that has everything to do with the guy in the car who continues to watch my every move. I don't have to glance at him to know that his eyes are pinned to me.

I can feel the heat of them.

With my purse clutched against my chest, I take a hasty step in retreat. "Good luck."

He cocks his head, eyes glinting. "Thought I didn't need it."

I take another step. It's the only thing capable of settling my racing heart. With the hungry look that fills his eyes, he reminds me of an animal on the prowl. "You don't, but I'm sending all my good vibes your way."

His expression softens until he looks more like the boy I grew up with. Not the handsome man he's become. "Thanks. I'll catch you in a couple of hours."

A shiver slides through me at the promise that fills his voice.

With a quick jerk of my head, I swing around and hightail it toward the back of the brick building before pushing through the metal door. I say a quick hello to the bouncer. Gerry is a mountain of a man with no neck to speak of and biceps that border on massive. There's no way I could wrap both hands around them. I know this because, much to his amusement, I attempted it the other night. He claims to be au natural, but I don't know how that's possible.

I wave to Sully, who's behind the bar, and Nathan, one of the barbacks. There's only a handful of people dotted around the space. As the night wears on, it'll only grow more crowded. Once the game is over, people will flood in, packing the place to the gills, waiting for the team to arrive.

So, I'll enjoy the peace and quiet while I can.

The last time I worked, it was so busy that I didn't realize the night was over until Sully flicked on the lights.

The tips have been surprisingly good. I didn't expect that from the number of college students that frequent the joint.

Will it pay my tuition bill?

Nope, not even close.

I'm using it to pay for rent and groceries so that my parents can't come back and tell me there's no longer room in the budget. Or that they want to sell Miles' car to help me out. As far as I'm concerned, that's off the table.

Added bonus, I feel good about being able to pay my own way and becoming more independent from my parents. There's a sense of accomplishment I've never experienced before.

I set aside those thoughts as customers trickle through the door. Most are college students who want to watch the game on one of the big screens and drink beer while they're doing it. As I bounce between the bar and my tables with a tray full of orders, my attention is continually drawn to one of the many television screens. It would be impossible not to watch Wolf.

Before the game, he went through a series of stretches in preparation. He's always been tall and broad in the shoulders. Decked out in all his padding, he looks even more menacing as he slides back and forth, making sure to stay limber.

Were my eyes glued to him the entire time he was warming up?

Guilty.

One covert glance around the bar proved that I wasn't the only one. Quite a number of girls found it necessary to wipe the drool from their chins.

Me included.

The crowd continues to thicken as the game gets underway. Raucous cheers go up when the first goal is scored against the visiting team. I watch as Ford Hamilton skates back to the blue line like it's no big deal. He stares toward the packed stands, and I'd lay odds that he's looking for his girlfriend. Those two are always all over each other.

And I love it.

Love that Carina found her happily ever after.

Especially with the way she devours romance novels.

Huh. Maybe that's what's missing from my life.

Seems to have also worked for Juliette McKinnon and Ryder McAdams as well.

I shake those thoughts away as a table full of guys catches my attention, and I take off in their direction. It's been a lot of shots and pitchers of beer. On game nights, both are half price. Which makes for a lot of drunk customers who think they're slick with the pickup lines.

Newsflash—they're not.

I haven't reached the level of annoyance, but it's slowly building.

Last week, during one of our shifts, Erin kneed a guy in the junk. As soon as she was done, Gerry stepped in and ran him out the backdoor by the scruff of his neck. Sully added to it by banning the jerk for life. It makes me feel better to know that the people I work with have my back in case anything happens.

A flash of caramel colored hair catches my attention from the corner of my eye.

"Hey!" Britt says with a wave.

As soon as she's close enough, I pull her in for a quick hug. "I didn't know you'd be stopping by tonight."

She jiggles the paper bag in her hand. "I can't stay long. My Aunt Mary baked a lasagna and packaged up a few pieces." She nods toward Sully. "My uncle brought it with him."

"Aww, that's so sweet. I bet you enjoy having family in the area."

"It's really nice. We've lived in California for the past ten years, so I haven't had the chance to spend much time with them until now."

I glance at my boss. "Sully's a great guy."

"He's the best." She nods toward the exit. "I should probably get going before the team gets here."

I pull a face. "I'm not looking forward to it."

She knows that there's one specific hockey player I've been trying to steer clear of.

"I bet. I'll catch you later," she says before taking off.

Unable to help myself, my gaze flickers to the television, and a wave of nostalgia crashes over me. Ever since I was five years old, I would sit in the stands and watch Wolf's and Miles' games. I've been at this school for two and a half years and have only attended one hockey game. And that was only because Madden made a deal with Viola when he was trying to win her back.

There was no way I could let her go alone.

Even after all these years, it was difficult to sit in the stands and watch Wolf on the ice without Miles. While Wolf has been a goalie for as long as I can remember, my brother was a defenseman. He took out anyone who skated too close to the crease. The two of them always played well together, feeding off each other's energy. It was as if they could read each other's minds.

"He's a real hottie, isn't he?" Erin says with a lusty sigh.

I drag my gaze away from the screen and jerk my shoulders, hoping the gesture comes off as indifferent. "He's all right." Then I tack on, "If that's what you're into."

She snorts as a wide grin lights up her face. "Ah, yeah. I'm totally into his brand of handsome." She glances around the bar. "And so are half the hoes in this place."

I can't help but reluctantly look at the girls that now fill the tables with their skintight jeans and cleavage bearing tops. More than a handful are wearing shirts with Wolf's name and number stamped across their backs or breasts. It's not like I haven't seen girls walking around campus decked out in his gear, but for some reason, in this moment, it eats at me.

And that bothers me more than anything.

Unwilling to dwell on the reason, I shove Wolf from my head and point toward a group of students who look like they could use a refill. "I'd better check on my tables," I mumble.

A rousing cheer goes up, and I glance at the television just in time to see Wolf pop up from his knees. A shiver dances down my spine as I stare at the screen.

"He's really on fire tonight," Erin says.

The next hour is filled with more of the same. Wolf's goaltending abilities are all anyone can talk about, along with his potential NHL career. By the time the team walks in after the game, the bar is packed, and my nerves are stretched taut. I feel the moment his gaze settles on me.

How could I not when a shiver races down my spine, and the tiny hairs at the nape of my neck stand to attention?

After all these years, Wolf Westerville has done the unthinkable.

Within a matter of weeks, he's managed to chip away at my defenses, and I have no idea how long it'll be before he obliterates what's left of them.

What I do know is that it's scary as hell.

CHAPTER 19

WOLF

The moment I push through the back door and into the dimly lit bar, my gaze scans the thick crowd with the need to find her. Even during the game, when I'm normally laser focused on tending the goal, Fallyn was front and center in my brain. All I could think about was her watching me on one of the big screens.

Would I have preferred for her to be in the stands cheering me on?

Fuck yeah, but I also knew that wasn't going to happen.

At least while working, she'd be forced to watch the game. Every time I saved a goal, the fans in the arena screamed my name and sang my praises. It only pumped me up. I didn't want her to walk more than ten feet without someone mentioning me.

And you know what?

I played the best fucking game of my life with twenty-six saves. Only two goals managed to sneak past me.

We won.

The moment my eyes lock on her, a sizzle of electricity arrows through me, nearly singeing me alive. The sensation is almost enough to stop me in my tracks. There's never been a girl who has affected me like this.

And it's doubtful there ever will be again.

For as long as I can remember, there's only been Fallyn.

She was my everything back then.

And she's my everything now.

Her inky black hair is pulled up into a ponytail, allowing me to glimpse the graceful line of her neck. Images of kissing my way down the long column pop into my head. My mind tumbles back to the other day in the Mustang when I'd dragged her onto my lap and buried my face in the crook of it. She smelled so damn good.

That memory is enough to have my dick stirring to life.

A smile tugs at her lips as she cocks a hip and nods at the guy who's chatting her up. The expression is like a gut punch. Almost enough to have me doubling over. It's been way too long since she looked at me like that. Once upon a time, all her smiles had been reserved for me. It was like pure sunshine in a bottle, and all I wanted to do was bask in it.

Jealousy roars through my veins, igniting my blood.

Unable to stop myself, I glare at the guy she's waiting on. He's leaning toward her, attempting to close the distance between them.

I snort.

Yeah, that's not going to happen.

Before I realize it, I'm on the move, plowing my way through the sea of students. Hands reach out, patting me on the shoulder, but I don't bother glancing their way.

How can I?

I'm unable to rip my attention away from Fallyn.

Or the douche who's under the delusion that his flirting will get him anywhere with this girl.

Move on to greener pastures, dude. Because it isn't happening here.

The moment I step behind her, my hands settle possessively on the tops of her shoulders before tugging her against my chest. It's only when she's in my arms that everything settles inside me, and I can breathe again. Even with the overpowering smell of hops and barley that permeates the air, I'm able to scent the rosemary mint shampoo she used on her hair. It's the same as it was when we were teenagers, and there's something calming about it as it slyly wraps around me, cocooning me in familiarity.

The dude attempting to shoot his shot frowns before flicking an irritated look my way. That one second of recognition is all it takes for him to blink and straighten on the chair like someone just shoved a two-by-four up his ass.

It's the precise reaction I was going for.

"Hey, Wolf. That was one hell of a game!"

"Thanks." My fingers curl into the skin beneath the black V-neck Slap Shotz T-shirt she's wearing. I hate how it hugs her body like a second skin, showing off every delectable curve.

Well…maybe that's not altogether true.

I actually love it. What I hate are all the dickheads who are leering, thinking they have a snowball's chance in hell of taking her home at the end of the night.

My grip tightens as I force her so close that her ass is nestled against my groin.

When an uncomfortable silence falls over the table, Fallyn clears her throat, attempting to break the awkwardness.

It doesn't work.

"I'll be right back with that pitcher of beer."

My hands drift down her arms and lock around her bicep before she can attempt to get away.

"I need to talk with you," I whisper against her ear.

A delicate shiver slides through her at my proximity. "Can't you see that I'm working?"

"It'll only take a moment."

Not bothering to wait for a response, I steer her toward a darkened hallway. We pass by the bathrooms before turning the corner where Sully's office is located. Across from it, there's a small storage room. Only then do I back her up until her spine hits the wall, and I'm able to cage her in with my bigger body.

I jerk my head toward the bar. "Were those assholes hitting on you?" My voice comes out sounding gruffer than intended.

With a lift of her chin, she straightens to her full height as a spark of anger ignites in her blue depths. "Probably."

"There's no *probably* about it," I growl. I swallow up the small amount of space that separates us, making it necessary for her to crane her neck in order to hold my gaze. "They shouldn't be harassing you. You're there to serve drinks and nothing more. I'll talk to Sully about it tonight."

"Please tell me that you're not serious." She shakes her head. "There's no need for you to get involved. Those guys were harmless. They were being friendly and nothing more. If there's a problem, I'll talk to Sully about it. I don't need you to fight my battles. I'm more than capable of doing it myself. I've had five years to practice."

My muscles tense as I inhale a sharp breath. Hurt thrums through me. I hate the reminder that I wasn't there for her.

When I remain silent, unsure what to say, she presses her palms against my chest and gives me a shove. Even though I've got muscle on top of muscle and weigh a solid seventy pounds more than she does, I fall back a step. The little bit of space she created is just enough for her to slip away.

Without another glance, she stalks toward the main area of the bar.

A potent concoction of desperation and jealousy spirals through me. It's a lethal combination, and the only logical explanation for the reason I blurt, "Miles wouldn't like it."

She screeches to a halt as her shoulders stiffen. She throws an icy glare over her shoulder. "Miles isn't here, now is he?"

Her words rob the air from my lungs. With that, she disappears around the corner.

No matter what I do or say, it's always the wrong thing. I'm no closer to chipping away at the armor that protects her than I was a few weeks ago.

It's so fucking tempting to smash my fist into the wall, but deep inside, I know it won't do a damn bit of good.

It won't change the past or anything between us.

CHAPTER 20

FALLYN

Four hours later and I'm still shaking with unspent anger. How fucking *dare* he bring up Miles!

Even thinking about my brother is like a knife through the heart. That's all it takes for pain to radiate throughout my entire being until it pulses with a life of its own. It's impossible to imagine a time when that won't be the case.

I avoid Wolf and the table of hockey players he's parked with for the remainder of my shift and allow Erin to wait on them. From the corner of my eye, I watch a ridiculous number of girls buzz around him like drunken bees, trying to capture his attention. Maybe if they did, he'd stop staring at me like I'm the only thing he's cognizant of. No matter where I go, his broody gaze is sure to follow.

It's a relief when Sully flicks on the overhead lights and tells everyone that they don't need to go home, but they can't stay here. Just like all the other nights I've been working, everyone groans. I think it's become more of a joke than anything else. A few guys mention an after party happening near campus and try to convince me to make an appearance. They joke about being the ones to serve me a beverage of my choice. Instead of giving them a flat-out refusal, I shrug and remain noncommittal.

After working a seven-hour shift, I have zero interest in hanging out or partying. I'm exhausted. What I'm looking forward to is taking a quick shower and falling face first into bed. The guy who was hitting on me earlier sidles up before glancing around.

"So…are you and Wolf a, you know, *thing?*"

I shake my head, wanting to quash that rumor that spread through the bar tonight like wildfire. "Nope."

Skepticism fills his narrowed eyes. "Are you sure about that? Because it kind of seemed like—"

"He's a family friend and nothing more."

With a nod, his muscles loosen. A small smile quirks the corners of his lips. "Okay, good. He's not a guy I want to piss off, you know what I mean?"

"Yup, I do," I say with an aggravated sigh.

Even though he's kind of cute with blond hair that falls over his dark brown eyes, the way he's been skulking about, glancing over my shoulder as if Wolf will pop up at any moment and take a chunk out of him with his teeth is enough to nip any possible interest I might have been feeling in the bud. Not that there was much to begin with.

He shifts from one foot to the other before raking one hand through his thick strands. "I was wondering if you might want to get together sometime. Maybe go to a hockey game or see a movie. Whatever you want."

The muscles in my belly contract with dread.

"Umm…"

He's not the first guy to ask me out tonight, and I've shot them all down with a pleasant smile pasted across my lips. "Thanks, but I'm taking a break from the dating scene." I clear my throat when he continues to stare and force myself to add, "Bad breakup."

He sidles closer and drops his voice. "We can just smash if that's more your style. I don't mind."

Ewww.

I take a hasty step in retreat, wanting more distance between us. And even then, it's not enough.

"Sorry, no." My voice grows cold.

"Oh."

Not wanting this convo to devolve any further, I point toward the door. "You should probably get moving before Gerry assists you with that." Although, after his last comment, I wouldn't necessarily mind watching him get run out of the bar.

His eyes fill with concern before he shoots a frown toward the back door. "That dude is a musclebound freak."

"Actually, he's really nice," I snap. I've had just about enough of this guy. My mistake was correcting the rumor he heard. Maybe I'm safer if these asshats assume I'm with Wolf. A shiver scampers across my skin. Although, the last thing I want people to think is that I'm one of Wolf Westerville's puck bunnies.

No thanks.

That thought pisses me off even more than this guy assuming he can fuck me and flee the scene of the crime.

What a jackass.

He needs to do everyone a favor and exit stage left.

Pronto.

Or I'll run him out of the bar myself.

When my gaze snags Gerry's, he arches a brow in silent inquiry before cracking his knuckles. His show of muscle is enough to dissolve my previous irritation.

"You need any help over there?" His deep voice reverberates across the space now that the music has been turned off.

Eyes widening, the guy who'd just propositioned me disappears without so much as another word.

A smile trembles around the corners of my lips as I shake my head. "Nope, it's all good. Thanks."

"No problem, sweetheart. All you gotta do is let me know when someone is bothering you." There's a pause before he adds, "The crowd was pretty tame tonight. Not one single fight broke out."

"I'm sure you'll get a chance to knock a few skulls together tomorrow," I joke.

He cracks the muscles in his non-existent neck. "Hope so."

As the crowd continues to thin, I search for Viola and Madden.

They were here earlier with the rest of the hockey players. I'm hoping to catch a ride home with them instead of Wolf.

After our earlier convo, I don't want to spend any more time with him.

My gaze slides around the room until it locks on the one person I was trying to avoid. He's leaning against the bar as a couple of my coworkers, and Sully, yap his ear off. His thickly corded arms are crossed over his broad chest as his attention stays pinned to mine. He's wearing a gray T-shirt that fits him to perfection. The way his biceps bulge is enough to have my mouth turning cottony.

One dark brow slinks upward as our gazes stay fastened. That's all it takes for heat to reluctantly burst to life in my core. The guy has an effect on me even when I'd rather he not. I stand frozen in place, unable to break free from the spell he's woven around me. It's only when he crooks a finger in my direction that I snap out of the mental fog that has descended and swing away.

I take my time gathering up stray glasses. Once the tray is stacked full of dirty dishes, I grudgingly return. His gaze stays fastened to me the entire time. As much as I want to beeline to the other end of the bar, I can't. It's probably not a coincidence that Wolf has taken up residence near the trash where the glasses are being washed. It's a constant battle to keep my attention focused on Victor, one of the bartenders, and not on the muscular goalie who invades all of my waking thoughts.

"Did you have a good night, Fallyn?" Victor grabs a few glasses and a pitcher.

"Yup," I say with a nod. "It flew right by."

"Always does on game nights. I'm giving Erin a ride home. Do you need one?"

Before I can respond, a deep voice cuts in, "I've got her covered. Thanks for looking out for my girl."

Grrrr.

Victor flashes a smile before holding up both hands in a gesture of surrender. "Sorry, man. I wasn't trying to step on any toes. Just wanted to make sure she got home safely."

My brows slam together as I glance at Wolf.

His girl?

No. I am most definitely not *his* girl. I will never be *his* girl.

And he should know that.

The smirk on his face dares me to argue.

"Actually, I was going to catch one with Viola and Madden," I snap, only wanting to shoot him down.

"That would be difficult since they took off an hour ago."

Crap.

I sneak a peek at Victor.

Well…he did offer before Wolf rudely cut him off.

It's as if Wolf knows exactly what thoughts are flitting through my brain because he shakes his head before crowding my personal space and whispering, "The deal was that I drive you to work and take you home."

I grit my teeth. "Does it really matter?"

His green depths spark with both heat and challenge. "Yeah, it does. I'll meet you at the car."

With that, he pushes away from the bar and heads for the back door before I can say anything else. My eyes narrow at his retreating form.

"I'd have to be a real dumbass to get in the middle of that," Victor says with a snort.

"There's nothing to get in the middle of," I grumble before taking off for more glasses and pitchers.

"Someone should probably tell him that."

It takes another fifteen minutes to clean the place up and get it ready for the next day. Then we count out the tips. I give a small percentage to the barback before snagging my purse and coat. My tummy trembles as I push through the metal door into the nearly deserted parking lot. Wolf's Mustang idles near the back as I burrow into the collar of my jacket. Even from here, I feel the heat of his gaze leveled on me. There's no way to escape it. No matter where I go, he's there, standing in my way, forcing me to acknowledge him.

Along with our past.

After nearly five years of silence, he refuses to be ignored.

My steps stutter to a halt as I return his penetrating stare.

Deep in my bones, I know that if I slide in beside him, everything will explode between us. Thick tension has been brewing for days.

I'm afraid of what will happen if it does.

I rip my gaze from his before swinging toward the alleyway. A heartbeat passes. Then another before a car door slams shut in the distance. I startle and quicken my step, knowing that he'll come after me. The frigid air crackles with tension as a mixture of nerves and excitement ignites at the bottom of my belly.

Even though I realize it's coming, a squeak escapes from me when his fingers tighten around my bicep.

His voice cracks like thunder in the velvety darkness that presses in on us. "Where the hell do you think you're going?"

Before I can respond, he turns me around and backs me up until my spine hits the rough brick of the building. Much like earlier, he presses his bigger body against mine, caging me in, making me feel small as I stare with wide eyes.

"Walking home."

"Like hell you are," he growls.

"You don't make decisions for me."

"Maybe not, but Miles would want me to look out for you."

Hearing him bring my brother up for the second time in one night is all it takes for the anger to bubble up like a geyser. My hands tighten into fists before I slam them into Wolf's steely chest.

A hiss of breath escapes from me as pain radiates throughout my knuckles, and I shake them out. I've probably caused more damage to myself than him, which only pisses me off more.

"Stop bringing him up! Stop trying to resurrect the past!" I hate the hot tears that sting my eyes.

His hands wrap around my clenched fists before lifting them to his lips and kissing each knuckle. A heartbeat later, he drags me closer. His arms band around me as I stare at the broad expanse of his chest and attempt to stave off the riotous emotion that is seconds away from clawing its way out.

"The last thing I want to do is hurt you, Fallyn."

The soft admission is all it takes for the dam to break as wetness slides down my cheeks. His arms tighten even more, crushing me as he drops a kiss against the crown of my head. Heat blooms at the bottom of my belly as strong fingers slide beneath my chin and lift it so he can rain kisses down upon my face.

As much as I try to hold it in, a whimper of need escapes from me right before his lips sweep across mine. His other hand rises until both are able to cup my cheeks, and I have no other choice but to meet his heavy-lidded stare. The heat that now fills his eyes is enough to scorch me alive.

He breaks the caress long enough to say, "Do you know how long I've waited to do that?"

CHAPTER 21

WOLF

The question hangs heavy in the chilled air between us.

A dazed expression fills her eyes as they silently sift through mine.

It's so damn tempting to crush my lips to hers for a second time this evening.

I'm starving for another taste.

Unable to resist the lure, I nip at her plump lower lip and am rewarded with a swift intake of air. Her unrestrained response is enough to turn my cock to steel.

"We can't," she whispers, eyes pleading with mine.

"Why not?" My voice is rough and animal-like. The beast I have forever tried to keep trapped beneath the surface where this girl is concerned.

My hands continue to cradle her cheeks. I don't want to ever let go. It's only when I'm touching her that I feel the blood rush through my veins and oxygen fill my lungs again.

It's been so long that I almost forgot what it felt like to be alive.

"Because there's no point."

When her tongue darts out to moisten her lips, a groan breaks loose from deep within my chest.

"We're not friends anymore."

I'm not sure if she's trying to convince me or herself of that.

"We've always been friends, Fallyn. There's never been a time when I didn't care about you or think about you." Obsessively. But I keep that part to myself, knowing it would probably push her even further away when all I want to do is tug her closer. I want her bound to me forever.

Instead of arguing, I lower my mouth and wait for her to either shove me away or protest the growing closeness. When she does neither, my tongue drifts across her lips, willing her to open and let me in.

That's all I've ever wanted.

For her to let me in.

It's almost a surprise when her fingers curl into the thick material of my sweatshirt and tug me closer. When I brush my tongue across the seam of her lips for a second time, she opens just a bit.

It might not be much, but it's more than enough for me to slip inside the warmth of her mouth and for our tongues to tangle.

She tastes so fucking sweet.

Just as I deepen the kiss, the chime of her phone penetrates the thick haze that has settled over me. When it happens for a second time, she breaks away and fishes the small device out of her purse with hands that tremble.

As soon as she glances at the cell, her muscles tense. She quickly withdraws, turning away so that I can't see the screen. Jealousy licks through me, thinking that maybe some guy from tonight is already texting, trying to shoot his shot.

"Who is it?" I rasp.

"My parents. I didn't text earlier, and they wanted to make sure I got home safely."

Her tight-lipped response is like a bucket of cold water dumped over my head. I didn't think anything could douse the flames licking like wildfire through my body.

I was wrong.

"We should probably get moving," she says in a clipped tone as if my mouth wasn't just roving hungrily over hers.

It doesn't escape me that every step forward with this girl is accompanied by three giant steps back.

CHAPTER 22

FALLYN

I release an unsteady breath and try to settle the jangled nerves that scatter across my skin as I key the entry for the hotel suite. As soon as the light flashes green, my heart lurches to the middle of my throat as I open the door. The air inside remains still. Untouched. There's a floral scent that fills the space.

Something familiar.

Like peonies.

It's strangely comforting when nothing about this situation should bring me a moment of relief.

As that thought races through my head, I slip inside the entryway and close the thick wood before leaning against it and squeezing my eyes closed. After a second or two, I force myself to move further into the suite.

Even though it's not the same one as before, it's almost identical. There are little touches that give it a different vibe. The paintings on the wall, the curve of the sleek furniture, and the palate of colors used to give it life.

This time, I don't bother to take in the view of the city or street below. I beeline for the sumptuous room with a king-sized bed that dominates the space. My feet grind to a halt when I find another robe folded on top of the comforter, along with a note and the satiny black blindfold.

After the way he'd caressed every inch of me last time, I wondered if he'd forgo the mask. As much as I want these encounters to remain anonymous, there's a part of me that is desperate to see the only man who has touched my body so intimately, stroking me to orgasm.

As soon as that sly thought pops into my head, I shove it aside.

It's better this way.

After the three encounters that he paid an exorbitant amount for, I don't ever want to think about this sad chapter in my life again. I'm ashamed this is what I've been forced to stoop to.

Unwilling to dwell on those dangerous thoughts, I pick up the thick card stock and find the same instructions as before. The fact that this "date" will go exactly the same way as the first one settles something deep inside me. I know what to expect, and there's a strange comfort to be found in that.

With the robe clutched in my hands, I head to the white and gray veined marble bathroom. It's bright and airy with a high ceiling. There's a massive picture window on the other side of the porcelain clawfoot tub that overlooks the town below. In a different life, one where I didn't need to hustle for my tuition, I could almost imagine relaxing in hot, sudsy water and soaking all my worries away.

I strip off my jeans and sweater before folding them neatly on the marble counter. Last time, I dressed up and took great care with my appearance, wanting him to like what he saw. This time, I didn't bother. Not even with the sexy underwear. There didn't seem to be a point. I shaved, straightened my hair, and applied some light makeup.

That's it.

Another wave of anxiety crashes over me as I tighten the thick sash around my waist and re-enter the room before crawling onto the bed and snagging the facemask. My hand trembles as I pick up my phone and text the number. Then I slip the mask over my eyes until blackness swallows me whole and settle against the pillows.

He doesn't make me wait. A few minutes later, the outer door opens and footsteps pad across the wood floor into the main area of the suite before crossing over the threshold into the bedroom.

That's all it takes for electricity to sizzle through the air until it feels like the tiny hairs on my arms are standing to attention. All of my senses sharpen to a fine point.

There's just him.

And me.

No one else in the world exists.

When he pauses, my heart thrashes painfully in my chest, and my mouth dries, making it necessary for my tongue to dart out and moisten my lips. He hasn't even touched me, and my breath has become labored.

That's when I recognize the feelings rushing through my veins.

Anticipation.

Fear as well, but excitement at this new experience.

My fingers curl, the rounded nails scraping across the comforter until I'm gripping it in my hands.

Will he say something, and I'll hear the sound of his voice?

Is it deep and husky?

Because that's the way I imagine it.

An image of Wolf pops into my head, along with the kiss we shared in the alley. As much as I want to banish it, that's impossible. I've spent way too much time thinking about it.

Thinking about what it would be like to go further with him.

Those thoughts are knocked from my brain when a heavy weight settles on the mattress. Even though I'm blind to everything around me, I turn my face in his direction. Like before, his fingers drift across my cheeks, tracing the line of my jaw before sweeping across my lips. Back and forth he strums as liquid warmth pools between my thighs.

One thick digit is pressed between my lips as if to test my response. Unconsciously they part, allowing him entrance. A slight saltiness floods my senses. The tip lays against my tongue and I don't realize that I've closed around him and drawn the finger in deeper until a pained groan rumbles up from his chest. The guttural sound is enough to have another round of arousal detonating in my core. The fact that I can turn him on by simply sucking on his finger feels heady and powerful.

I can't deny that it turns me on.

His finger slips free before both hands drift to the tie cinched around my waist. He pauses for a heartbeat. Then another. When I writhe beneath him, he loosens it, drawing both sides open until I'm fully exposed.

It's so tempting to rip the mask off my face so I can finally see who this man is. The one who bought my virginity. The one who is showing me more pleasure than he's taking. Instead, my arms stay pinned to my sides.

Not more than a handful of seconds later, he presses his lips to the ugly scar that has always made me shrink and hide within myself.

But here's a man who isn't repulsed or disgusted by my physical imperfection. The permanent reminder of the worst night of my life. The one that changed everything.

It's strange to realize that he's giving me so much more than money.

He kisses every millimeter of it, laving his tongue over the old wound. When there can be no denying his feelings about it, he straightens to a seated position. His fingers pluck at my nipples in tandem, tweaking and playing with them until they're both hard little points that beg for his attention. My spine arches, seeking out more of his touch.

When his fingers disappear from one breast, a protest escapes from me just as he draws one pert tip between his lips and sucks it deep into the warmth of his mouth. Need explodes inside me like a firework, and I gasp at the sensation that ricochets through my entire being. It's as if there's an invisible string connecting the tip of my breast to my pussy. As soon as sensation flares to life in one, the other throbs with arousal.

Another groan breaks loose from me as he pops one tip free before giving the same delicious attention to the other side. I can't help but twist beneath him.

I never imagined this experience would give me so much pleasure.

I thought it would be something I needed to endure to pay my tuition bill.

But that hasn't turned out to be the case.

I want this.

I want him.

Whoever he is.

I've spent time daydreaming about two men this week.

The one who bought my virginity.

And Wolf.

Guilt spirals through me, tempering some of my arousal. In my innocent fantasies, I always imagined that he would be the one to touch me for the first time. Even after the fallout, he still managed to sneak into my dreams.

If there's anything good that will come out of this, it's that this man will erase him from my thoughts once and for all. Maybe then I'll be able to finally move on and stop thinking about him.

That's the hope anyway.

When he nips at the tip of my breast with sharp teeth, I gasp. That's all it takes to knock thoughts of Wolf from my brain and focus on the pleasure that blooms from the bite of pain. He quickly licks my nipple before sucking it into his mouth.

A whimper breaks loose. There's no way for me to keep it trapped inside as desire rushes through my veins.

He licks and kisses his way down my ribcage, worshipping every inch of flesh until reaching the V between my legs. For just a heartbeat, he buries his face against my slit. Air gets trapped in my lungs as he inhales me like a drug.

A low rumble resonates from his chest, and it sends a thousand shivers racing down my spine as he presses my thighs apart until I'm spread wide. Embarrassment crawls up my neck and cheeks. All I can imagine is this faceless stranger staring at me, devouring me with his eyes.

He trails one finger across my delicate lips, from the top to the bottom, before finally dipping it inside my heat. Once buried to the hilt, he holds it perfectly still as if allowing me time to adjust to the intrusion. Pleasure unfurls within my core as my muscles clench with newfound need. Another groan falls from his lips as he drags it from my body.

I shift on the mattress, wanting to feel the delicious sensation again. Instead, I startle when his large hands settle on my inner thighs, unbearably close to my center. His fingers tease the edges before stretching both lips wide. In my mind's eye, I can imagine them gaping open, revealing everything hidden inside.

My heart slams against my ribcage as his warm breath ghosts over the most intimate part of me. Even though I'm blindfolded and can't see what he's doing, my other senses feel alive and heightened. My fingers twist the luxurious material in an effort to contain myself, but it's difficult.

The first brush of his lips has a ragged cry escaping from me. His fingers tighten around my thighs to hold me in place as he spears the velvety softness inside my pussy.

My brain short circuits as sensation rushes through my veins.

He stretches me even wider and continues to lick until I'm reduced to something I never thought I'd be.

A shuddering mess of hormones.

The tip of his tongue lazily circles my clit. The delicious sensations brewing inside are almost too much to wrap my brain around. My spine arches off the mattress as he continues to lap and suck my flesh. Before I realize what's happening, I come with a heady rush. The wave crashes over me before dragging me out to sea where I'll never be found again.

As good as the last time was, it's nothing compared to the orgasm that rips through me, leaving me breathless.

Mindless.

My muscles are as limp as an overcooked noodle. He continues to nibble as if he'll never get enough.

It's so tempting to bury my fingers in his hair.

Is it long or short?

Dark or light?

I have no idea.

An image of Wolf nudges its way back into my brain.

It's all too easy to imagine him touching me like this.

My tongue darts out to moisten my lips as a million different thoughts circle through my head.

Should I say something?

Thank him, maybe?

He's paid all this money and he's gotten nothing out of it. Even though I shouldn't feel guilty, it eats away at me.

I'm robbed of my decision as he rises to his feet. My ears stay perked for the slightest sound. That's when I hear his footfalls echo off the wood as he walks out of the bedroom. Before the outer door slams shut, I rip the mask from my face and rush to the main living area, but it's too late.

He's gone.

The only thing that lingers is a woodsy scent in the air.

I hurry to the door and fling it open, stepping outside and staring down one long stretch of hallway before swinging around to do the same on the other side, but it's empty.

Almost as if this entire episode was a figment of my imagination.

My head continues to spin as I slip back inside the suite and walk to the bedroom. As soon as I cross over the threshold, my phone chimes. It's jarring in the silence that surrounds me. I glance at the screen only to find that another ten thousand dollars has been deposited into my account. Dropping onto the bed, I stare at the total sum.

Between that and the first amount, I have more than enough to pay for this semester's tuition along with my rent for the next few months.

Relief washes over me.

But there's something else buried beneath that as well.

Something undeniable.

Something I'm not proud of.

Anticipation.

Because the next time I meet with my mystery man, he'll take my virginity.

CHAPTER 23

WOLF

$\mathcal{I}$ loiter against a red brick half wall with my arms crossed over my chest and search each new face for Fallyn as students pour from the glass doors. I shift, growing impatient for the sight of her. It's been three days since our second meeting at the hotel. All I have to do is lick my lips and I can still taste her faint flavor there.

I'm so damn hungry for more.

The course I've set is a dangerous one. If I were smart, I'd rethink each decision before making it.

But let's be real, I'm way too far gone and that's not going to happen.

"Hey, Wolf."

My head snaps to the side only to realize that a pretty girl has sidled up next to me when I wasn't paying attention. My gaze flickers to her for a second or two before returning to the entrance of the building. I've seen this chick around campus and at the bar, but I have no idea what her name is off the top of my head.

"Hey, how's it going?" Even though I toss out the question, I don't really give a shit about the response.

Unfortunately, she takes that as a green light to proceed and sidles closer.

A little too close for comfort.

"It's good. What are you up to? Are you finished with classes for the day?"

My gaze flickers toward her for a second time. "Um, yeah. I'm waiting around for a friend."

I wish there were a way to stop this convo in its tracks. In my mind, I can already see how it'll play out. She'll ask me to do something (probably head back to her place), and I'll turn her down flat.

"Oh." She tucks a stray lock of shoulder-length blonde hair behind her ear. "I thought maybe if you weren't busy—"

I straighten to my full height as Fallyn steps into the sunshine. Her long, inky-colored hair falls around her shoulders as she scans the thick crowd. Her lips look as if she's wearing stain on them, but I know it's just their natural color. She's never been one to wear a lot of makeup.

And damn if that isn't sexy.

The sheer force of her beauty hits me like a punch to the gut every single time. It's been that way since we were kids. Back then, I was too young to understand what it meant.

All I knew was that I wanted to protect and watch over her.

Be as close as possible.

There's a natural pull between us.

Like an invisible string slowly being reeled in.

At least for me there is.

And it's only deepened with time.

Keeping my distance all these years has been torture. Now that she's back in my life, these little snippets of time I've been able to snatch are nowhere near enough to satiate the beast that lives deep within.

I crave more.

I crave everything.

Especially now that I've tasted her silky flesh.

I won't be satisfied until every piece of her belongs to me.

Until I'm all she sees.

All she can think about.

Until her need is as ravenous as mine.

I have no idea if that's even possible.

"Sorry, I gotta take off," I mumble before the blonde can push out the rest.

The moment I step in Fallyn's direction, her gaze slices to mine and she stumbles to a halt. A few people knock into her in their haste to escape the building before she explodes into movement. Her gaze shifts to the girl left behind in my wake before resettling on me again with narrowed eyes. People scatter out of my way as I move through the congestion that clogs the walkway until finally reaching her.

With a tilt of her chin, she holds my gaze. "What are you doing here?"

Now that she's in front of me, close enough to wrap my hands around and haul against my body, it takes effort to keep my muscles loose.

Especially when the scent of her rosemary and mint shampoo teases my nostrils.

I want to breathe her deep into my soul and hold her captive until she no longer finds it necessary to fight the inevitable.

"I've got a little bit of time between class and practice. I thought maybe we could hang out." I keep my voice casual so it comes out sounding like no big deal when nothing could be further from the truth.

"Where?"

Her response throws me off. I was expecting a flat-out denial and that I'd have to cajole her into spending time with me. I had a whole spiel worked out in my head.

Is it possible that I'm making a little bit of headway with her?

One side of my lips quirk. "It's a surprise."

The less she knows right now, the better.

When indecision flashes across her features, I realize she's thinking about our last meeting set up for later this afternoon. As stupid as it sounds, I don't want to have sex with Fallyn without spending more time together.

Anytime I shoot her a text, she barely responds.

So here I am…stalking her movements across campus.

It's tempting to drag a hand down my face.

Is this really what it's come to?

"I don't know…"

The urge to reach out and touch her throbs through me. When it becomes almost too much to resist, I clench my hands at my sides.

"It'll be fun, I promise."

She releases a steady breath before jerking her head into a tight nod. "All right."

As soon as my brain gives the command to touch her, my fingers lock around hers as I navigate the sea of students. When she tenses, I wait for her to untangle herself from me and sever the connection. If I'd been thinking clearly, I would have kept my distance. Maybe placed my hand against the small of her back to steer her through the thick crowd.

It takes no more than a couple steps before her muscles lose their rigidity.

Even though I'm afraid to push for too much, too fast, I can't help myself. It's only now that she's back in my life again that I realize how lonely I've been without her.

And Miles.

They were my entire world for more than a decade.

They were all I needed.

All I wanted.

They completed me in every sense of the word.

And then, one day, they vanished.

There wasn't a damn thing I could do about it.

Over the years, my teammates at Western have become like brothers to me, but it's not the same. There's no way for these guys to know me the way Miles and Fallyn did, because I'm not the same person I was back then.

How could I be when the most important people were ripped away?

That's something that changes you for the worse.

The entire time we move across campus, her fingers stay ensconced in mine. I couldn't be more hyperaware of their softness and warmth if I tried.

"People are staring," she mutters from the side of her mouth.

Unaware of the students who surround us, I glance around and realize that she's right. People *are* staring. Well, chicks are staring with wide, disbelieving eyes. A few have their mouths hanging open in shock.

Good.

Maybe now they'll finally get the hint that I'm not interested. I have zero interest in anyone other than the girl at my side. I want everyone to know that Fallyn DiMarco belongs to me.

Whether she understands that or not.

My fingers tighten around hers as those thoughts roll through my head. I can't say they don't fill me with genuine pleasure.

"Who cares? Let them stare."

She presses her lips together, uncomfortable with the attention.

When the arena comes into view, she grounds to a halt and glances at me. I keep my fingers locked around hers, unwilling to give her the chance to take off.

"What are we doing here?" There's a scraped raw quality to her voice. Almost as if I've betrayed her and it makes me feel like shit.

But we need to do this.

She needs to do this.

I keep my tone casual. "There's an open skate, and I thought it might be fun if we dropped in for a bit." There's a beat of silence. "When was the last time you were on the ice?"

Her other hand rises to rub at her chest as she turns ashen.

My attention drops to the movement. Only now do I realize that she's rubbing the scar. The one I didn't know she had until I pulled the edges of her robe apart and stared at her chest. It fucking tore me up to see that her body bears a constant reminder of the worst day of our lives. I couldn't help but lean down and press my lips against the puckered flesh as if it were possible to take away all the pain that lives inside her.

The text she sent after our first meeting asking if it repulsed me shattered my heart into a million jagged pieces. I had to stop myself from swinging around, stalking back to the suite, and gathering her up into my arms.

My guess is that it's the reason she's still a virgin at twenty years of age.

I hate that she's embarrassed about her body. If it were possible for me to leech away her pain and take it onto myself, I'd do it in a heartbeat.

"I haven't skated since before..." her voice trails off.

"You used to love it," I remind softly.

She gnaws her bottom lip as her gaze slides back to the massive structure.

"It's time, Fallyn. Time to move on and stop allowing the accident to control every aspect of your

life. Miles wouldn't want that for you."

Her muscles turn rigid.

Just when I think she'll pull away and tell me to fuck off, she says instead, "I don't know. Maybe you're right."

CHAPTER 24

FALLYN

Angel

As soon as the words escape from my lips, I want to stuff them back inside and tell him to forget it. I've only stepped foot inside this building one other time. And that was for my cousin, Viola.

When I'd agreed to attend the game so Vi could watch Madden, I hadn't expected all those old memories and feelings to get dredged up and churn inside me. For the most part, hockey rinks are all the same.

The same feel and smell hangs in the air.

The people.

Athletes, fans, family.

Kids racing around, either stopping at the arcade to spend their parents' money or at the concession stand for popcorn, warm pretzels, and fizzy drinks.

Sitting beside Viola and watching Wolf in goal had been even more painful than I'd anticipated. A physical ache had bloomed to life in my chest until it was impossible to ignore. By the time the game was over, it felt like I was suffocating and couldn't breathe.

"Are you sure?" he asks quietly, his fingers tightening around mine. "Because we can go somewhere else. I just thought it was something fun we could do. Happy memories from our past."

I suck an unsteady breath into my lungs before ripping my gaze away and staring at the building that looms in front of us. "No, it's fine." I pull out my phone before glancing at the screen. "I have somewhere to be in three hours, so I won't be able to stay long."

Emotion flashes in his eyes before it's quickly masked. "That won't be a problem." He nods toward the building. "Should we head inside?"

My teeth scrape across my lower lip. "Yeah."

With our hands clasped, he tows me toward the wide stone steps that lead to the front entrance. The one time I was here, it was packed with people, and everyone had been decked out in Wildcats colors. Some had painted their faces orange and black. Most were wearing player jerseys. It hadn't escaped me that a lot of them had been sporting Wolf's.

We push through the glass door and into the spacious lobby. Banners hang from the ceiling with photos of Wildcats players. That's all it takes for a wave of emotion to crash over me, threatening to suck me under. A thick lump rises in my throat as I take in the space.

Other than a few people milling around, the place is quiet.

"Let's grab a pair of skates for you."

Wolf tugs me toward a window where a guy our age lounges, reading a textbook. It's only when he glances up that I realize it's Anthony. He pops to his feet as his face lights up with recognition.

"Hey, Fallyn! It's good to see you."

"Hi. I didn't know you worked here."

"I've been doing it since freshman year. It's only a handful of hours a week, but the extra cash helps."

Now that I have to pay for groceries and necessities myself, I totally get it.

I glance at the man at my side, and a shiver of awareness dances down my spine because that's exactly what he's become.

A man.

All of Wolf's boyishness has disappeared. The fullness of youth no longer fills his cheeks. Instead, his face is all hard lines and angles. Dark stubble coats both his chin and cheeks. His green eyes suck me in, reminding me of the forest near our cottage in the summertime.

Bright gold color rings the pupils. There are so many varied flecks that make up the shade.

As a kid, I would sit on his chest and stare into his eyes, trying to count all the varying hues. He always laid perfectly still and allowed me to do it.

I blink away those memories and refocus my attention on Anthony. I haven't run into him since he asked me out again.

Wolf eyes him up with a frown. "You two know each other?"

I shift. "Um, yeah. We've had a couple of classes together."

Anthony takes the opportunity to add, "We also went out a few times last year."

Wolf raises a brow and steps a little closer so that our bodies are touching. "Is that so?"

I clear my throat, hoping to change the subject. "We should probably get our skates."

"Are you still the same size as before?" When I nod, Wolf says, "Can I get a pair in a size eight?"

Disappointment flashes across the other guy's face as his gaze bounces between the two of us. "Sure. Do you need anything else?"

"Nope." Wolf nods toward the rink. "Are there a lot of people here for open skate?"

Anthony looks away just long enough to flick a quick glance toward the sheet of ice. "Maybe four or five. It's been pretty slow this afternoon." He hands over the skates. "Let me know if these don't work."

Wolf grabs them before inspecting the blades. "They'll be fine."

"So, Fallyn...have you given any more thought—"

Wolf throws an arm over my shoulder, steering me away from the counter and toward the arena before Anthony can finish.

"It was nice running into you," I call out before turning to Wolf with a glare. "That was rude."

"Trust me, it was in his best interest that I get you out of there before he asked you out." His voice dips. "*Again.*"

"It was just a few dates," I mutter, hating that I feel the need to explain the situation.

We push through the heavy doors into the chilled air. I inhale a lungful as the scent of the ice hits me full force, and another wave of nostalgia crashes over me. All the times that Wolf, Miles, and I were dropped off at the rink near our house for open skate push in at the edges of my brain. We spent so many hours fooling around at the arena. The boys would shoot on goal while I twirled around and pretended to be the next Gracie Gold.

We walk around the curve of the ice to where the locker rooms are situated. He points to a bench shoved up against the wall. "Why don't you sit there and change."

It never occurs to me not to follow the directive. Once I drop onto the bench, he hunkers down before picking up my foot and slipping off one shoe. A million goose bumps prickle along my arms as his thumb slides across the arch of my foot.

Startled by the physical contact along with my reaction, I whisper, "What are you doing?"

He flicks a glance up at me. The second our gazes collide, my belly hollows out. "Helping with your skates."

"I'm more than capable of doing it myself." My voice comes out sounding raspy as if I'm being strangled from the inside out.

With a shrug, he slips off the second one and loosens the worn laces of the skates before carefully working it onto my foot. "Never said you couldn't."

My mouth dries as he laces up the second skate. Then he picks up my shoes and straightens to his full height before taking a step in retreat.

My brows draw together as I watch him. "Where are you going?"

He jerks his head to the left. "To the locker room to grab my skates."

"Why are you taking my shoes?"

His lips quirk at the corners. "Just making sure you don't take off on me."

"Seriously?"

The playful look disappears as his stare intensifies. "As a heart attack."

Unsure what to do with myself, I fold my arms across my chest. "I'm not going to leave. You can put them back now."

"Nope." He gives them a little shake. "We'll just consider this insurance. I'll be back in a sec."

Before I can argue, he swings around and heads to the locker room, pushing through the metal door and disappearing inside. I stare at it for a moment or two before glancing at the ice. There's an older couple holding hands and a woman with a small child wearing snowpants who's using what looks like a chair made out of PVC pipes. A smile springs to my lips as I watch him push the chair across the smooth surface, chasing the lady. At the other end of the rink is a blonde, probably around our age.

There's a natural grace about her movements that tells me that she's had years of training. I used to pretend I was Gracie Gold. This girl actually resembles her in the ability department. She circles the ice before leaping into a jump and then spinning so fast I wonder how she doesn't get dizzy. She's a pleasure to watch, and I lose myself in the flowing movements.

"All set?"

Startled from my thoughts, I find Wolf standing in front of me, looking taller than before on skates. I have to crane my neck even more to meet his steady gaze.

I rise to my feet. When I wobble, my arms spring out in an effort to steady myself so I don't go down like a ton of bricks. Wolf's hands lock around my ribcage to hold me in place. Even though there's a few layers of clothing to separate his palms from my skin, awareness shoots through me as his face hovers inches from mine.

It wouldn't take much to close the—

As soon as that sly thought invades my brain, I jerk back and nearly stumble. His fingers tighten around me.

Electricity crackles in the air that surrounds us.

"You good?"

"Yup. Just not used to this. It's been a while." I clear my throat and glance away from the intensity that fills his eyes and blurt, "See? I'm still here. I didn't take off."

"I would have chased you down if you did."

The dark promise in his voice has my attention snapping back to his. A quick glance at his eyes tells me that he's not joking. Possessiveness fills them. It's the same look I noticed the night after the game when he showed up at the bar. I've tried so hard not to think about what happened in the alleyway after my shift.

Unfortunately, it's been replaying in my brain on a constant loop.

That's all it takes for butterflies to explode at the bottom of my belly and wing their way to life.

"Ready?"

I jerk my head into a nod, all the while pretending that his comments haven't set fire to something deep inside me. "As I'll ever be."

It's a relief when his hands loosen from around my waist. I don't think I could take another moment of his touch.

Just as a sigh escapes from me, his bare fingers wrap around mine. And then he's tugging me toward the gate that separates us from the ice. With one swift movement, he yanks the handle and shoves it open before stepping onto the smooth surface.

He swings around and extends his hand. It's not even a question in my brain to take it. More like instinct. His grip tightens around me as I step onto the ice and glide across the smooth surface. Tension vibrates through every muscle.

It's been a long time since I've done this, and it no longer feels second nature the way it did when we were younger. My other hand tightens in an effort to stay upright so that I don't end up on my ass. If I was worried when I first rose to my feet near the bench, it's nothing compared to the unease I feel right now.

It's as if Wolf can read my mind. He tugs me forward until his arm can slip around my waist to steady me.

"See? Easy peasy. Just like riding a bicycle."

"I wouldn't go that far," I say with a snort. "In fact, if this is the same as getting on a bike again, then I probably shouldn't attempt that either because it feels like I'm seconds away from breaking a few bones."

"I would never let that happen."

With his arm banded around my middle, he tugs me closer. I'm more or less being propelled forward as my feet stay firmly planted on the ice.

Well, as firmly planted as they can be.

It takes one full lap around the oval before the stiffness filling my muscles gradually dissipates and I begin to enjoy myself. I stop focusing on the possibility of face planting and become more aware of the guy at my side. Even after the trauma of our past, I still trust Wolf to keep me safe. That thought continues to circle around in the back of my mind.

Only now am I able to fully acknowledge it.

When we were children, Wolf went to great lengths to protect me.

He'd take a hit for me.

Or Miles.

I suppose that's why the loss of his friendship had been so devastating. Or that I was so hurt by the way he disappeared from my life without a word.

Other than my brother, I've never trusted anyone more than Wolf.

"Penny for your thoughts?" he asks softly, knocking me from the past that continues to slyly wrap around me.

Instead of admitting the truth and delving headfirst into something so painful, I keep it light. "The pond near our house and how we'd skate there in the wintertime. You and Miles would clear off the snow and set up goals at each end."

"And we wouldn't go home until our fingers and toes were numb, and our teeth were chattering," he adds with a twitch of his lips.

I can't help but smile because it was one hundred percent true.

Snow days were the best days. The boys would play hockey. Sometimes other kids from the neighborhood would join us, but I always liked it best when it was just the three of us.

"Those are some of my favorite memories," he says softly.

"Me, too." Nothing since then has ever compared.

How could it?

Before I realize what he's doing, Wolf spins me around so that I'm skating backward in front of him with our hands tightly clasped.

"Relax," he whispers, continuing to steer us. "I've got you."

His eyes bore into mine as I force my muscles to loosen.

If I'm being completely honest—Wolf has always had me.

He's forever possessed the power to suck me in and hold me captive.

When we were growing up, I didn't want to break free. It was never a thought in my head.

Now I'm no longer sure.

The more time we spend together, the harder it becomes to keep my distance. Both physically and emotionally. It's all too easy to remember everything that drew me to him in the first place, like a moth to a flickering flame. I couldn't stay away even if I tried.

The longer his green eyes bore into mine, the more the world shrinks around us until he's all I'm cognizant of. It's as heady as it is dangerous.

It's almost a relief when he breaks eye contact and gives someone a chin lift in greeting. I force my gaze away and find the figure skater I'd been watching earlier. Up this close, she's even more beautiful than I'd imagined.

Petite.

Blonde and blue-eyed like a porcelain doll.

Jealousy bubbles up within me before I quickly stomp it out.

Do they know each other?

Intimately?

That thought pisses me off.

Because they probably do.

I'm sure she's just one of the many girls on campus that he's slept with.

My gaze slices to his, only to find him watching me with an intensity that nearly steals my breath away.

"Do you know her?" It takes effort to keep my voice level. The last thing I want is for him to think that I'm jealous.

A spark of humor ignites in his eyes. Somehow, he knows exactly what thoughts are running rampant through my brain. The longer he stares, the more heat gathers in my cheeks until it feels like they've been set ablaze.

I press my lips together so I don't dig myself any deeper into a hole. One that I won't be able to climb out of.

His gaze never deviates from mine as he leans closer and drops his voice so that only I can hear. "There's nothing for you to be jealous of."

The words, so like the ones from our past, echo in my ears.

With that comment, my humiliation is complete.

I clear my throat. "I'm not."

His attention stays focused on me as he nods toward the girl who has disappeared from the ice, leaving us alone.

"That's the new coach's daughter."

"Oh." Now I feel like an idiot.

A jealous idiot when that's the last thing I should be. It shouldn't matter who Wolf dates or sleeps with.

We're no longer friends.

We're...nothing.

Damn it. I knew spending time alone with him was a disastrous idea.

I'm so focused on my thoughts that I don't realize that Wolf has maneuvered us to the team benches until his hands encircle my waist, hoisting me onto the half wall before setting me down so that we're eye level. My heart picks up tempo as our gazes cling.

It's slowly that he swallows up the space between us until his warm breath feathers across my lips. I can't help but inhale a big breath of him, taking him deep into my lungs.

"Fallyn," he groans, sounding as if he's in distress.

As if his insides are twisted up into painful little knots.

Maybe I haven't wanted to admit it, but I know exactly how he feels because I'm experiencing it as well.

My body gravitates toward his until his mouth can drift across mine. Even when my lips part, opening in silent invitation, he doesn't lose control like he did the other night. His movements are measured as if we have all the time in the world to explore.

My brain clicks off as need spirals through me and I twine my arms around his neck before drawing him closer. In this moment, nothing matters more than the feel of his mouth coasting over mine.

Not the heartbreak of our past.

Or the uncertainty of our future.

It's only when someone clears their throat that we splinter apart. Our heads twist until a middle-aged guy with a clipboard comes into view. He stares at us with a raised brow.

"Hey, Coach."

Well, hell…

"Wolf." His gaze slices to me before bouncing back to his goalie. "Have you seen my daughter around? I thought she was here practicing."

"I think she took off about ten minutes ago."

"Thanks."

Without another word, the older man disappears into the locker rooms, leaving us alone in the frigid rink. I glance at Wolf only to see a smile trembling around the corners of his lips.

I whack his chest before burying my face against his jacket and mumbling, "I'm so embarrassed."

That's all it takes for his shoulders to shake with silent laughter. He slips his arms around me before dropping a kiss against the crown of my head. As I burrow against his comforting strength, I realize that I could stay here forever. Wolf has always been my safe space.

Just as I sink further into his touch, my eyelids fly open, and I quickly untangle myself from him. My fingers wrap around my cell before slipping it from my pocket so I can glance at the screen.

Crap.

I didn't realize how much time had slipped by.

"What's wrong?"

My gaze jerks to his as regret crashes over me.

How could I kiss Wolf when I'm about to meet with the man who'll take my virginity?

I glance away and mumble, "Nothing. I have someplace to be and need to get moving."

Silence descends as thick tension vibrates in the chilled air.

"Where?"

I open my mouth, but not a single sound escapes from it. The longer I remain silent, the more tense the atmosphere turns. There's no way I can tell him the truth. That I sold my virginity in order to pay my tuition bill for the semester. I can't imagine what his reaction would be.

Or maybe I can.

His likely response is more than enough to dissolve the laughter bubbling up in my throat.

My tongue flicks out to wet my lips.

It's difficult to force out the excuse. "I have an appointment downtown."

More awkward silence stretches between us as he sifts through my gaze as if trying to get at the truth. There's no way I can allow him to do that. I'd rather die than tell him what's going on.

It's a relief when he drops the topic and says instead, "I'll drive you so you're not late."

Unwilling to consider the offer, I shake my head.

I need time away from Wolf before I meet my mystery man. I sneak another peek at my cell. Even if I set up a ride right now, there's no way I won't be late. The probability of a car making it here in less than ten minutes is low.

I chew my bottom lip with indecision.

My attention gets pulled back to him when his fingers slide across my cheek. There's something comforting about his gentle touch. It's tempting to sink into it and squeeze my eyes shut, blotting out the world around us.

"Just let me drive you," he murmurs.

It's such a bad idea…

But what choice is there?

"Yeah, okay," I say, giving in. "Thank you."

"It's not a problem."

Ten minutes later, we're in his Mustang and heading downtown. Every couple seconds his gaze flickers in my direction. I feel the heat of his probing stare like a physical caress. I couldn't be more aware of it—or him—if I tried.

Unable to meet his searching gaze, I stare out the passenger side window. Once upon a time, I thought Wolf would be the one to take my virginity. How weird is it that he's driving me to have sex with another man?

Even if he doesn't realize it.

I chew my lower lip and stare blindly out the passenger side window. Only now do I realize that allowing Wolf to drive me here was a mistake. I hate that he'll forever be tied to this experience.

When we're a couple blocks from the hotel, I point to a medical center. "You can drop me off right here."

He glances at the three-story brick building on the left side of the street. A light snow drifts from the sky and dusts the sidewalk. "Should I wait?"

Absolutely not.

How horrific would that be?

To see him after…

Would he take one look at me and realize what happened?

"No. I'm not sure how long the appointment will last."

"I don't mind. I've got time to burn before practice."

My fingers shake as they wrap around the door handle before jerking it open so I can slip from the vehicle. "I'll find my own way home. Thanks."

His gaze bores into mine, holding it ensnared. "Are you sure?"

"Yup."

There's a pause as his dark brows draw together. Emotion flashes across his features as his tongue darts out to moisten his lips. "Fallyn, there's something I need—"

I can't do this with him.

Not now.

My head is already messed up. I need to see this through and get it over with. Maybe, at a later date, we can sit down and discuss what happened between us. But that's not something I can do right now. I can't think about Wolf when I'm about to have sex for the first time with another man.

The thought turns my stomach.

"Please," I whisper. "I can't do this right now. Just give me a little time."

Storm clouds gather in his eyes, turning them vibrant. "I know but—"

"We'll talk tomorrow."

Before another word can escape from him, I slam the car door and twist away, taking off at a brisk pace. I'm so afraid that he won't accept my answer and will try to follow me. With my shoulders hunched, I slip inside the building and head toward the back, searching for an exit that will lead to the alleyway. My heart thrashes as I glance over my shoulder to make sure that I'm still alone.

A potent concoction of confusion and sadness swirls around inside me. I hate that this is the way our lives have played out.

But there's nothing I can do about it.

I have to see this through.

Only then will I be able to move forward.

CHAPTER 25

WOLF

Even after Fallyn disappears through the glass doors and into the building, I stare at the last place I saw her before dragging a rough hand over my face and slamming my fists against the leather steering wheel.

Fuck.

I should have come clean when I had the chance and admitted that not only am I the one who bought her virginity, but that I know why she's so desperate for cash.

One call to my asshole father filled me in on the situation. He'd crowed about finally stealing the company from Hugo and bankrupting the DiMarcos.

It had made me gut sick.

But how could I reveal the truth without her hating me even more than she already does? Only now am I starting to make progress where Fallyn is concerned. There's no way I can go back to a life she isn't a part of. These past years, I've been living in black and white. Her presence has filled my world with so much vibrant color. There's no way I can go back to existing in the darkness.

Whatever I have to do to keep her, I'll do it.

No questions asked.

It's only when the burner phone I bought chimes with an incoming message that I pull into traffic and drive to the hotel. I park in the underground structure so that my Mustang isn't in plain sight and head to the bank of elevators.

Indecision spirals through me as I drag a hand through my short strands. Part of me wants to go through with this and then carry on afterward as if nothing happened. As if I'm not the one who awakened her body and gave her pleasure.

Is there really anything wrong with that?

I'm pretty sure there is. And if she ever finds out that I'm behind this, she'll never speak to me again.

Is that a chance I'm willing to take?

Once I step out of the elevator and find the suite, I hesitate outside the door.

In that moment, it occurs to me that I could walk away right now. It would be easy enough to transfer the remaining money into Fallyn's account and simply disappear. She'd never know it was me. We could continue spending time together and see where our relationship goes from there.

Then it would be her decision to sleep with me.

Deep down, I know it's the right thing to do.

Instead of backing away, I swipe the card against the lock. The light flashes green, and the door buzzes, announcing my arrival.

As much as I want to do the noble and honorable thing, I can't.

Not where she's concerned.

I want her too damn much.

I always have.

Fallyn DiMarco belongs to me.

She's always belonged to me, and there is nothing that will ever change that.

I slip inside the suite and close the door before beelining to the bedroom. Even in the entryway, I could smell the lingering scent of her floral perfume that permeates the air.

That's all it takes for me to stiffen right up.

When I arranged this through Chloe, I had every intention of taking her virginity. I made sure it was stipulated that we would meet three times so I'd be sure to get my fill of her.

Enough to last for the rest of my life.

That first time, after staring down at her wrapped up in the thick white robe, I couldn't bring myself to do it. Especially after pulling the edges apart and catching sight of the scar that mars her chest. I traced over it with my fingertips, wishing it were possible to take away all the hurt I caused with the accident.

Instead of taking my own pleasure, I adored every inch of her body, making sure she understood through my reverent touch just how gorgeous she was. Both inside and out.

Watching her fall apart is an experience I'll never forget.

The second time, I cherished her with both my lips and tongue.

My footsteps pause over the threshold, and my breath catches at the sight of her. Unlike the previous two encounters, the robe I left out is neatly folded at the edge of the mattress, and she's stretched out in the middle of the king-sized bed with the mask covering her eyes.

Naked.

All I want to do is stand here and soak in the sight of her, committing it to memory.

Her inky black hair is draped across the white linen of the pillowcase and her scars are prominently on display. Her rosy-tipped breasts are hard little points that beg for my attention. My mouth waters at the sight of them.

Fallyn has grown even more curvy than when she was a teenager, and I can't help but revel in them. Her pussy is clean shaven. If I swiped my tongue across my lips, I'd still taste her there.

One lap of my tongue and I was addicted.

Fallyn will never realize just how deep my love for her runs.

I'm not even sure I understand it myself.

There has never been anyone other than this girl. As I stare down at her prone form, I realize that no matter what happens between us today, there'll never be anyone else again.

How could there be?

I gravitate to the bed before settling beside her on the mattress.

Her chest rises and falls in rapid succession with each shaky inhalation. As brave as she's trying to be, her anxiety is like a living, breathing entity.

My fingers rise, circling one puckered nipple, giving it a gentle tweak before doing the same to the other. Her hands twist into the thick material of the comforter as she arches into my touch as if silently seeking it out. I close the distance between us before pressing my lips against the scar, kissing the length of it.

I just want her to realize how fucking beautiful she is.

I hate that it's even a question in her mind.

Another wave of uncertainty crashes over me as I rest my forehead against the valley between her breasts. She lays perfectly still, her heart beating a steady rhythm beneath me. When I remain frozen in place, her arms hesitantly rise before slipping around me, pressing me closer until I'm surrounded by her.

Until she's my entire fucking world.

The beginning and end of it.

The way it was always meant to be.

"Take off the mask," I whisper.

When she doesn't move, I say more firmly, "Take it off, Fallyn."

Her muscles turn rigid as her arms drop to the mattress as if weighted down by bricks. As soon as they do, I force myself to straighten. She rips off the black mask and blinks at the weak sunlight that filters in through the gauzy curtains covering the windows.

The moment her gaze falls on me, her eyes widen in shock as she shakes her head. *"No."*

Air leaks from my lungs as I shove my hand through my short strands. I knew she'd be angry, and I wasn't wrong.

Her eyes flash as her face turns ashen.

When I remain silent, her voice escalates with each bitten out word. "It was *you* the entire time?"

I force myself to hold her furious gaze. "Yeah."

She scrambles off the bed and snags the robe, turning her back before shaking it out and wrapping it around her naked body. Only when she's covered head to toe does she swing around to face me again.

Rage vibrates off her in heavy, suffocating waves as she folds her arms tightly across her chest. "I can't believe you would do something like this!"

Her voice quivers with unspent emotion.

"I'm sorry." As much as I want to eat up the distance between us and take her into my arms, I remain still. "It might not seem like it, but I was trying to help."

"By purchasing my virginity?" Disbelief rings throughout her voice as it echoes off the ceiling and walls.

"Would you have really preferred that a stranger take it? Some old man?" Even the thought of that pisses me off. I'd rip apart anyone who dared to touch what's mine.

"Yes! I would have preferred it be a faceless stranger that I'd never have to see again."

I shake my head and take a tentative step toward her. The truth is out of my mouth before I can stop it. "How could I let another man touch you?" There's a pause before I force out the rest. "You were always meant to be mine."

"I was *never* yours." Her blue eyes flash with fire and rage. "Not after the accident."

I take another step, steadily stalking her throughout the room. "No matter what happened, I've been here waiting. If you needed money, I should have been the first person you asked for help. You and Miles were my family. Sometimes it felt like you were the only ones I had. You should've realized that I would have given you anything you needed. It wasn't necessary to sell your body to the highest bidder."

As soon as the last sentence shoots out of my mouth, I realize it's a mistake.

Her face drains of color as a mixture of hurt, anger, and embarrassment crashes over her features. "I didn't want your help," she whispers thickly.

When I reach out, only wanting to pull her into my arms and

soothe the fury rushing through her veins, she jumps away as if my touch has the power to burn.

"But you needed it." I can't resist adding, "You needed *me*."

Sparks fly from her eyes as she tears off the robe she'd just wrapped around herself minutes ago. The fluffy material falls, puddling at her feet as she glares. "Then you should take what you paid for." When I remain frozen in place, she angles her head and straightens her shoulders. "You want my virginity so badly? Then take it!"

My hand rises to massage the back of my neck as every muscle vibrates with pent-up tension. It's so fucking tempting to spring forward and accept what she's offering.

Instead, I force myself to stay still and shake my head. "No. Not like this."

A strange calm falls over her as she thrusts out her breasts and arches a brow. "What's wrong? Isn't this how you imagined the scenario playing out?"

Instead of waiting for an answer, she spins around and stalks to the bed before climbing onto the king-sized mattress and settling in the middle of it. My gaze stays pinned to her the entire time. There's no way I could look away even if I wanted to. Especially when she arches her back and spreads her legs so wide that I can see every delicate inch.

A tortured groan rumbles up from deep within my chest as confusion circles through my brain.

"Come on, Wolf," she taunts. "Take what you bought."

CHAPTER 26

FALLYN

air gets trapped in my lungs, making it impossible to breathe as I wait for his reaction. My brain reels as I stare at Wolf. It's almost impossible to reconcile that it's been him all along.

Is this something he does often?

Buys virgins?

The thought sickens me, and bile rises in my throat.

My attention stays locked on him as he swallows up the distance and settles at the end of the bed between my spread thighs. Any moment my heart will explode from my chest before thrashing around on the hardwood floor as a fresh wave of nerves crashes over me.

I steel myself as he reaches out and slides his fingers from my ankle to my knee. Even though it's tempting to squirm beneath his gentle touch, I force myself to remain perfectly still. Just when I think his hand will drift higher, it glides back down to my ankle.

Tremors rack my body as his heated gaze flickers to mine before returning to the V between my thighs.

"You're so fucking beautiful." The hunger lurking in his eyes has them turning shades darker. "You know that?"

I shake my head and press my lips together. If I try to speak, it'll come out sounding more like a squeak.

"Well, you are."

This time when his fingers glide upward, they don't stop at my knee. They inch higher until the soft pads graze the delicate skin of my inner thigh. My teeth sink into my lower lip in an effort to keep the whimper of arousal trapped inside where it belongs. I don't want him to realize how much he affects me.

His movements stall for a second or two before he uses his other hand to press my thighs wider. Never have I felt so exposed in my life. Even during our previous two encounters. With the blindfold covering my eyes, blotting out the world around me, I could almost trick myself into believing that what we were doing was hidden away in the darkness, and the man touching me couldn't inspect me with such thoroughness.

It's no longer possible to believe that lie.

Not when he's sitting in front of me, staring so intently.

What I can't deny is the worshipful expression on his face as he drags his thumb across my slit. That's all it takes for sensation to burst in my core before fanning outward to the very tips of my fingers and toes. He gently spreads my lips before swaying closer. When I squirm beneath the intensity of his stare, he glances at me as if to gauge my reaction.

His voice drops a few octaves, turning gruff. "Did you like it when I touched you before?"

I press my lips together, refusing to give him anything more than what I already have.

Eyes locked on mine, he slowly strums my flesh again. Delicious sensation ripples throughout my being and a reluctant response erupts from me. "Yes!"

My breath catches when his thumb drifts upward, and he rubs soft circles against my clit. "What about when I licked you?"

The avalanche of pleasure is enough to make my eyes cross. "I liked it."

He tilts his head. "No one else has ever touched you like this?"

I can't help but arch into his hand, unconsciously seeking out more delicious sensation. "No. Never."

A puff of air escapes from him as he refocuses his attention on my pussy. "I can't say that I'm not happy about that, but you shouldn't have allowed the scar on your chest to hold you back." His gaze collides with mine again as he presses one finger into my softness until he's buried knuckle deep. "You're so damn gorgeous, Fallyn." His eyes darken as he remains perfectly still. "I can feel how tight you are. Do you have any idea how fucking sexy that is?"

It's a potent combination of his gruff voice, the words coming out of his mouth, and the feel of his finger inside my heated body where no other man has been that leaves me squirming.

"Please." The word escapes before I can stuff it back inside.

"Please what? Tell me what you want."

He tosses out the question as his finger retreats until only the tip remains pressed against my entrance. My inner muscles contract, desperate for the same delicious fullness. Before I can say anything, he surges forward again.

I groan as pleasure crashes over me. "You bought my virginity." My tongue flicks out to wet my lips as I force myself to say, "I want you to take it."

His green eyes spark with so much heat that it's almost a surprise when I don't burst into flames. He withdraws before pressing back inside.

"You're right, I did. But it doesn't need to be this afternoon. We can wait."

The idea of stopping is a painful one.

Especially since I've never been more turned on in my life. Even though I'm loath to admit it, knowing that Wolf is the one toying with my body only pushes me further to the brink.

His attention drops to the V between my legs. "I have no problem licking that sweet little pussy so you can get the pleasure you're so desperate for."

Wolf's dirty words add a whole new level to the need thrumming through me. I don't understand how that can be the case when I'm already dancing on the edge.

I arch into his touch. *"Please."*

Satisfaction flashes across his face before he settles between my bent knees. Instead of attacking my flesh and shoving me over the precipice so I no longer have to think, his eyes stay locked on mine as he softly presses his lips to my leg. His touch is worshipful, as if he has all the time in the world to explore. The velvety softness of his tongue flicks over me before he sinks sharp teeth into my inner thigh, slowly working his way toward my center. But it's not enough. All he's doing is stoking flames that are already burning out of control. I'm a writhing mess as I watch him draw closer to the part of me that throbs with newfound awareness.

Hot licks of anticipation sizzle through my veins as memories of what it felt like to have his mouth feasting on me roll through my brain. I'm so fucking needy.

Air hisses from between my parted lips the second his mouth settles over my delicate flesh. My eyes feather shut as sensation consumes me. Nothing in my life has ever felt so amazing. His tongue swipes over me for a second time, and my spine arches in an attempt to get closer to the heat of his mouth.

When it disappears, a tortured groan breaks loose. It's tempting to scream out my frustration.

"Open your eyes," he growls. "I want you to see who's between your legs, giving you all this pleasure."

The command detonates another chain reaction within me. It's only when my eyelids spring open that his lips resettle on my pussy. Our gazes lock as he continues tonguing me. The sight of his dark head between my spread thighs is so damn erotic. I couldn't look away even if I wanted to.

Before the accident, I'd imagine what it would be like for Wolf to touch and kiss me, but it was never anything like this. My daydreams were far more innocent and chaste.

His fingers bite into my delicate skin as he presses my legs apart. I'm at his mercy. In the morning, there'll probably be bruises. I can't resist thinking of the contrast we make. His darker, tattooed flesh against my creamier, unblemished complexion. Where his palms are calloused and rough, mine are soft and more pampered.

In the past, he's always been careful to treat me gently, as if I were fragile. Made of spun glass. That's no longer the case. Somewhere in the back of my brain, in a place I don't want to inspect, I'm grateful for it.

When he spears his tongue deep inside, a whimper slips free from my lips. He does it for a second time before circling my clit with lazy strokes. Pleasure crashes over me in heavy waves before dragging me out to sea. I want to find a way to hang in this moment of blissful suspension forever. When my muscles tighten, and the intensity in my core becomes too much to bear, I splinter into a million jagged pieces. Knowing that Wolf is buried between my outstretched legs is what finally pushes me past the point of no return until I'm in free fall. My fingernails claw at the thick material of the comforter as I scream out my release.

It blows apart the two other orgasms.

That's when I realize that nothing in my world will ever be the same.

Every molecule has shifted, morphing into something new.

It's both frightening and thrilling all at the same time.

He continues to lap at my drenched flesh as I crash back to earth with a painful thud. My muscles have never felt so pliant. My breath comes out in harsh pants that fill the silence of the room. I stare at the ceiling for long minutes, trying to corral my disorganized thoughts, before forcing my gaze to the man buried between my legs, licking and kissing me. My flesh now feels over sensitized and swollen. His eyes stay fastened to mine. There's no escaping the hunger that glows within them.

There's nowhere for me to run and hide.

I'm naked and vulnerable. Spread out like a feast he's intent on devouring while fully dressed in the same clothing we'd been skating in little more than an hour ago.

The sight is jarring.

When I remain silent, unsure what to say, he presses one final kiss against me before raising his head. He never looks away or breaks eye contact. It would be a relief if he did. Instead, I remain pinned in place like a butterfly against a foam board.

Everything within me stills as he kisses his way up my belly and then ribcage, adoring every inch of flesh as he makes his way to the jagged scar that bisects my chest. My lungs flood with oxygen as he presses his lips to the imperfect and puckered skin. Warmth gathers inside me, heating me up from the inside out. Other than my doctors, he's the only one who's ever touched me there. I want to squirm and push him away before curling in on myself, but I realize that Wolf won't allow it.

Not anymore.

Those suspicions are confirmed when he rises and presses his mouth against mine, nipping at my lower lip before his tongue delves inside my mouth.

Just as I sink into the intimate caress, he pulls away enough to growl, "Make no mistake, Fallyn. You belong to me now just like you belonged to me then. You will *always* be mine."

A shaky breath leaks from my lungs as I study him. The possessiveness that shines from his eyes has my heart doing a painful flip flop beneath my breast.

"Now get dressed and I'll take you home."

CHAPTER 27

FALLYN

"We have an interested buyer," Mom announces. "They just submitted an offer."

"Really?" Even though I know that selling the house is for the best, I still have mixed feelings. "That's good news."

"Yeah, it is." There's a sigh. "I just wish that none of this were necessary."

"I know."

She drops her voice to more of a hushed whisper. "And your father is still trying to figure out a way to reverse the decision. He's contacted a few different lawyers and spoken to the board members. I don't think there's anything he's going to be able to do."

I swing away and stare out the window. "Maybe cutting ties completely with the Westervilles is what needs to happen."

It should have occurred years ago. Then my father's anger and rage wouldn't have continued to simmer. We could have all healed instead of being forever stuck in this purgatory.

"I don't know, Fallyn. I really don't." There's a pause before she changes the subject. "How's your job at the diner?"

I wince, knowing that at some point, I'll have to confess the truth. "Um, it's good."

"I realize you're happy about the loan coming through for the semester, but I wouldn't have minded if you'd returned home for the spring. It would make all of this a little easier to deal with."

"I really don't think that's the case, Mom. It's better that you only have to worry about the two of you right now."

"I suppose that's true."

When my phone dings with a text, I pull the cell away from my face to glance at the screen.

> I'll pick you up in ten.

My belly spasms.

"Fallyn? Are you still there?"

"Sorry! I need to get going, Mom. But we'll talk soon, okay?"

"Sure. Love you, honey."

"Love you, too."

I stare at the text from Wolf and contemplate my options. After yesterday, I'm nowhere near ready to see him. There are so many conflicting emotions that war inside me. I have no idea what I want.

Or need.

Although, I'd be lying if I didn't admit that the pull I feel for Wolf is even more consuming than when we were younger.

Decision made, I pop my head into Viola's room. "Hey, would you mind driving me to work?"

She glances at me from where she's studying at her desk before leaning back and stretching her muscles. Since living together, I see how hard she works to get top grades in school. It also makes me doubly glad I didn't major in engineering.

Although, it's not like I was ever in danger of that.

I've helped quiz her for a few tests. It's like staring at a foreign language.

One I never want to learn.

"Sure, I could use a break."

When she doesn't rise from her chair, I glance at my phone and clear my throat. "I don't mean to rush you, but I need to get moving."

"Oh, sorry!"

I force a smile. "No worries."

"I wouldn't want you to be late for your new job."

And I wouldn't want to run into Wolf on the way out. He'd probably demand that I go with him, and then he'd let it slip that I sold my V-card to pay this semester's tuition.

That's not something I've worked up the courage to mention to my cousin.

I know that I should, but still…

It's humiliating to be in this position.

We both snag our jackets before heading into the hallway. When we pass the stairwell door that leads to the lobby, I shove it open.

"Let's take the stairs instead. It'll be faster."

She shrugs. "Sure."

As soon as we make it to the first floor of the building, I glance around, relieved that Wolf has yet to arrive. There's been a few times when he's been heading up the sidewalk as I'm leaving the complex. I hold my breath as I push through the glass door. Cold air strokes over my cheeks as I burrow into the collar of my jacket. My gaze flies over the parking lot, relieved that his vehicle is nowhere in sight.

With my arm looped through Viola's, I drag her to her white Jeep.

"Jeez. You really are in a hurry," she mutters, hastening her pace to keep up with me. "You must really enjoy waitressing there."

"Yup. Don't want to be late."

Less than two minutes later, we pull onto the street and leave the apartment building behind in the rearview mirror. Just as we turn the corner, I catch sight of Wolf's electric blue Mustang and quickly duck down.

Viola glances at me with a frown. "Are you all right?"

I take a second or two to fumble around on the floor. "Um, yeah. Just dropped my phone under the seat."

With a shake of her head, her gaze slices to the windshield. "Don't take this the wrong way, but you're acting weird. Is there anything you want to talk about? I feel like it's been a while since we hung out.

Maybe we should get Juliette, Stella, Carina, and Britt together for another girls night. The last one was so much fun."

I chew my lower lip, trying to decide if I should tell her the truth. It would feel so good to finally get it all out in the open. Even though I'm not technically lying to my cousin, that's the way it feels, and I hate it. By the time the shock wears off, we'll be at Slap Shotz and I can jump out of the car, escaping any questions.

"Yeah, that sounds like a plan. I'll check my schedule and let you know when my next night off is."

She flashes a smile. "I'll text the girls."

Just as I'm about to admit the truth, a message pops up on my phone.

> Hey, I'm downstairs waiting.

The muscles in my belly contract as I stare at those four little words.

Rather than respond, I tuck the cell into my jacket pocket for safe keeping.

Every new message that dings only heightens my anxiety.

Viola shoots me another look as we pull up in front of the bar. "Seems like someone's trying to get a hold of you. Maybe you should see who it is."

"Nah. It's just spam."

"Do yourself a favor and block the number."

"Yeah, I will." My fingers grip the handle as I jerk it open and slip from the Jeep. "Thanks again for the ride. I appreciate it."

"Anytime."

As soon as the door closes with a resounding thud, she takes off and I hustle inside the bar like the hounds of hell are nipping at my heels.

Well…maybe just one hound.

CHAPTER 28

WOLF

With a frown, I stare at the apartment building. There's no sight of Fallyn. Then I glance at my phone for the umpteenth time. Every text message I've sent within the last fifteen minutes has gone unanswered.

Her phone is either dead or...

She's ignoring me.

After yesterday's shocking reveal at the hotel, I probably should have expected her to go into avoidance mode. For fuck's sake, after the uncomfortable ride home, I'd slipped my fingers beneath her chin and forced her to meet my gaze before she could bolt from the vehicle.

Then I told her not to bother trying to avoid me.

Just as I'm about to head inside the apartment building, Viola's white jeep pulls into the parking lot. When she exits the vehicle alone, I realize that she probably dropped Fallyn off at work.

Son of a bitch.

After she disappears inside the lobby, I roar out of the lot and head to Slap Shotz. I make it there in less than ten minutes before parking and stalking inside. It's still early in the evening and there aren't many customers.

The moment I walk through the door, my gaze slides around the space until it lands on Fallyn's dark head. Only then does everything settle inside me.

"Hey, Westerville," Gerry says, greeting me with a fist bump.

"What's up?"

"Not much." He cracks his neck one way and then the other. "Unfortunately."

I snort.

"I suppose you're here to see your girl?"

My gaze flickers to him. "Yup."

A small smile slides across his face. "Figured that was the case."

Her long ponytail swings behind her as she stops at a table of dudes. That's all it takes for jealousy to spiral through me as I cut a path directly to her. Her laughter drifts in the air before scampering down my spine.

"So, what can I get for you guys?" she asks, her tone sounding shades lighter than I'm used to hearing. "Another pitcher? A round of shots?"

"We'll do a shot if you—"

Just as my fingers wrap around her bicep, she glances my way. Her eyes widen when she sees me.

"Wolf," she says with a gulp. The barest hint of a tremor threads its way through her voice.

"Don't look so shocked, angel. My guess is that you were expecting me."

Before she can say anything else or these guys can decide to involve themselves in our business, I steer her away from the table and into the dark hallway where the bathrooms are located. We turn the corner near Sully's office until we're tucked away from prying eyes. I force her spine against the wall before caging her in.

With our faces inches apart, I search her wide blue eyes.

"I'm here to stay, Fallyn. I'll be damned if I let you push me away after all these years."

When her tongue peeks out to moisten her lips, I lose total control and my mouth crashes onto hers. As soon as my tongue sweeps across the seam, she opens, and I delve inside. All I want to do is subdue her into submission until she stops fighting me.

Stops fighting *us*.

She needs to realize that it won't do her a damn bit of good.

Everything I've done has been for her.

The kiss turns frantic as our teeth scrape. My cock is so hard. Any moment, I'll come in my jeans.

That's what this girl does to me.

A whimper explodes from her and shatters the silence that has settled around us. Only then do I pull away enough to rest my forehead against hers. We're both breathing hard as our gazes stay locked.

"Are you going to keep running from me?"

She remains still for a second or two before shaking her head. "No."

My muscles loosen with relief. "Just know that there's nowhere you can run that I won't give chase."

A fine tremble slides through her as she whispers, "Wolf."

"Yeah, angel?"

"I just wanted a little bit of time to sort everything out in my head. Is that really so much to ask?"

Maybe not. But my answer isn't going to change.

"I've given you as much as I can. I won't allow any more distance between us." I press another kiss against her lips before drawing away. "I need to get to practice. I'll be back later to take you home."

She nods, giving me exactly what I want.

What I need.

"All right. I'll see you then."

That settled, I press one last kiss against her mouth before swinging around and walking out of the bar.

CHAPTER 29

FALLYN

Angel

It's almost comical the way my cousin's jaw comes unhinged and hangs open as she stares at me with wide, disbelieving eyes. Kind of like I just blew her mind.

Then she whacks my arm.

Hard.

"Ow!" I rub the spot. "What was that for?"

"Not telling me about all this!" Her dark blonde brows pinch together in consternation. "How could you keep this from me?" Hurt seeps into her tone.

That's all it takes for guilt to swallow me whole. I glance toward my bedroom window that overlooks the courtyard beyond the glass. Even from here, I'm able to see the bare tree branches and crisp layer of snow that coats them.

My shoulders collapse under the heavy weight of her accusation before I jerk them in a tight movement.

Her question circles around in my brain before I admit softly, "I just couldn't."

"Wolf bought your virginity!" she whisper-yells as if I'm not aware of the development.

Heat and humiliation crawl up my neck before flooding my cheeks. "I need to give the money back."

Except…half of it has already been spent and there's no longer a hold on my school account. I paid for the spring semester in full since registration for summer and next fall are right around the corner.

It was only when I was walking into the building after we made that silent—and fairly awkward—ride home from the hotel that my phone chimed with an alert that the final payment had been deposited into my account.

When I'd whipped around to stare, he'd met my eyes briefly before squealing out of the parking lot and onto the dark street, disappearing around the corner.

"Would he even accept it?" she asks cautiously.

"Nope."

Within seconds, I'd shot him a text demanding that he reverse the funds. At the very least, what he'd just deposited, and he'd flat-out refused.

"I honestly don't think I could be more shocked."

I snort. "Join the club."

For the first time since I sprang the news on Viola, a slight smile quirks the corners of my lips.

"And now you're going to—"

She breaks off when my phone chimes with an incoming message. I don't have to glance at the screen to know who it is. We have another driving lesson this afternoon. As much as I want to cancel, how can I do that when Miles' car hangs in the balance?

"Hang out with him like nothing happened?" she finishes in disbelief.

"Yeah, that's the plan," I mutter before gradually rising to my feet and heading to the dresser to snag my purse.

Just as I cross over the threshold, she says, "Growing up, Wolf was such a big part of your life. Does it help to spend time with him?"

My footsteps falter as that question spirals through my brain. It's one I've been secretly asking myself. I throw a glance over my shoulder until our gazes can fasten. What I find is genuine curiosity mixed with concern.

There were times when it felt like Wolf eclipsed everything else in my world. The sun rose and set on him. And then the worst happened. The two most important people disappeared, leaving me alone. Even though I always had Viola, my world shrank over the years, becoming a pitiful shadow of what it once was. Now that Wolf has forced his way back into my life, it feels like I'm attempting to fight my way free of the suffocating darkness that descended after Miles' death.

There's nothing good about my parents losing everything they've worked so hard for over the years, but it's forced me to wake up and become more of an active participant in my own life. I didn't realize that I was operating on autopilot and allowing things to just happen until I was forced to figure out my shit.

It's taken me a long time to do that.

Wolf will forever be intertwined with my best and worst memories.

In my descent into darkness and subsequent rise.

His explosion back into my life has only proven that our relationship, what there is of it, is complicated and not easily untangled.

"I think it has." My voice softens as I attempt to keep my emotions in check. "In a strange way, I feel closer to my brother when we're together. I've spent so much time trying to bury the past, it's kind of nice to remember and talk about it with someone who loved him just as much as I did."

Viola nods, emotion flooding her expression. "He loved you so much." There's a pause before she murmurs, "They both did. If I had to hazard a guess, I'd say that Wolf still does."

My heart clenches painfully until it feels impossible to suck in a lungful of air. "I know."

"Just know that I'm always here if you want to talk."

"Thank you." Viola isn't only my cousin, but my best friend as well. I'm lucky to have her in my life. She was my rock during a turbulent time. The only person I could cling to and retain a small bit of my sanity with. "I appreciate it."

The corners of her lips tip upward. "Love ya, cuz."

Some of the heaviness that has been pinning me to the earth lifts. "Love you, too."

I blow her a kiss before disappearing through the apartment door and into the hallway. Everything we discussed somersaults through my brain as I take the elevator to the first floor and walk through the lobby. As embarrassed as I was to tell Viola, it's a relief that she knows.

I hate secrets.

As I push through the glass doors into the waning afternoon sunlight, I spot Wolf's electric blue Mustang idling near the curb. A shiver dances down my spine as our gazes collide. That's all it takes for the air around me to heighten and turn charged with irrepressible energy.

My mind tumbles back to the other night at the bar.

Was ditching him a smart move to make?

Probably not.

Deep down inside, I knew he'd come for me.

Once he'd secured my agreement that I wouldn't try to avoid him, he'd walked out before returning a few hours later after practice. My skin had buzzed with awareness the entire time he was there.

Nerves wing their way to life at the bottom of my belly, threatening to escape as I pop open the door and slide onto the leather before giving him a bit of side eye. There are times when staring full on at Wolf is just too much. It sends my senses into overdrive. His green eyes hold a wealth of secrets now that we're older.

Much like me, he's no longer the open book he once was. The tattoos that decorate his arms, neck, and hands are all new, making him look like an entirely different person. As tempting as it is to inspect every single one of them, I haven't. That would require me to get up close and personal.

How can I do that when I'm trying to keep him at a firm distance?

My gaze settles on his fingers that grip the steering wheel.

It seems like the safest place.

Except...as I continue to stare, all I can think about is what it felt like to have them stroking over my flesh and buried in my body. That's all it takes for a tidal wave of heat to crash over me before pooling like warmed honey in my core. When I shift on the seat, attempting to alleviate the growing discomfort, a growl rumbles up from deep within his chest.

My eyes widen at the animalistic sound that escapes from him before slicing to his face. The heat darkening his eyes is enough to have my heart skipping a painful beat before pounding harshly beneath my breast.

He wraps his hand around my jean clad thigh. The fingers that I had just been staring at tighten, sinking into my flesh. They keep me tethered to the earth, so I don't float off into the atmosphere never to be heard from again.

I force out an unsteady breath, trying to dispel the arousal rushing through my veins, suffusing every cell of my being. I've never felt attraction like this before, and I'm unsure what to do with it.

Maybe that's not completely true.

I know exactly what to do with it, but I'm unsure how to take that next step. Or even if I'm ready for it. I'm a twenty-year-old virgin with no real idea how to proceed.

I'd meant it when I told Viola that our relationship was complicated.

"Are you ready to do this?" he asks, breaking into the chaotic whirl of my thoughts.

When I blink, unsure what he's asking, a slow smile spreads across his lips as the look of intensity is taken down a few notches, making it possible for me to suck fresh oxygen into my lungs.

His voice dips. "I'm asking if you're ready to drive."

Heat slams into my cheeks that he's able to read me so easily. When my tongue darts out to moisten parched lips, his gaze drops to the movement. As he stares, his teeth scrape across the plump lower lip as his lids turn heavy.

Any moment, I'll self-combust.

He doesn't say another word before shifting toward the windshield and pulling away from the curb and out of the parking lot.

I couldn't be more aware of the man beside me if I tried.

By the time we reach the church parking lot, I feel like all of my out-of-control emotions are back under submission. At the very least, I'm hoping to fake it until I make it.

He parks in the middle of the vacant lot and another round of nerves detonates at the bottom of my belly but it's for an entirely different reason. If I was desperately searching for something to dampen all the arousal careening through my system, the idea of sliding behind the wheel does it.

Without a word, he jerks the handle open and slips out of the muscle car before walking around the shiny hood. It's only when he opens my door that I realize I'm frozen in place, terrified to move a single muscle.

I squeeze my eyelids tightly closed and attempt to fight back the terror. I wish the idea of driving wasn't so paralyzing. Millions of people do it every day without issue.

And yet, here I am, trapped in the past. Reliving the worst day of my life whenever the idea of starting up a car and pulling onto the road pops into my brain.

How will I ever conquer this fear?

Gentle fingers slip beneath my chin. "Open your eyes, Fallyn."

The sound of his soft yet commanding voice has my eyelids fluttering open, and I find him hunkered down in front of me so that we're eye level. "I don't blame you for being scared, but you need to work through it. And we'll do that together, okay? I'll be here beside you the entire time. Miles would be proud of you for taking this step."

Tears prick my eyes at his heartfelt promise. A long moment stretches between us as I search his green depths and find nothing but sincerity. It wouldn't take much to get lost in them.

As easy as tumbling down the rabbit hole.

My heart thumps a painful tattoo against my ribcage.

His face looms close enough for his minty breath to ghost across my parted lips. "I won't let anything else happen to you."

There's a savagery to the words as his fingers tighten around my lower jaw. The pressure isn't enough to cause pain. More like ground me in the moment and dispel the hurt and anger of our past as it slyly tries to weave its way around us.

His gaze sifts through mine. When he's satisfied with what he finds, he asks, "Are you ready?"

I jerk my head into a tight nod.

What other choice is there but to soldier on?

When I remain frozen in place, he reaches in, brushing against me as he unclicks the seatbelt, causing the protective strap to release. The woodsy scent of his cologne cocoons me in comfort, making me feel strangely safe in his presence.

He retreats before straightening to his full height as I force myself to climb out of the car. Electricity sizzles through my veins as he nabs my fingers and pulls me into the comforting circle of his arms before wrapping me up tight in their strength. Any distance I've forced myself to maintain collapses like a flimsy house of cards as I burrow against his broad chest. It takes a few minutes for my anxiety to dissipate until it becomes easier to breathe.

Wolf drops a kiss against the top of my head and whispers, "You got this, Fallyn. I believe in you."

With one last squeeze, he unwinds his arms and takes a step in retreat.

I slip around him and head to the driver's side before sliding inside the expensive vehicle and fastening the seatbelt with hands that tremble. Since the engine was never turned off, the car continues to idle. One foot settles tentatively on the clutch and the other on the brake as my fingers wrap around the gear shift. I release a shaky breath and attempt to settle everything that vibrates like a live wire inside me. Even though I miss the way his hand had settled over mine, guiding it during our last lesson, I don't ask for him to do it again.

I run through a mental checklist and adjust the mirrors before sliding the seat closer to the wheel since Wolf is taller than I am. Then I gently press the clutch and gas pedal as I shift into first gear just like he taught me. The car jerks forward before stalling.

Everything inside me deflates. If this isn't a sign from above, I don't know what is.

He lays his large palm over my hand. "It's fine. Shake it off. Turn on the engine again and let's start over."

"All right," I mutter, repeating the process.

When he doesn't pull away, leaving me to my own devices, some of my anxiety dissolves. This time, the Mustang doesn't immediately die. When it begins to shutter, I step on the gas and the engine revs as the car jerks forward. Picking up speed, I shift into second.

He gives my hand a little squeeze. "Good job. See? It's not so hard."

I snort.

Ha! It's surprisingly more difficult than it looks when someone else is doing the driving. Why would anyone bother with a manual when automatic is so much easier?

We circle the deserted lot at least a dozen times until I'm in third gear and somewhat confident that I won't lose control and end up crashing into the front of the church.

"Okay. You've mastered this part." He nods toward the street. "I think you're ready to hit the road."

I flick a nervous glance at him before my attention arrows back to the windshield. "Please tell me that you're not serious."

"Of course I am. You're doing great." His hand stays wrapped around mine. "I wouldn't suggest it unless I thought you were ready."

I circle the paved lot a few more times, trying to work up my courage to leave it behind.

"Come on, Fallyn," he cajoles. "You can do it."

"Don't push me," I grumble, reluctantly turning out of the lot and onto the city street.

My pulse leaps, skittering beneath my skin as my fingers lock around the steering wheel. He rubs soothing circles across the back of my hand. The caress is just enough to get my attention and dissolve the iciness that coats my insides.

"Relax, angel. You're doing great. Take a left turn at the next light."

As we approach the intersection, I downshift and crank the wheel before expelling a harsh breath from my lungs. Then I'm back in third. Wolf turns on the radio until indie rock fills the small cabin. After a few minutes, I find myself humming along with the music.

When 'Mr. Brightside' by The Killers pours through the speakers, my mind tumbles back to when he sang it during karaoke at Slap Shotz. His gaze had slid over the crowd of rowdy college students before fastening onto mine. I should have realized then that everything was about to change.

Whether I was ready or not.

"Told you I was coming out of my cage," he murmurs, as if he understands the thoughts running rampant through my head.

It's disconcerting.

We've always had that kind of uncanny ability with each other. That's what happens when you've known someone your entire life.

My eyes dart to him for just a heartbeat before returning to the black ribbon of road stretched out in front of me. A shiver shimmies down my spine as I rack my brain for something to say. My tongue feels thick and useless in my mouth. Tension continues to ratchet up until it turns explosive. It wouldn't take much to blow us both to smithereens.

It's almost a relief when he says, "Turn left here."

I pull into a semi-crowded parking lot and realize that we're at the same diner as the first time we went out driving. I ease into a spot near the back where it's less packed and turn off the engine. All of the tension gripping me loosens as I relax against the seat and release an unsteady breath into the atmosphere.

"I did it." My voice comes out sounding shaky.

"Yes, you did. You should be proud of yourself." His lips curve. "I'm proud of you, Fallyn. Even though you were scared, you fought through it."

Pleasure bursts inside me like an overinflated balloon. His praise shouldn't have the power to affect me, but it does, and I refuse to lie to myself and pretend that's not the case.

It's only when he flexes his fingers that I realize they're still wrapped around mine and have been there the entire time in a silent show of support.

"Are you hungry?"

After that, I'm famished. It feels like I've scaled a mountain and lived to tell the tale.

With a nod, we exit the vehicle before meeting in front of the hood. When he slips my fingers into his hand, I can't help but glance down at them. After all the intimacy we've shared, holding hands is nothing.

And yet, the contact feels unbearably intimate.

As I contemplate tugging them away and putting some much-needed distance between us, I'm slammed with the realization that I don't want to. I like the feel of his hand wrapped protectively around mine. It's been a long time since I felt safe and secure.

Those disturbing thoughts circle through my brain as we settle at a table inside the diner. I glance at the plastic-coated menu even though I know exactly what I'm going to order. A few customers and staff greet Wolf, calling out his name and telling him that he had a great game the other night along with how much they're looking forward to the next one.

A different waitress takes our order. She looks older. Maybe college-aged like us. The entire time she attempts to flirt with Wolf, his eyes stay locked on mine.

He's in no way rude, but he doesn't go out of his way to encourage her chatter either. It doesn't take long for her to realize that she won't be able to draw his attention away from me and her behavior turns brisk before she finally disappears. Barely does she say a word when dropping off our drinks.

Two waters along with chocolate milkshakes.

I shift on the red vinyl seat as his gaze remains fastened to me. The intensity of his undivided attention is as flattering as it is alarming. When I bring the straw to my lips, his gaze drops to the movement and his eyes darken, the pupils swallowing up the green of his irises. He draws the corner of his lip into his mouth before slanting a heavy-lidded look my way.

The heat in his eyes is enough to reignite the arousal that's been simmering in my core since our last meeting in the hotel room. I haven't been able to stop thinking about what it felt like to have his mouth on me. Sure, I've heard my friends talk about sex, but I never imagined it could feel so amazing.

It was like the world detonated around me.

And I didn't give a damn.

I can't help but long for more.

With Wolf.

He cocks his head, all the while sifting carefully through my eyes. Keeping all my private thoughts locked away is impossible.

"What are you thinking over there?" His voice sounds as if it's been scraped raw.

My guess is that he already knows.

I drag my eyes away as heat floods my cheeks.

"Answer me, Fallyn." There's a sharpness to his voice that has my attention snapping back to him.

"What?"

"Tell me what you're thinking."

My teeth scrape across my lower lip as my pulse skitters. I shouldn't bring it up as if I'm eager for him to lay hands on me again.

Except…that's exactly what I am.

Eager.

Needy.

I'm a ball of sexual tension waiting to explode at the tiniest spark.

It's demoralizing.

And by the intensity written across his face, he understands it.

I'm ashamed to admit that it was so bad the other night, I closed my eyes and conjured up a mental image of what he looked like between my outstretched thighs. Then I touched myself. It didn't take long until I was a slippery mess. Unfortunately, the orgasm was a pale imitation of what it felt like to have Wolf bury his finger inside my pussy or run his lips over my aching flesh.

When I remain silent, he reaches across the table and snags my hand, wrapping his larger one around it. His thumb rubs soft circles against my palm. The innocuous caress sends shockwaves throughout my body.

"There's no more running away," he murmurs as if I'm in need of the reminder.

After the other night, I've already figured out that much.

"Now tell me what's going through your head because, whatever it is, I can see it written clearly across your face."

"Then it seems like you already know. I shouldn't have to say a word."

He leans closer, bridging the divide between us. "I do, but it's important that I hear it from your lips, angel."

The endearment goes straight to the heart of me before exploding upon impact.

I straighten my shoulders and force out the question. "Are you still going to take my virginity?"

His nostrils flare as something dark and possessive leaps into his eyes. "Yes, but not because I paid for it. I want you to give it to me of your own free will."

Even though it's tempting to run and hide from the earnestness of his expression, I'm powerless to do so.

"I want you to be my first," I whisper, telling him what he's so desperate for me to acknowledge.

"Good, because that's exactly what I want."

With a gulp, I attempt to swallow down the nerves that vibrate in my chest at the blunt conversation we're having in the middle of this diner. "Is that something you've thought about over the years?"

He leans as close as the table will allow. "Of course it is. I've always wanted to be your first. Just like I wanted you to be mine."

My mouth falls open as his words somersault through my brain and I shake my head, wondering if I've misunderstood the admittance.

From the intensity of his expression and the muscle that ticks a mad rhythm in his jaw, my guess is that I haven't.

Which means that like me, Wolf Westerville is still a virgin.

CHAPTER 30

WOLF

Fuck.

I didn't mean to blurt out the truth like that.

By her slack-jawed expression, I've shocked the hell out of her.

It's tempting to plow a hand through my hair and glance away, but I refuse to do that. My gaze stays pinned to Fallyn. I've been waiting years for a chance to slip back into her life and there's no way I'm going to be anything less than honest.

Even if it means embarrassing the fuck out of myself.

There's nothing I wouldn't do for the dark-haired beauty sitting across from me. She's so stunning, both inside and out, that it robs me of breath and makes my heart ache.

After the accident, I never thought I'd get this chance again.

Now that I have, wild horses couldn't drag me away.

"Are you saying…" Her voice trails off as her narrowed eyes search mine.

I lift my chin, all the while rubbing soft circles against her palm. "Go ahead. Get it out."

"Are you trying to say that you've never had sex before?" There's a beat of strained silence. "Is that what you're telling me?"

I jerk my shoulders and try to keep my voice level. "Would that really be so hard to believe?"

Her eyes widen as if I've just said something outlandish. "Yeah, it is."

"Why?"

She blinks before muttering, "Because...well, look at you."

Heat suffuses her cheeks.

It's fucking adorable.

"What's that supposed to mean?" I ask, a slight quirk on my lips.

"You're gorgeous. Ever since stepping foot on campus, I've heard how girls talk about you. The hot, tatted up goalie." Fallyn rolls her eyes, letting me know what her thoughts are on the matter. "You can't be that oblivious."

"You're right. I'm not."

She straightens and lifts her chin. "So then, the answer is no. I don't believe for a minute that you haven't had the chance to hook up with all the groupies that throw themselves at you."

I shift closer until the hard edge of the table presses into my chest. "You're talking about two different things. One is opportunity. The other is desire." When she blinks again like I've complicated a mathematical equation she's desperate to solve, I continue. "I've had plenty of opportunities to have sex. The problem is that I've never wanted anyone as much as I want *you*."

That slack jawed expression returns full force.

It's so damn tempting to slide from the booth, scoop her up into my arms, and carry her ass out of the restaurant, but there's more that needs to be hashed out between us before that can occur.

My grip tightens around her fingers as my eyes probe hers, sifting through the disbelief. She needs to understand just how serious I am.

This matters.

She matters.

"You're the only one I've ever wanted, Fallyn. It's been that way for as long as I can remember. How could I think about screwing another girl when none of them were you?"

That question hangs heavily in the air.

"Your parents wouldn't allow you to date until you were sixteen. So, I waited. I wanted to ask you on your birthday but..."

Grief flashes across her face. "The accident."

"Yeah." I can only imagine that the very same expression is etched across mine. Fallyn turned sixteen a month after her brother died.

When she leans closer, it feels as if we're both straining toward each other. Like two magnets intent on being together.

"You've really never had sex?" Confusion flickers across her face as her voice dips to a whisper. "Like ever?"

"I tried to fool around with a couple of groupies freshman year, but it didn't feel right." Memories flash through my brain. "It was awkward. Every time I closed my eyes, you were the one I imagined. But none of them smelled or felt like you. Their lips weren't plush like yours. So, I didn't bother. I focused on school and hockey." Before I can stop myself, I blurt, "And you."

She tucks an errant lock of hair behind her ear. "Me? What do you mean?"

I jerk my shoulders, not wanting to come off like a stalker.

Although...

Maybe that's exactly what I am.

Even when I thought Fallyn was lost to me, there was only ever her.

"I kept tabs on you. When you were in the hospital and then when you started at the new high school. I knew a few guys who played hockey there, and they watched out for you. Made sure no one gave you problems."

I examine her face for clues as to what she's thinking. The last thing I want to do is creep her out.

"You did?"

"Yeah."

When I squeeze her fingers, she glances down and stares at them for a long, silent moment. With every heartbeat, the tension ratchets up until there's a good possibility I'll choke on it.

Nerves get the best of me. "Fallyn?"

"I just can't believe all of this," she whispers before chewing her lower lip. "Were you serious when you said that my parents wouldn't allow you to see me? When I asked them, they said you didn't bother reaching out." Her voice thickens with unspent emotion. "That it was Miles you were friends with, not me."

Anger rushes through my veins. It takes effort to keep my voice level, but it still comes out sounding like a feral growl. "I always cared about you. I was friends with you just as much as I was with Miles."

Her shoulders fall forward as if there is a thousand-pound weight forcing them down. "I don't know what to believe. I hate the idea that they might have lied to me." Her voice dips. "That they kept you away on purpose. Especially when I needed you more than anything else."

My heart twists beneath my ribcage. I hate that I wasn't there for her and couldn't help her to heal.

"But I also realize how much they blamed you. And your family. It's consumed them this entire time."

Unable to help myself, I scoot from the booth. Two long-legged steps are all it takes to bring me around to her side. Her wide blue eyes track my every movement as she stares up at me. Before she can ask what I'm doing, I slide onto the seat and gather her up into my arms. I can't stand the physical distance for another second and need her close. I wasn't able to be there for her after the accident, but I'm here now.

It's a relief when she doesn't shove me away. "I'm sorry, angel. So fucking sorry. I should have fought harder." But I'd been sixteen years old and lost in my own despair. My parents had agreed that giving the DiMarco family space to grieve was the right thing to do.

That space then turned into an impenetrable fortress impossible to breach.

The first time I mentioned it, I don't think Fallyn believed me. Or maybe she didn't want to accept that her parents were capable of lying to her and would deliberately keep us apart.

The last thing I want is for her to have issues with them. Deep down, I realize they were only trying to protect her after the loss of Miles, but I won't allow the distance to linger any longer. I can't continue to stand on the outside and watch her.

Fallyn belongs to me.

Hugo and Eleanor won't like it, but at some point, they'll have to come to terms with it. Because I refuse to live another day without her by my side.

I won't.

A heavy silence descends as I press her close.

For the first time in years, it feels like I can breathe again.

That's what this girl does to me.

Breathes life into my lungs.

I lose track of how long we sit in the restaurant clinging to one another like survivors lost at sea. All I know is that I'll never get enough of her. I press my lips against the shiny black strands of her hair before inhaling the rosemary and mint scent. She's like a drug careening through my veins. I just want to snort her up and feel the rush.

A growl of displeasure escapes from me when she wiggles out of my embrace and tips her chin upward to meet my gaze. Everything within me stills as emotion flickers across her features. She's so damn expressive. One look and I know what she's thinking.

When so much has changed over the years, it's a relief to see that some things are still the same. I search her eyes, needing her to work through all the silent questions circling around in her brain so we can finally move forward.

"Ask me, Fallyn. I'm an open book where you're concerned. I'll never be anything but truthful with you."

Color rises in her cheeks as she glances away.

When she remains silent, I urge in lower tones, "Whatever it is, ask me."

The breath she releases escapes from her lungs like a slow leak. "It's difficult to believe that you've never done anything before."

I drop my voice, needing her to understand just how much she means to me. Even when she thought I'd moved on. "Your pussy is the only one I've tasted. It's the only one I want."

Forever.

But I'll keep that tidbit to myself for the time being.

She sneaks a peek at the customers that surround us, but none are paying any attention to our conversation.

Her brows rise as she mumbles, "You've never had a blowjob?"

I shake my head. "Nope."

It's like she can't wrap her brain around the fact that I have as little experience as she does. While the scar on her chest is what held her back from getting physical, mine was by design.

With a smirk, I shrug. "I've jacked off plenty of times."

Heat gathers in her cheeks as she whispers, "Have you ever thought about me when you, um, do it?"

"Every fucking time," I growl. "And I've read a shit ton of romance novels because I wanted to understand what would feel good for you." There's a pause before I add, "How I could give you the most pleasure."

Arousal sparks to life in her eyes before she glances away and tucks her chin close to her chest.

Unwilling to let her pull away from me—*from this*—I slip my fingers around her jaw and force her to meet my gaze.

"Don't do that, angel. Don't hide. Not when I've finally found you." I search her eyes. "There's no reason to be embarrassed by what we do alone or together. Just know that I have no regrets about waiting. I want to do everything with you. *Only you.*"

A smile tugs at her cupid's bow of a mouth. "I want that too."

All I can say is thank fuck.

"If you wanted me so badly, why didn't we have sex in the hotel room?" More color stains her cheeks. "It's not like you didn't buy my virginity."

Did I think about doing it with her each and every time we were together?

Damn right I did.

"After all these years, I wanted our first time to be special. And I wanted you to know exactly who was taking your innocence and making love to you." I shift on the seat as thoughts of what she looked like spread out on the king-sized mattress press in at the edges. So fucking beautiful. Like a goddamn angel. "And it had to be your choice. No matter how it was supposed to play out."

"Yes," she whispers.

My brows rise as my cock twitches. "Yes, what?"

"I don't want to wait any longer. I want you to be my first. *Now.* Too much time has already been stolen from us."

Thrown off by her response, I release an unsteady breath. I thought she might need time to process everything we've discussed this evening. Even though I don't want to, I pump the breaks before excitement can crash through my system and I scoop her up, throw her over my shoulder, and carry her out of this restaurant like a caveman.

"I don't want you to think that we have to jump into bed and have sex. We can take as much time as you need and get to know one another again."

It's a surprise when she shakes her head. "I don't want to wait. I want to be with you now."

That's all it takes for my erection to press painfully against the zipper of my jeans.

But still...

"There's no pressure. I need you to be sure, Fallyn."

"Maybe you're the one who's having second thoughts."

That ridiculous comment is all it takes for me to slide from the booth and rise to my feet before pulling her along with me. Before she can ask any questions, I give into the impulse that's been pounding through me since she stalked across the distance that separated us on campus and slapped me.

I scoop her into my arms and carry her out of the diner.

CHAPTER 31

FALLYN

Wolf's hungry mouth roves over mine as the elevator rises to the third floor. There's nothing gentle about the caress. And I wouldn't want there to be. He's already spent time kissing me softly, licking and sucking at my mouth in a worshipful way, conveying just how much he wants me.

How much he's *always* wanted me.

But this feels different.

If he could eat me alive, he'd do it in a heartbeat.

And I'd love every minute of it.

The need that vibrates off him in heavy, suffocating waves is nothing short of intoxicating.

My arms tangle around his neck as I cling to him, rubbing against his muscular body like a cat in heat. We're pressed together so tightly that I feel the thick jut of his arousal against my lower abdomen. A whimper of need escapes from me as the car jolts and a bell signals our arrival.

All I can think about is what it'll feel like when he finally slides deep inside the heat of my body. The only thing I have to compare it to is when he pressed his finger inside me.

Except it'll be thicker.

Much thicker.

As anxious as that thought makes me, it also fills me with anticipation and excitement. I've dreamed about this moment since I was fifteen years old. I want to experience that kind of closeness with Wolf.

And the fact that he saved all his firsts...

A bubble of giddiness bursts within me. It's almost too much for the confines of my skin.

The metal doors slide apart, and a shocked gasp penetrates the thick haze that surrounds me. I reluctantly crack open an eyelid, only to find three girls standing in the hallway with their mouths hanging open.

One of them clears her throat. "Hi, Wolf." Envy brims from her voice.

His grip intensifies as if he's afraid I'll flee. He should realize that I'm not going anywhere. An unintelligible response escapes from him before he drags me out of the elevator and down the hallway. Their high-pitched laughter chases after us.

I should be embarrassed by the PDA.

But I'm not.

At all.

I don't give a crap about those girls or the gossiping that will inevitably follow. Any of them would trade places with me in a heartbeat.

His long legs eat up the length of the hallway faster than I'm able to keep up with. It's only when he grounds to a halt outside his apartment and fishes out a key from his pocket that I'm able to catch my breath.

When he shoves open the door, it hits the interior wall with a shudder. A growl escapes from him as he swings toward me and nibbles at my lips before lifting me into his arms. His eyes flash with so much heat and hunger as he tips his chin upward to hold mine. The sheer force of it arrows straight down to my core before exploding like a firework. The need to feel more of him spirals through me as I tangle my legs around his waist. His large hands palm my ass, squeezing and kneading the flesh.

That's all it takes for arousal to burst to life within me as a groan breaks loose and my grip around him intensifies. Even though there are way too many layers of clothing separating us, I grind against his hard abdominals, desperate for friction.

I'm so damn needy for what only he can give me.

He kicks the door shut before stalking through the living area and then down a short hallway to the bedroom. Once closed inside his private space, we stay locked together. The way our mouths are fused, and our tongues tangle is nothing short of intoxicating. As much as I don't want to break the contact, I can't bear the layers of clothing that keep me from his naked flesh.

I wiggle around until he realizes that I'm trying to escape his hold before sliding against his muscular body until my Chucks touch the carpet.

Only then do I break our kiss.

A growl rumbles up from deep within his chest as he stares at me. The heated look he slants my way is almost menacing. The saliva dries in my mouth as hot licks of need pool in my core.

Without a sound, my shaky fingers tighten around his sweatshirt, dragging it up his torso until I can pull it over his head. There's a black Western Wildcats hockey T-shirt that quickly meets the same fate.

A gasp escapes from me as I stare at his bare chest.

Not only is he heavily muscled and thickly corded, he's covered in tattoos. There's so much color decorating his flesh that I'm unsure where to look first. I don't realize that I've reached out to touch him until my fingertips ghost over his chiseled pectorals.

When we were kids, I caught sight of him all the time when we'd hang out by the pool. There wasn't a single mark on him. That he's had all of this color and artwork tattooed on him in the span of five years seems almost unbelievable.

Just as I open my mouth to fire off a barrage of questions, my gaze falls on my brother's full name with the date of his birth and subsequent death. Wolf stills as my fingers drift over the swirling ink. A thick lump forms in my throat as hot tears prick the backs of my eyes, making it impossible to breathe. It takes effort to blink them away as I force my gaze to his.

"You marked yourself with him."

His fingers wrap around mine before drawing them to his lips and brushing a soft kiss against the knuckles.

"How could I not?"

Heavy emotion swamps me as I refocus my attention on the sun-kissed flesh that has been turned into a canvas of precious memories. There are hockey sticks in an X with Miles' number on it and the perfect illustration of his beloved Porsche.

My heart stops before pounding into overdrive when I see my name framed by peonies. Ever since I can remember, Wolf would give me a vaseful of bright pink peonies on my birthday. They were always my favorite. In the summer, our gardens would overflow with their wild blooms.

My shaking fingers drift over each letter.

I just…

Can't believe this.

More wetness gathers in my eyes as I lift them to meet his. "When did you get all these?"

"The year after he died, I inked his name on my chest. And then each anniversary, I've added to it. No matter what, he'll always be with me."

I brush my lips across my brother's name, completely blown away by what I've discovered. If I didn't realize it before, I do now.

This man holds so much love for me.

That knowledge crashes over me like a tidal wave, threatening to suck me under.

For so many years, I felt lost and adrift without the two most important people in my life.

Only now does it feel like I've been found.

He threads his fingers through my hair before tilting my face upward so that I have no other choice but to meet the steadiness of his gaze. "You know that I've always loved you, right?"

I nod. My heart feels as if it's on the verge of exploding.

"It's always been you, Fallyn. Always."

It's only as I stare into his eyes and the sincerity that brims from them that I wonder if my love for Wolf is what kept me from getting involved with other guys. Sure, the scar marring my chest bothered me. But deep down, I suspect it was more than that.

I love you, too," I whisper, needing him to know that I feel the same.

No matter what happened in our past, this was meant to be.

We were meant to be.

Fate would have continued to nudge us toward one another.

The need to see all of him, to be as close as possible, spirals through me. My fingers settle on the button of his jeans before flicking it open and lowering the zipper. More colorful tattoos decorate his abdomen. The thick length of his cock presses insistently against the denim. I slip my hand inside the cotton and drag it down until his erection can spring free.

It's not like I haven't seen photos of penises before, but it's quite another thing to see one up close in real life.

And Wolf is...*big.*

Both thick and long.

I shove the jeans along with the boxer-briefs down his thighs before sinking to my knees and glancing up until my gaze can fasten on his. Sparks of heat flash from his eyes as his hands stay tangled in my hair. The firm pressure is what grounds me in the moment.

My tongue darts out to lick the bulbous tip, and a burst of saltiness explodes in my mouth. It's strange to realize that I like the way he tastes. When I take another greedy swipe, a guttural groan escapes from him.

"You don't have to do that, Fallyn. It's not something I expect."

"I want to."

My tongue flicks out to wet my lips before I wrap them around the mushroom-shaped head and suck him into the warmth of my mouth.

Even though I've never done this before, and I'm not quite sure how to go about it, I keep my eyes pinned to him in order to gauge his reaction as I take him as deep as I can before retreating. His fingers tighten around the sides of my scalp with each pass I make.

Just when I find my rhythm, his cock swells, growing impossibly hard. A few seconds later, he pushes me away. His dick is released with a soft pop as my brows furrow. One hand stays wrapped around the side of my head as the other drifts across my jaw before grazing my swollen lips.

"Did I do something wrong?" How embarrassing would that be?

With a snort, he shakes his head. "No, you did everything right. A little *too* right." His voice sounds as if it's been roughed up by sandpaper, and it scrapes something low in my belly. He leans down until he can wrap his hands around my ribcage before lifting me to my feet and pressing a hot kiss against my mouth.

He breaks away just enough to whisper, "When I finally come, it's going to be in that sweet little pussy of yours. I want to feel your tight heat wrapped around my hard cock, strangling the life out of it. It's all I've been able to think about."

More arousal pools in my core as those images flash through my head like a slow-motion picture show.

Before I can agree with the sentiment, he shoves both the jeans and boxers down his legs until he's completely naked. He doesn't give me the chance to take in his male beauty as he scoops me into his arms and carries me to the queen-sized bed. It's gently that he lays me down, hovering over me and caging me in with his bigger, muscular body. His gaze searches mine as his mouth descends. When his tongue sweeps across my lips, I open, allowing him entrance. And just like in the elevator, our kiss is deep and all encompassing. It's as if he can't get close enough.

As if he wants to devour me.

It wouldn't take much for him to swallow me whole.

My arms twine around his neck to draw him closer.

Just as I lose myself in the caress, he pulls away. "I want to strip you bare."

His fingers tangle in the hem of my sweater before dragging it up my chest and over my head. The pale pink bra with a tiny bow in the center is the next garment to be shed. Love shines brightly from his eyes as he stares down at me before lowering his face to my chest and pressing his lips against the scar. My fingers slide through the short strands to hold him in place.

"You're so fucking perfect." He rains soft kisses down on me before admitting roughly, "I waited so damn long for you that I almost gave up hope of this—*of us*— happening."

My arms tighten around him as tears spring to my eyes. "I'm so sorry. For everything you went through."

He tilts his head until our gazes can catch and lock. "We should have been able to lean on one another and be there for each other."

That comment is like a dagger to my heart because he's right. The three of us were so tight. Wolf and I should have been allowed to grieve together. Instead, my parents kept us apart and started a war between our families. I understand their pain and anguish. It's one they continue to breathe life into each and every day, but what they did was wrong. And at some point, we'll be forced to have an honest conversation about it. There's no other way for the four of us to move forward.

Unwilling to take anything away from this moment with Wolf, I focus on the gorgeous man looming over me.

He's the only one I want to think about.

"I'm just thankful that you're here with me now."

He presses one last kiss against the jagged flesh before sinking further down my body. The scrape of his teeth leaves me shifting as my core dampens with need. When he reaches the waistband of my jeans, he flicks open the metal button before drawing down the zipper. The sound of metal teeth grinding against one another is the only one that fills the room.

He presses his lips to the exposed skin above my panties before shimmying the material over my hips and thighs until I'm just as naked as he is. He rises to his knees on the mattress so he can stare down at me for a long stretch of minutes. His hot gaze licks over every inch. The heat of it slides over my curves. As much as I want to cover myself and shield his view, the worshipful look that brims in his eyes is what keeps my arms pinned to my sides.

"I know I keep saying it but it's true—you're so fucking beautiful. There's no way I could ever get tired of looking at you like this."

I release an unsteady breath and allow my thighs to fall open so that he can see every inch. A tortured groan escapes from him as his gaze arrows to my core. He wraps strong fingers around one bare ankle before lifting it so that he can settle between them.

Instead of delving in and stroking his fingers over me like I expect, he murmurs, "I need another taste of your honey. I'm so fucking addicted to it." His gaze slices to mine. "To you."

As the heat of his mouth settles over me, my eyelids feather shut. He licks my slit from the top to the bottom with the flat of his velvety soft tongue and then back up again before circling my clit. Arousal explodes within me, ricocheting through every cell of my being.

Even though he's only begun to touch me, I already realize that I won't last long. It's as if I'm on sensory overload. My back bows off the mattress as his large hands lock around my thighs to hold me in place as he spreads me even wider and continues to eat at my delicate flesh.

Just as my muscles tighten and I'm about to splinter apart, he retreats and leaves me hanging. A gasp escapes from me as my eyelids fly open. A knowing smirk curls the edges of his lips as he crawls up my body until the blunt head of his cock is nestled against my soaked entrance.

My eyes widen as they hold his gaze.

"I've waited too damn long for us not to come together."

As he mutters the rough words, I realize that it's exactly what I want. "Okay."

His face lowers until our mouths can align. Only then does he slip his tongue between my lips to dance with my own.

A few heartbeats later, he pulls away just enough to growl, "Can you taste yourself on me? Best fucking flavor in the world. If I ate your pussy every single day, it still wouldn't be enough."

His heated confession has arousal flooding my core and I widen my legs, wanting him to sink further inside my body. It's almost a surprise when he stops.

"I should grab a condom."

I shake my head. "You don't have to. I'm protected."

He searches my eyes. "Are you sure?"

"Yes. Please."

"Okay." With gritted teeth, he presses forward. The muscle in his jaw ticks as he flexes his hips.

"Fuck, baby. You're so damn tight. It's like a fist clenched around me. I've never felt anything so amazing." Concern flickers in his eyes as they search mine. "Does it feel good for you?"

"It does." It's not a total lie. I refuse to tell him that there's a bite of pain because I don't want him to stop. And I certainly don't want anything to ruin this moment that's been years in the making.

As he props himself up on his elbows, the muscles of his biceps bulge, caging me in with his strength. I've never felt more cherished or protected. And that has everything to do with the man who is making slow love to me.

He advances an inch or so before withdrawing, only to repeat the movement until he's buried inside my body. As he steadily rocks against me, my inner muscles stretch around his girth, and pleasure gradually blooms to life. It's almost a surprise when a moan escapes from me and I flex my hips to meet his careful thrusts.

Intensity fills his eyes as he slides into my tight heat. I arch, wanting more.

Wanting everything he has to offer.

"You understand that it was always meant to be like this, don't you?" He withdraws only to glide back inside.

I nod. Even when that wasn't a concept I was able to acknowledge to myself, deep down I realized Wolf was my other half.

He grits his teeth as if in pain. "I can't go any further without hurting you, Fallyn. And I fucking hate that it needs to happen. But I promise this will be the last time."

My hand drifts upward to cup his shadowed jaw. For just a

moment, he squeezes his eyes tightly shut before pressing into my palm.

"Just do it. I'll be fine." His concern is sweet. How many guys would hesitate when they're this turned on? Only Wolf. "You don't have to worry about me."

His ridiculously long eyelashes flutter open.

"You're mine to take care of and that responsibility weighs on me. I hate that this will cause you even a moment of agony."

"It's okay. I'll be fine because I'm here with you."

Determination fills his eyes as they stay locked on mine. He withdraws before sliding back inside my body with more force. The moment he breaks through the fragile barrier, a scream tears from my lips, and his mouth crashes over mine, swallowing down every single cry. Now that he's buried to the hilt, he holds himself perfectly still, allowing my inner muscles the time it takes to adjust.

He pulls back just enough to search my eyes as a silent tear treks down my cheek. He kisses the wetness away before doing the same to the other side.

"I'm so sorry, angel."

"It's all right." My voice wobbles. "It wasn't so bad."

With his hips pressed against mine, it feels as if I'm pinned to the mattress by his thick cock. I have no idea why that thought turns me on so much. As my body stretches around his girth, the pain of his intrusion recedes and arousal once again sparks to life. I can't help but squirm against him.

"Are you ready for me to continue? Or should I stop?" The muscles of his throat constrict with the question. His jaw is still clenched as if it'll shatter into a million jagged pieces. "Because I will if that's what you want."

"Please don't stop."

He releases a steady stream of air from between his lips as he squeezes his eyes closed for a second or two. "You're so warm and wet. *Tight*. It's almost too much to take. It's too damn good." His teeth scrape across his lower lip. "There's no way I'll last long."

Just as he pulls all the way out, a sigh of relief escapes from me before he surges forward again.

A tortured groan escapes from him. "How am I going to live outside your body now that I know how damn good it feels to be buried inside it?"

Even though I can hear how tightly strung his voice is and feel the tension quivering through every hard muscle, Wolf takes it slow, making sure every movement is gentle. By the sixth stroke, there's no denying the pleasure that's unfurling inside me.

It doesn't take long for us to find a rhythm. With a whimper, I arch. It's as if I'm chasing the same pleasure as when his face was buried between my thighs.

"Do you feel it, baby?" When I nod, he says, "I want us to come together."

"I want that, too."

His lips lift into a tortured smile as he rocks against me. When my muscles fill with tension, I know I'm close to careening over the edge and into oblivion.

Just as my inner muscles spasm, he groans, and the warmth of his release paints my womb. He throws his head back until I can glimpse the thickly corded muscles of his throat. It's only when his body turns slack that he huffs out a satisfied breath. The warmth of it stirs my hair and feathers across the delicate skin near my ear and neck.

"I love you, Fallyn."

He lifts his head to search my eyes. His expression turns serious as if he wants me to know that it's not the orgasm talking but that he truly means it.

"I love you, too."

He rests his forehead against mine and stares into my eyes. "I'm never letting you go."

"I really hope you don't."

After finding each other for a second time, I don't think I could live through the loss of him again.

CHAPTER 32

WOLF

*B*y the time we emerge from the bedroom, it's after ten o'clock. Her smaller hand is safely ensconced in mine. Exactly where it belongs. The last thing I want to do is take her home. As soon as we step foot into the living room, my roommate and his girlfriend stare at us. Viola's eyes widen as a knowing expression lifts the corners of Madden's lips.

"Well, well, well. Isn't this an interesting turn of events," the fucker sing songs.

With a glare, I pull Fallyn a little closer. "Get used to it."

He snorts and lifts his hands as if in surrender. "Never said that it wasn't a good one, just interesting."

Viola pops to her feet. Her comically wide gaze flickers to me before homing in on her cousin. "I was just about to head out." She stares at her as if trying to execute some sort of Jedi mind trick before annunciating carefully, "Do you need a ride home?"

Fallyn squirms under the intensity of her stare. "Yeah, that would be great."

The blonde pops up from the couch and picks up her purse from the table before beelining toward the door.

As soon as Fallyn takes a step, I tug her back into my arms. The last thing I want to do is let her go. Not when I just got my hands on her after all these years. Not when we're finally on the same page. But I sense that she still has a few things to work out—namely her parents. They went to great lengths to keep us apart. It's doubtful they'll be thrilled that I'm back in her life again.

Especially after the way my father went behind Hugo's back and ousted him from the company. If anything, they'll despise me even more now than they did after their son's death.

Regret and grief spiral through me.

I wish it were possible for the two of us to hole up in my bedroom for the rest of our lives. Unfortunately, that's not an option. The only way for a relationship to work between us is if we're open and honest with the people in our lives. My parents don't give a shit if I'm with Fallyn. They're too wrapped up in themselves to care.

My gaze searches hers, attempting to sift through all the thoughts circling around in her head. Instead of finding confusion and doubt, there's a softness that fills her deep blue eyes that wasn't there before.

"Text me when you get home?" Even though my attention is trained on her, I feel the intensity of Madden's stare burning a hole through me. This is the first time he's seen me walk out of my bedroom with a girl. I'm sure he'll be filled with questions.

When she nods, I brush my lips across hers. It takes effort to rein in all of my baser instincts. It's so damn tempting to throw her over my shoulder and carry her back into my bedroom, but she's probably sore and needs a chance to work through everything that's happened between us.

"I love you," I whisper against her lips, needing her to know exactly how I feel. How I've always felt. And how goddamn good my life feels with her in it.

With that admittance, her body softens against me. "I love you, too."

The fist clenching my heart loosens just a bit. I stare into her eyes, feeling like I could get lost in them forever.

Viola clears her throat from the small entryway. "We should get moving. I still have a lot of reading to plow through."

A dull blush hits her cheeks.

Damn but she really is adorable.

"Okay."

I press my lips to hers one last time before setting her free. My gaze stays pinned to Fallyn as she heads to the door where her cousin waits with a hand planted on her hip.

And then they're gone, both of them disappearing into the hallway. I fucking hate how my world goes dark when she's not around.

"FYI—staring at the door isn't going to bring her back, Romeo."

I force my attention to my roommate and good friend before releasing a steady breath.

Before I can tell him to shut it, he says, "So…I guess you two are together now, huh?" It's not really a question.

"Yup." I drop down onto the chair situated across from him.

Madden has always been a pretty easy-going guy. Nothing ruffles his feathers. It's one of the reasons I agreed to live with both him and Ford instead of at the hockey house where Ryder, Maverick, Riggs, Colby, Hayes, and Bridger are.

It's nonstop chaos over there. Parties, girls, younger teammates crashing on the couches when they don't want to go back to the dorms. More parties.

I like the quiet.

He shifts on the couch. "And her parents?"

I stare at him for a long, drawn-out minute. Sometimes I forget that Madden was with Viola before the accident and is aware of our backstory.

"They don't know." It's tempting to tack on *yet* but part of me is afraid to. I'm terrified of losing Fallyn. Not when we've just got together, and everything is so new and fresh.

"Seems like it could be an issue," he says quietly.

With a nod, I drag a hand over my face. He's not telling me anything I don't already know. Hugo and Eleanor won't be pleased with this development. They went to great lengths to keep us apart.

As if to reinforce that thought, he adds quietly, "We got together with them over the break. Even though years have gone by, nothing has changed for them. They're still living in the shadow of Miles' death, and they want to keep Fallyn there as well." There's a pause. "Was there anything else that happened?"

Fuck.

"Yeah, my father got fed up with Hugo's bullshit and forced him out of the company they founded," I admit.

A low whistle escapes from Madden as he leans toward me, resting his elbows on outstretched knees. "How the hell are you going to overcome *that* obstacle? Don't you think they'll have a problem with you and their daughter being together?"

"Of course they will."

It's slowly that he shakes his head, staring at me like I'm crazy. "You realize this isn't going to end well, right? Did you ever think that maybe it's not worth it? That maybe the best thing you can do is let sleeping dogs lie?"

Tension floods my muscles.

Madden isn't telling me anything that hasn't already been secretly gnawing at the back of my brain.

And yet...

"How the hell am I supposed to do that? I love her. I've *always* loved her. For the past five years, it felt like a chunk of me was missing. I lost it the night of the accident. Now that Fallyn is back in my life, I feel whole again." I search his eyes for a sliver of understanding. "How can I just let that go?" Before he can respond, I lift my chin and say in challenge, "Is that something you could do? Just walk away from Viola?"

Even as I fire off the question, I already know the answer.

"Fuck, no." A steely expression enters his eyes. "Letting her go the first time was hard enough. I would have found a way to win her over and I wouldn't have stopped until she was mine."

"Exactly."

He shakes his head. "All I have to say is that you've got your fucking work cut out for you, man."

I snort.

Don't I know it.

CHAPTER 33

FALLYN

It's the bright winter sunlight streaming through the window that has me surfacing from a deep sleep. It's only when I stretch my muscles that I realize I'm not alone.

I don't have to turn my head to realize who I'm curled up against. I might have driven home with Viola last night and slipped into bed by myself, but as soon as I texted Wolf, he said he didn't want to sleep alone. That he'd spent enough nights without me.

Even though I'd told myself that a little bit of distance would do me some good, the thought of being snuggled up next to him was one I couldn't resist. Fifteen minutes later, I'd quietly let him into the apartment. I thought we'd make love again, but he'd pulled me into his tatted arms, and we'd drifted off to sleep.

A contented sigh escapes from me. It's been a long time since I've felt this kind of peace. So long that I almost didn't recognize what it was at first. That thought is quickly followed by one of my parents. As soon as they pop into my head, I force them out. I don't want to dwell on them when I'm wrapped up in Wolf's arms and just had the best night of my life.

After all this time, it finally feels like a tiny piece of the puzzle has fallen back into place again.

Wolf.

He was the missing piece. As much as I didn't want to believe it was true, he's made me feel whole again. The scar on my chest doesn't throb quite so much when we're together. The old wound isn't a constant reminder of everything I lost.

I crack open my eyelids and stare at the man next to me.

He's gorgeous.

I've heard girls gush about his dark green eyes, buzzed hair, bulging muscles, and tattoos. He's a menace in the crease and I'm sure that's part of his allure. He looks like a bad boy.

A player.

Except…

Turns out looks are deceiving.

And gossip is nothing more than meaningless chatter.

Up until last night, he was just as much of a virgin as I was.

There's something special about being able to share that kind of intimacy with the person you love.

My gaze drifts over his handsome face.

His features are prominent.

Chiseled cheek bones.

Dark lashes that are long and thick.

And his lips are…

I squint and attempt to come up with an adjective.

Plump.

Pillowy.

Plush.

Something along those lines but still ridiculously masculine.

And they're capable of way more pleasure than I imagined possible. The feel of his lips and tongue, not to mention the scruff of his shadowed jaw against my delicate flesh is enough to send a shiver of desire scampering down my spine. Not to mention, liquid arousal pooling in my core. If I were wearing panties, they'd be drenched from those delicious memories alone.

Even though we didn't have sex last night, he stripped me bare and ran his hands over every single inch until I was begging him to take me again.

He refused, instead saying that my little pussy needed time to heal. Then he kissed and licked me until I came with my hand pressed against my mouth so that my cousin would be none the wiser.

Afterward, I promptly passed out.

Who would have ever suspected that an orgasm could sap every ounce of energy?

So, yeah…pillowy, plump, and plush are all perfect descriptors of his lips.

My hungry gaze slides past his strong jaw and down the thick column of his neck with its colorful tattoos decorating his sun-kissed flesh. It's tempting to reach out and stroke my fingers over every single one of them.

But I don't.

It's not often that I get the chance to study him while he's unaware of my perusal. I've always felt like Wolf was watching.

Patiently waiting.

He has way more control than I've ever given him credit for.

What would it be like to unravel him in the same manner he does me?

It's an interesting question.

My attention licks over every gorgeous inch as it continues its descent. I try to remain perfectly still, barely breathing, but my thorough inspection has need pooling like warmed honey between my thighs. And clenching them has done nothing to alleviate the dull ache that has throbbed to life like a steady drumbeat.

Above one chiseled pectoral is a little red heart. Unable to help myself, I strain closer for a better look and realize that my initials are inked there. It's enough to bring a sting of tears to my eyes. Even when he assumed I was lost to him, he still branded my name on his skin. And he didn't sleep with other girls because I'm the only one he dreamed about.

Wanted.

Needed.

How could I have been so blind for so long?

How could I let my parents lie to me for all these years without questioning it?

I should have realized that the bond Wolf and I shared—*still share*—was stronger than that.

Unbreakable.

It's only when his large hand drifts across my cheek that I realize he's woken up.

"What's wrong, angel? Why are you crying?" His voice is all growly, and it strums something deep inside me.

"I'm not."

He captures one tear with the pad of his thumb before bringing it to his face and inspecting it. His tongue darts out to lick away the wetness.

"Tastes like tears to me."

I release a steady puff of air into the atmosphere as I give in to the urge to touch him now that he's awake. My fingers drift over the heart.

"My initials are here."

He rolls closer. "Baby, you only have to look and see that you're inked all over my body. If I couldn't be with you, I wanted you with me." His fingers toy with mine before lifting them to his mouth and brushing his lips across my knuckles. "Always."

My heart stutters at his soft words before thumping into overdrive.

How is he this amazing?

How is this really happening?

My head continues to spin, trying to play mental catchup.

It all feels surreal.

A thick lump of emotion settles in the middle of my throat, making it impossible to speak.

"I've always loved you. Even when you didn't love me back."

Another tear treks down my face. I need him to understand what's in my heart. "I love you more than anything. More than life itself."

"Stop it, angel. Your tears are killing me." He drags me on top of him until I'm straddling his naked chest. My pussy is splayed wide against all those thick slabs of muscle. That's all it takes for a shiver of awareness to dance down my spine as I shift. It's quickly followed by a tidal wave of arousal that's almost enough to blot out my grief.

When a whimper escapes from me and I squirm around, trying to find more of the delicious friction that sends shockwaves zipping through every nerve ending, his hands tighten around my hips to hold me in place as his eyes spark with heat.

"You're so damn beautiful. Especially with that expression filling your eyes. The one that tells me you need to be fucked."

My teeth scrape against my lower lip as I arch. That's when I realize it wouldn't take much to come.

With a groan, he moves beneath me. "I love the way you soak my chest."

His hands slide upward before tightening around my waist. Before I can question what he's doing, he lifts me up. His biceps bulge with the movement and if that isn't sexy, I don't know what is. I get the feeling he could bench press a small vehicle if he wanted.

My fingers tighten around his forearms in an attempt to balance myself as I'm hoisted in the air and set gently down on his mouth. His green eyes glow as they hold mine captive from below.

"Now you're exactly where I want you."

Even though I can't see the lower portion of his face, I hear the sexy smirk woven through his deep voice.

I release a shaky exhalation as his tongue slides deep inside my pussy. Pleasure explodes in my core before fanning outward. I can't help but widen my thighs, needing more of what only he can give me.

There's no way another man could satisfy me the way he does.

His hands stay locked around my waist, the fingers curling into my bare flesh, as he continues to lick and nibble. As much as I want to bow my spine, stretching my taut muscles, I don't.

I can't look away from the heady mixture of heat and tenderness that floods his eyes as he continues tonguing my shuddering softness.

That expression alone is enough to trip my pulse until I see stars.

No one has ever stared at me with so much love and adoration.

What makes it even more special is that it's Wolf.

The boy I was secretly in love with my entire childhood.

A moan escapes from me as he continues to eat at my flesh. There's nothing frenzied about his movements.

He breaks away long enough to ask, "Are you ready to come for me, angel?"

"Yes," I say with a needy whimper as my muscles turn whipcord tight. "Please."

"I love the sound of that word falling from your lips."

"Please. Please. Please."

He spears his tongue deep inside me before nibbling at my clit.

That must be the magic combination because I splinter apart while riding his face. The feel of his soft lips along with the shadow that covers his jaw is ridiculously delicious. His hands slide upward from my waist to my breasts. With nimble fingers, he tugs and pulls at the hard little nipples as an orgasm tears through my body.

I'm left with no other choice but to scream out my pleasure. It never occurs to me to cover my mouth. I can only hope that Viola has already left for class and we're alone in the apartment.

Every time he makes me come, I think it can't possibly get better. Then he proves me wrong and shows me exactly how amazing it can be.

He continues to lick me until my muscles turn lax and are no longer contracting.

"Fucking delicious," he growls. "My new favorite thing is to make you come. Especially when it's all over my face. I'll be able to taste you there for the rest of the day. Do you have any idea how much I love that?"

Embarrassment crashes over me as I shift to get a better look at him. Heat scalds my cheeks because he's right. The lower part of his face is wet and shiny with my arousal.

"I'm so sorry," I whisper, mortified by the sheer force of my own need.

He blinks as his dark brows slide together. "What are you sorry about?"

"Getting so carried away."

He barks out a laugh. "Don't ever apologize for being turned on. Especially when it's by me. I fucking love it. All I want to do is lap up your cream. Have I made myself perfectly clear?" Heat ignites in his eyes until they blaze with need. "All your orgasms belong to me. When you lose control, it's because of me. There's nothing sexier in this world than being able to turn my woman on and hear her scream out my name."

Oh god. That's exactly what I just did.

My face is on fire as I glance toward the wall that separates my room from Viola's. "I really hope she left for school, or I'll never hear the end of it." Especially after I heard her with Madden.

Wolf grins as if ridiculously proud of himself. "Let her hear just how good I made that sweet little pussy feel. I don't give a shit."

I swat his chest. "I don't think that's necessary, do you?"

"Maybe we can make a game of it. We'll see just how many inventive ways I can make you lose control and scream out my name."

"Umm…no, thank you."

He waggles his brows. "We'll have to read some of those romance novels together. I have to admit, there's some pretty creative stuff in there. Stuff you seem to enjoy."

Consider my curiosity piqued.

Carina reads a ton of smutty books. I'll have to borrow a few from her. I want to give Wolf just as much pleasure as he gives me.

"Maybe we should."

I scoot backward until I'm able to sit on the center of his chest before leaning down and pressing my lips to his. When I make a move to retreat, one hand snakes around the back of my head to hold me in place.

"Oh? Did you actually think we were done?" He shakes his head as his gaze stays fastened to mine. "I'm just getting started with you, angel."

That's when I realize Wolf hasn't gotten off yet. I sit up and glance over my shoulder at the erection he's now sporting.

My thighs clench with the need to feel his hard length deep inside me again. I slide down his muscular body before rising to my knees until I can hover over his morning wood. My gaze dips to his cock as I run my fingers up and down the straining shaft, from the tip to the root and then back again where pre-cum beads the slit. The more I rub it into the velvety soft crown, the more fluid leaks from him.

"Fuck, that feels good." His eyelids drift shut as he arches into my hand. After flexing his hips a few more times, he cracks open his eyes and meets my gaze. "But not as good as being inside your sweet cunt."

His dirty words send a thrill shooting through me as I tighten my fingers around his thick erection and carefully guide it to my entrance. As drenched as I am from him eating me, his girth still stretches my inner muscles.

He stacks his hands behind his head and stares with heavy-lidded eyes. "Watching you try to fit my cock inside your pussy is so damn hot."

I shoot him a frown and grumble, "Maybe if you weren't so big, it would be easier. You'd just slide right in. No problemo."

He snorts. "Are you really trying to tell me that you'd prefer I had a teeny tiny dick for you to play with? I'm willing to bet that it wouldn't satisfy you for long. Just give it time, angel. You'll see that your pretty little pussy was made just for my big cock."

He flexes his hips and I swear his dick swells in size. I have no idea how that's possible but it's exactly what happens. My attention falls to his abdominal muscles and the way they stretch and tighten. Desire hits me like a punch to the gut, making my core throb with even more awareness. Every part of him is hard and chiseled.

He's the perfect specimen of a man.

And he's mine.

Just like I'm his.

My gaze falls to the small red heart with my inked initials and a burst of love rushes through my veins and fills me up until it feels like I might explode.

When he rocks his hips for a second time, the head of his cock slides a little deeper inside my core. The stretch is dizzying. It's mind-boggling how he fit the first time.

I suck the corner of my lower lip into my mouth and chew it as my brows slant together in concentration. Drawing a deep breath into my lungs, I hold him with one hand all the while working myself down his thick length.

When a pained groan escapes from him, my gaze flickers upward.

"Am I hurting you?" For all I know, my grip is too tight or I'm bending his boner in a way it shouldn't be.

He shakes his head. "Your pussy feels amazing. It's so damn wet and tight. Someone should have warned me what a lethal combination that is. I'm going to end up coming before you're even fully seated on me."

It's thrilling to know that I turn him on just as much as he does me. That doesn't seem like it should be possible.

A fresh wave of arousal dampens my core. With another groan, he flexes, continuing to inch his way into my body. I glance down at the place we're intimately connected and realize that he's only halfway inside me.

He shifts and slides his hands from behind his head until his palms are wrapped around my hips. His fingers sink into the flesh. It's slowly that he lifts my lower body so that he's no longer buried inside me. Then he carefully brings me down on his cock. He repeats the movement over and over again until we find a rhythm. Somehow my body loosens and becomes even more slippery, allowing him to slide deeper with each pass. I can't help but stare at the way he flexes his hips, canting them, the muscles of his lower abdomen bunching as he works his way inside my body.

"Are you watching how nicely you take me? How greedy that little cunt is for my dick?"

A whimper escapes from me.

I never would have imagined that Wolf would be such a dirty talker, but I love it. The rumble of his deep voice turns me on even more. Or maybe it's watching the way his cock glistens when he pulls out before driving inside again.

The sight of our fucking is so sexy.

"You're so wet," he says with a groan. "It feels so damn good. I can't imagine anything feeling better than this. I'd stay buried inside your softness forever if it were possible."

My core clenches at the idea.

"Mmm." He arches his hips. "I just felt your pussy tighten around me."

I do it again.

"Tease," he growls.

He continues to bounce me on his cock. By the time he's buried balls deep, there is such a feeling of fullness within my body that I might just burst from it. It's such a delicious sensation. His gaze locks on mine as he grinds his pelvis.

"Fuck, baby. I'm going to come."

When his erection swells, growing impossibly hard, my inner muscles spasm around him, clenching the thick length in order to milk every last drop. His jaw locks as he groans out my name.

Unlike the first time, I bite my lower lip, so I don't scream my head off. After the last shudder racks my exhausted body, I collapse against the broad expanse of his chest. My breathing comes out in short, sharp pants as I lay my head against him and listen to the sound of his steady heartbeat. He wraps me up in his strong arms and presses me close before dropping a kiss on the top of my head.

"Told you I'd fit," he says with a gruff chuckle.

I melt against him as contentment steals over me. My brain wanders as I hover in that in-between space of wakefulness and slumber. Both my mind and body are exhausted. Deliciously pliant. It wouldn't take much to drift off for an hour or so stretched out along Wolf's muscular form. Even though his cock has softened, he's still nestled against my entrance as if he can't bear to leave it. And I find that I don't want him to.

His hand strokes over my hair. "Will you come to my game tonight?"

Even in my relaxed, sleepy state, I hear the need that weaves its way through his voice.

My eyelids flutter as I stifle a yawn. "Is that what you want?"

"Of course it is." His voice dips, turning gruff. "But I understand if it's too painful. I would never force you to do something that made you uncomfortable."

And just like that, I'm wide awake.

I lift my tousled head and rest my chin against the solid strength of his chest. "I'll come and watch."

He searches my eyes carefully. "Are you sure? My feelings won't be hurt if you're not up to it."

I take a moment, allowing his comment to circle around in my brain before nodding. "It's time to leave the past where it belongs and move on. I can't live there anymore. And Miles wouldn't want that for me either."

"No, he wouldn't." His fingers thread through my hair before he closes the distance between us so that his lips can slant over mine. The velvety softness of his tongue dips inside my mouth to tangle with my own.

He pulls away before whispering, "He loved you so much."

"He loved you, too. You were his brother in every way that mattered."

Emotion flickers in his eyes. "I felt the same."

"I know."

He shifts me around until my back hits the mattress and he's rolling from the bed and rising to his feet. My gaze slides down the length of his impressive form before settling on his cock. Even in his softened state, he's still imposing. A little shiver dances down my spine as I track each movement. He hunkers down near my desk where he dropped his black Wildcats team backpack after arriving last night.

In silence, he tugs open the zipper and rifles around inside the bag before pulling out something orange and black. It only takes four long-legged strides for him to reach the bed. Curiosity gets the better of me and I pull myself up to a seated position as he resettles on the mattress and shakes out the thick material.

That's when I realize he's holding a jersey.

His jersey.

"I want you to wear it to my game. Just like you used to."

A thick lump of emotion swells in my throat as a sheen of wetness blurs my vision. It takes effort to blink it away.

"Fallyn?" His voice dips, turning raspy.

I drag my gaze to his before jerking my head into a nod. "Thank you. I'll wear it tonight."

Air escapes in a rush from between his parted lips as he searches my eyes. "Are you sure you're good with this? The last thing I want to do is pressure you."

"You're not." I hug the material to my chest. "I want to be there for you in all the ways I wasn't these past years."

His hand snakes around the nape of my neck before dragging me to him and pressing his lips against mine.

"That means everything to me, angel."

CHAPTER 34

WOLF

I slide from one end of the goal to the other, warming up my hips before dropping to my knees and quickly popping back up again as my teammates circle their half of the ice. The puck drops in thirty. Even though I should be one hundred percent focused on the upcoming game, my gaze continually drifts to the stands, searching for Fallyn as warmups get underway.

A pit the size of Texas settles at the bottom of my gut.

What if she's a no show?

What if she changed her mind at the last minute and doesn't want to watch me play?

Or...

Maybe she changed her mind altogether and doesn't want anything to do with me.

Maybe I came on too strong, and it freaked her out.

After everything I revealed, there's no way to walk it back again. No way to put all the emotions I feel for her in a box and pretend they don't exist.

She finally understands just how obsessed with her I am.

Have always been.

Fuck.

I hate this.

Hate how it makes me feel. I don't get nervous before games. I'm focused on our adversaries and taking home another win. One that will bring us that much closer to a national championship.

I resettle my attention on Ryder and Maverick as they take their positions in front of the goal. The puck is passed to Ford by one of the assistant coaches and he skates forward, attempting to outsmart the two defensive players. As soon as he rips off a shot, Ryder blocks it, and the drill ends. Maverick gives Ford a little crap and I can't help the smile that lifts my lips. I love playing with these guys and will miss them next year.

Instead of dwelling on that, I focus on the three new guys who move into position to execute the same drill. I keep my attention focused on Colby. The guy is a talented fucker with a bag of tricks up his jersey sleeve. Like Maverick, his father was a star player in the NHL. There's been a lot for him to live up to but so far, he's done it. In typical Colby fashion, he fakes one way and then another before ripping off a shot. I slide and reach toward the left corner, but it hits the bar and goes in.

Colby flashes me a shit-eating grin as he skates by.

Asshole.

Midway through warmups, I glance at the bleachers and find Fallyn sitting with Viola, Juliette, Stella, Carina, and Britt. The first four have become known in the locker room as the girl-friends.

I love seeing Fallyn with them.

That's exactly what I want.

For her to be my girlfriend.

She's wearing a cream-colored knit hat with a pompom on the top over her long dark hair. Her jacket has been shed, revealing my orange and black jersey with a pair of dark wash jeans that hug her curves. As corny as it sounds, the sight of her is almost enough to knock the air from my lungs. After all these years, it finally feels like the tumblers of a safe falling into place. I can almost hear the click as an imaginary door opens.

As soon as our gazes collide, her lips hitch into a small smile and she gives me a wave.

I've never been so tempted to skate out of goal and off the ice as I am now.

All I want to do is get my hands on her again.

And then never let go.

Not ever.

It takes effort to shake that thought away and refocus my attention on warmups. Ten minutes before game time, the players from both teams vacate the ice. The lights in the arena are dimmed and the music is cranked up as the players from the Richfield U Railers are announced. The same is done for the Western Wildcats to even more fanfare. The crowd goes crazy as my name is called, and I skate to the goal. Even though I'm unable to see Fallyn with the spotlight in my eyes, I feel the warmth of her gaze. It's like a living, breathing entity.

And I feel Miles.

His presence is all around, blanketing me in calm. It's been a long time since I've felt him with me, and I know that has everything to do with his sister.

I can't help but glance up at the arena ceiling.

This game is all for you, buddy.

After the remaining players are announced, the first line takes their places. Bridger makes a quick stop in front of the net before searching my eyes behind the cage.

"You good, man?"

I jerk my head into a tight nod. "Yup. Never felt better."

He grins around his mouth guard. "Great. Then let's kick some Railer ass."

With a laugh, I agree with the sentiment, and we knock gloved fists before he takes his position near the blue line.

Hayes skates to center ice as Colby and Ford flank him at the red line. The puck gets dropped. Hayes battles the other team's center for possession before passing the black disc to Ford, who takes off toward the other team's goal like his ass is on fire. As soon as he crosses the blue line on the other side of the ice, two burly defensemen sweep their sticks in front of them, waiting for Ford to make a move. One rushes him while another protects their goal. Ford fakes one way before shooting it to Colby. When the defensemen swarm, Colby loses the puck. It gets passed up to an attackman who crosses the center line and makes a drive toward me.

I lower my center of gravity, sliding back and forth in front of the goal as I watch the play unfold. Maverick and Ryder are all over the attackman. When he turns, looking like he'll pass off the puck, I know he's going to rip off a shot instead. I've played against this guy plenty of times.

He's a glory hound.

He wants the goal.

I focus on his hips to see which way he'll move and then slide to the right and drop to my knees. When the puck flies toward me, I catch it with my glove.

As I drop the disc, Bridger races past and scoops it up, taking off toward the other side of the ice. I point to Fallyn in the stands before twisting my hand toward the ceiling. With a nod, her fingers drift to her lips and she blows me a kiss.

That's all it takes for everything within me to settle. The nerves eating away at my insides thirty short minutes ago have completely disappeared. As the first period turns into the second and then the third, I'm having the best fucking game of my life. I feel invincible with Fallyn watching me, cheering me on each time I save a goal.

If I have my way, it'll be a shutout.

And that'll be for both Fallyn and Miles.

By the time the final buzzer rings signaling the end of the game, I'm exhausted.

But happy.

So fucking happy.

I did exactly what I set out to and didn't allow the other team to score. They must have ripped off at least thirty shots. Probably more. I didn't keep track. As soon as I saved one goal, I focused on the next one.

Each time I passed off the puck, I looked up at Fallyn and made the same gesture with my gloved hand.

My teammates clear the bench and swarm me, patting my back and shoulders. The music that blasts through the sound system echoes in my ears as the fans clap and stomp their feet. Air horns blare as the crowd roars their approval. It's pandemonium in the arena.

Even though I realize there are going to be some major celebrations happening tonight, all I can think about is getting cleaned up and finding Fallyn. I want to wrap her up in my arms and hold her close. I want to bury my face in her hair and inhale the rosemary mint scent deep into my lungs.

More than that, I don't ever want to let her go.

I search the stands as I skate off the ice but don't find her anywhere. Over the din, my name is shouted.

More like chanted.

With a laugh, Colby knocks me on the shoulder and points toward the first row behind the plexiglass. There's a group of girls who are waving crazily with signs that have my name written in orange and black on thick posterboard. As soon as I glance their way, they raise their jerseys and shake their bare tits.

Jeez.

Ford and Ryder laugh their asses off before skating to the benches.

"If Carina even catches me looking in their direction, she'll cut my junk off," Ford jokes.

Or maybe he's not joking at all.

They've been together for about two months and from what I can tell, he has absolutely no interest in other girls.

I don't think he ever did.

For him, it was always Carina.

His ex-stepsister.

Ryder's the same way. He's totally wrapped up in Juliette.

More like they're wrapped up in each other.

Hayes claps me on the shoulder and nods to the girls who are still shaking their titties like their lives depend on it. "Looks like someone's getting lucky tonight."

"Nah. But you go for it."

He gives them a considering look before flashing a grin. "I just might do that."

It takes roughly twenty minutes to remove my pads and another ten to shower and get dressed. By the time I head out of the locker room, I'm one of the last stragglers. I push out through the metal door and into the hallway, intent on finding Fallyn.

Now that she's back in my life, I hate being without her. Even though I knew she was sitting in the stands, watching every move I made, it wasn't enough. I'm hoping it'll just take a couple weeks or maybe even a month to chill out, but deep down I know that's not going to happen. How can it when I've spent the past five years feeling like a vital piece of myself was missing?

The first time she slid inside my Mustang, I knew I'd found the reason for my existence. The purpose for drawing air into my lungs. It's an odd, unsettled feeling to realize that your heart no longer beats within your own chest but is buried deep inside someone else's.

I don't step more than a foot into the corridor before grounding to a halt. The tension filling my muscles dissolves when I find Fallyn leaning against the wall, waiting for me.

Without a word, I drop the athletic bag to the floor and eat up the distance between us with three long legged strides before dragging her into my arms where she belongs. My lips crash onto hers, devouring them with all the pent-up hunger that swirls through me. As soon as she opens, my tongue delves inside her mouth to tangle with her own. The emotion rushing through my veins is almost too much for the confines of my skin. Any moment, I'll come undone at the seams.

That's exactly what this girl does to me.

Tears me apart before putting me back together again.

My hands cup the sides of her head to hold her in place as I pull away and search her eyes.

"Missed you, angel."

"I missed you too," she says with a husky laugh. "Congrats on the game. You were amazing out there. Nothing got past you."

I rest my forehead against hers. "I was amazing because you were there, wearing my jersey, cheering me on. I always played better when you were in the stands watching."

I press my lips against hers. "Everyone's heading over to Slap Shotz to celebrate. Any interest in going? Or would you rather head home?" I waggle my brows. "We could always chill out and watch a movie."

She snorts. "Why do I get the feeling that we would never get around to the movie portion of the evening?"

"Because even after all these years, you still know me."

"I do." Her expression sobers. "Just like you know me."

"I've always known you, Fallyn. Even when you wanted nothing to do with me."

She buries her face against my chest as I wrap my arms around her and hold her tight. It's the closest my heart will ever come to being inside my body again.

She raises her face before stretching up onto the tips of her toes and pressing her lips to mine. "We should probably make an appearance at the bar, or everyone will wonder what happened to you."

"I don't give a shit about that."

"I know." Her lips lift into a smile. "Then we can take off and I'll congratulate you in private."

I raise a brow, warming to the idea. "Exactly what would that entail?"

"Whatever you want," she says with a smile.

"Hmm, I can think of a couple things that would keep you busy for quite a while. And then maybe you can sit on my face again because I fucking love having your pussy hovering over my mouth."

Heat floods her cheeks as she groans and buries her face against my chest. "Stop."

"Never," I say with a chuckle.

Instead of scooping her up in my arms and carrying her home, I reluctantly take a step in retreat and pick up my athletic duffle. Then I throw an arm around her shoulders and haul her against me.

It's exactly where she belongs.

"Let's get out of here. The sooner we make an appearance, the sooner you can make good on all those promises."

CHAPTER 35

FALLYN

Gerry flashes a shit-eating grin as Wolf ushers us through the back door of the bar.

"Well, well, well…isn't this a nice surprise to see you here on your night off." He flicks a glance at Wolf as they bump fists. "Looks like you aren't the only winner tonight, Westerville. I'm suddenly two hundred dollars richer."

When my mouth tumbles open, he actually laughs before jerking his head toward the man at my side. "Oh yeah, everyone saw the way this guy was constantly hovering. FYI—it was Erin who started the pool."

When I find the other waitress in the crowd, she smiles before shrugging. "If you'd held out for another week, that money would be mine," she calls out from a few tables away. "But I won't hold that against you. I'm not sure how you managed to go this long without giving in."

"I want my winnings by the end of the night," Gerry tells her.

She waves him away before taking off for the bar.

I groan, unable to believe that my new co-workers were betting on my relationship with Wolf. Before I can say anything, he whisks me away.

"Did you know about this?" I ask as we wind our way through the crush of bodies, unsure if I'm irritated or just plain embarrassed.

"Nope. And I wouldn't have cared if I had."

His smooth voice has the power to mollify me.

Since we're late getting here, the place is already packed to the gills. Hands reach out, congratulating Wolf on what a great game he had. Girls gravitate to him, attempting to stroke his chest and strike up conversations. It doesn't matter if I'm tucked securely beneath his arm. They'd happily steal him away—or join us, if that's the only way they can have a small piece of him.

I glance over to see if he notices the attention, but he doesn't bother making eye contact with any of them. His gaze is locked on the tables shoved together in the back as he presses me closer.

Realizing every seat is occupied, Wolf taps a younger player on the shoulder and tells him to move it. The kid scrambles out of his way without question. After dropping down onto the chair, he pulls me onto his lap before wrapping his arms around my waist and brushing his lips over mine.

"An hour," he grumbles. "Then we're out of here."

I can't resist the smile that curves my lips. "Oh? You have big plans for later?"

He flexes his hips until his thick erection can nudge me. "The biggest." One brow lifts in askance. "Wouldn't you say?"

I shift as heat pools in my core. "Maybe too big?"

I'm joking.

Sort of.

He smirks. "Nah. It's the perfect fit." His voice turns into even more of a growl. "It'll just take a lot of stroking and licking to get that sweet little pussy ready. And I'm more than willing to do it. In fact, I'd be upset if I couldn't."

All this talk of foreplay has even more arousal sparking to life inside my core, and I shift on his lap.

His hands tighten around my hips. "You need to stop squirming, or I'll drag your ass out of here right now."

Erin stops by to take our order before sending a little wink my way. "Looking cozy over there, Fallyn."

She's not wrong.

Britt took off and headed home after the game, but all the other girls are seated around the table. Like me, Juliette is perched on Ryder's lap. I've noticed that he doesn't like her to be very far. He's always touching her as if he wants everyone to understand that she belongs to him now. I glance around the table and realize that all the guys are like that with their girlfriends. Ford's arm is casually slung around Carina's shoulders. The same with Stella and Riggs.

And Vi and Madden?

My heart actually melts because they have such a long history. I never expected to see them together again, but I've been pleasantly surprised by how easily they've fallen back into a relationship.

My cousin and I share a look before she snuggles against her boyfriend. I love seeing her so happy.

Contented.

Those thoughts are enough to have my gaze shifting back to Wolf.

Not once did I ever think we'd speak again, much less get together. No matter how much I longed for this when I was a teenager, those fantasies crumbled to dust after the car crash. The crazy part is that all the years sitting between us have melted away like snow in the springtime.

"Tell me what you're thinking," he whispers, warm breath feathering across the outer shell of my ear. It sends a delicate shiver dancing down my spine. I'm still getting used to the way he affects me.

"Just that I really missed you being in my life."

His expression turns sober. "You know that I feel the same, right?"

I nod.

He's been very clear about his feelings for me. There haven't been any of the usual games people our age play. With Wolf, there never were. Not where I was concerned. When I think back to our youth, I realize that his intentions were always there.

I was just too naïve to recognize them.

Just as he brushes his lips across mine, Sully lumbers onto the stage and raises his hands to be heard over the laughter and chatter that hums around us.

He brings the microphone to his lips. "Our boys brought home another win tonight!" He searches the thick crowd before pointing to Wolf. "In large part to our talented goalie!"

Applause and catcalls break out, vibrating off the walls.

A reluctant smile lifts Wolf's lips as he gives him a nod of acknowledgment but nothing more. Unlike some of his teammates, he's never been one to soak up the accolades and bask in the attention.

Even when he has every right to do so.

He played an amazing game tonight. Everyone seated around me couldn't stop talking about it. He was like an unstoppable brick wall. Nothing got past him.

And I couldn't be prouder.

"Get up here, Westerville. You're starting us off tonight!"

Wolf shakes his head and pitches his voice just loud enough to be heard over the dull roar of the crowd. "Nah, that's all right. I prefer to watch the show rather than be part of it."

Everyone gets in on the action, hounding and harassing until he finally grumbles, "Fine."

His fingers tighten around my waist as he lifts me to my feet before rising to his.

With a quick kiss pressed against my lips, he whispers, "This one's for you, angel."

And then he's gone, parting the sea of people like Moses as he makes his way to the stage. As soon as Wolf jumps onto the platform, Sully throws an arm around his shoulders like he just found his long-lost son.

It's kind of adorable.

The older bar owner has so much genuine affection for the hockey players and the Wildcats program. I used to think it was because he was trying to live vicariously through the younger guys but it's so much more than that. It goes back to them all being one big family.

Once a Wildcat, always a Wildcat.

Even though Wolf's placid expression never falters, I realize that he doesn't enjoy the limelight. When his gaze settles on mine, I blow him a kiss. From across the space that separates us, I see the way his eyes darken with need and a little thrill shoots through me knowing that I'm the one he'll be taking home at the end of the night.

Sully says something in his ear that I'm unable to hear before clapping him heartily on the shoulder and handing off the microphone. Wolf swings around to pick out a piece of music. He flips through the list on the computer screen before choosing a song and returning to the stage. As soon as the first notes of the guitar riff fill the air, recognition slams into me, making the tiny hairs on my arm prickle with awareness.

Wolf's attention stays locked on mine as he holds the microphone to his mouth. His tongue darts out to moisten his lips as the instrumental continues and the crowd quiets to a hush. The drums come in, joining the guitar, and adding to the harmony, as he croons the lyrics of 'Maps' by Yeah, Yeah, Yeahs just like he used to when we were teenagers.

My heart constricts as I realize he's pouring out his heart for everyone to witness.

That's all it takes for tears to prick the backs of my eyes as the crowded bar fades to the background until it's just the two of us. My heart slams against my ribcage as it fills with so much love that it feels like it'll burst.

Only now do I realize the gigantic void my life had become without him in it. As if I wasn't really living. Or breathing. I was walking around in a catatonic state where I didn't feel anything too deeply.

And now…

All that has been ripped away.

And rebuilt into something stronger.

Lasting.

He continues to hold my gaze as the electric guitars play and the song ends much in the same way it began.

His eyes hold mine captive as he murmurs into the microphone, "No one will ever love you the way I love you, angel."

It's only when the thunderous applause erupts around me that I blink back to the present as Wolf passes the mic to Sully. The second he steps off the stage, the crowd swarms, swallowing him up.

When my phone vibrates in my pocket, I fish it out before glancing at the screen.

> Made reservations at The Cellar for lunch next week Tuesday. See you then.

The text from Mom is like a gut punch and sends me into freefall.

A thick shudder slides through me.

How could I have forgotten the anniversary of Miles' death?

I've been so wrapped up in Wolf and the financial aid issues I've been dealing with that it must have slipped my mind.

I'm jerked out of those thoughts when Wolf slips his arms around me and tugs me close before pressing a kiss against my lips. "That was all for you."

"Thank you. I loved it."

When I paste a smile in place, he pulls away just enough to study my face. Concern flickers in his eyes. "What's wrong?"

Sometimes I forget just how well he knows me. After all these years, he still has the uncanny ability to read me with just one look.

I shake my head and up the wattage of my smile, hoping he'll let the topic drop. The last thing I want to do is ruin what an amazing evening this has turned out to be.

It's almost a shock when he jerks to his feet and wraps his fingers around my wrist before dragging me out the back door of the bar. Before I can ask any questions, we rush past the bouncer.

"Yeah, I was pretty sure that song was gonna clinch the deal," Gerry calls after us with a laugh. "Should have bet money on it!"

It's only when we're outside and the cold breeze slaps at our cheeks that he jerks to a halt before spinning me around to face him. The noise and music from inside fades to the background as his eyes narrow. "Tell me what's going on." His gaze stays pinned to mine. "Because I know something's not right."

The steely look of determination in his eyes tells me that he won't drop the subject until he uncovers the truth.

My shoulders collapse as air leaks from my lungs. "Mom just texted about meeting at a restaurant next Tuesday."

Emotion flickers in his green depths as grief crashes over his features. "The anniversary."

It's not a question. More of a statement.

I nod and press closer to his bigger body, needing his strength.

"I've been thinking about it a lot lately," he admits.

I draw away just enough to meet his gaze. "You have?"

"I always do this time of year. Mostly, I wonder what life would have been like for your family if I'd died that night instead of him."

My heart stops before thrashing painfully beneath my breast. "Please don't ever say that again," I force out, gut sick he would ponder the possibility.

"Why not? It was my fault." Anguish fills every line of his features.

With a shake of my head, I dig my fingers into the thick cotton of his sweatshirt before dragging him closer. "It was an accident, Wolf. You loved Miles more than anyone and would have never hurt him on purpose."

His arms hang limply at his sides instead of banding around me, holding me close. "If I hadn't talked Miles into going to that party, it wouldn't have happened. He would have had a chance to live out his life. We both know that he would have done amazing things. He was the best person I knew."

Hot tears prick my eyes as I nod. Miles was handsome, smart, and athletic. Ever since he was a kid, he had a natural charisma that people gravitated to. If you knew him, you couldn't help but love him.

"It wasn't just you. I wanted to go to that party as well. He did it for both of us. So stop blaming yourself."

"But I'm the one who was driving. I'm the one who lost control of the car. It should have been me. If life were fair, it would have been me."

I shake my head, refusing to let him heap all the blame onto himself. "It was an accident. That's it." A tear trails down my cheek as I admit, "To hear you talk like that breaks my heart more than it already is because I can't imagine a world where you don't exist."

The fierceness of my words is what ends up jackhammering through the haze of pain that cocoons him and his arms snake out, wrapping around me before dragging me against the steely strength of his chest. He squeezes me so tight that it feels like I'm being crushed alive, but I don't care. In this moment, it's what we both need.

Miles is no longer here, but we are.

For the first time in years, I feel like I'm alive and I don't want to squander a single moment of it because my brother wouldn't want that for me. Or Wolf. And he certainly wouldn't want our parents to continue living in the shadow of his demise. Eaten up by grief and bitterness. He would be furious that they blame Wolf for his death and that the grudge they've held against him, and his family has, in the end, destroyed ours. He'd be so disappointed in all of us.

Wolf sucks in a harsh breath before slowly releasing it back into the atmosphere. "The last thing I want to do is hurt your family more than I already have."

More wetness falls from my eyes because I realize what he's going to say before the words escape from his lips.

"There's no way your parents will ever accept me in your life."

His grip tightens as if he's afraid I'll be ripped away at any moment.

Instead of trying to ease his concerns, I stare into the surrounding darkness and remain silent because deep down, I know he's right.

My parents will *never* approve of him.

Or us.

CHAPTER 36

FALLYN

My palm flutters to my lower abdomen as if that alone will settle the nerves that eat away at my insides.

It does nothing.

I stare at my reflection in the mirror, taking in my outfit—soft gray sweater, black skirt, and matching black boots. My appearance is as somber as my current mood.

Instead of getting together and celebrating my brother's life, the three of us gather and grieve every year over the unfairness of it being cut short and how Miles never had a chance to fulfill his potential. I always come away feeling depressed.

If the previous years are any indication, it'll take a few weeks before I can lay all the heartache to rest. Up until now, I never considered how unhealthy the tradition we've created is. Viola has cautiously tried to broach the subject, but I've always shut her down. It's only now that I've spent more time with Wolf that I see it. I can't get sucked back into that bottomless pit of despair. Each year it becomes more difficult to fight my way back out again.

The three of us haven't moved on the way we should have.

And my parents are the reason for it. They're so comfortable cocooned in their grief.

Barely living their own lives.

The only thing that keeps them going is their feud with the Westerville family. Without that, what would they have?

Who would they be?

I have no idea.

It's a disturbing realization.

There's a soft knock on the bedroom door before Viola peeks her head inside. "Are you ready?"

I suck in a deep breath before forcing it back out again. "Yeah."

Pushing the door wider, she wanders further inside the space before coming to stand next to me. Her arms slip around my body as she tugs me close.

"I'm sorry, Fallyn. I still miss him like crazy."

My shoulders wilt. "Me, too." I don't think that will ever change.

Instead of giving into the comfort, I break away and snag my purse off the dresser. The sooner I get this over with, the quicker I can put it behind me and move on. I wince because there will never be a time when I'm able to put Miles behind me. He'll always be beside me, cheering me on.

I wish my parents could understand that and make their peace with it.

Maybe they could even find happiness again.

They deserve that.

We all do.

We need to celebrate Miles' life instead of grieving his death as if it's still fresh and new.

"If you're ready, we can get moving," she says.

We slip into our winter jackets before heading for the apartment door. My parents offered to pick me up, but I didn't want to spend any more time with them than necessary.

Guilt pricks at me for those uncharitable thoughts.

Wolf offered to drop me off for lunch, but the farther he stays from the restaurant and my parents, the better off we'll all be.

At least for the time being.

It's all about baby steps.

Today, the plan is to broach the subject of therapy. Then, down the road, I'll bring up that Wolf is back in my life.

Fifteen minutes later, Viola pulls into the restaurant parking lot before rolling to a stop near the front entrance and shifting into park.

She twists around and studies me for a few silent moments. "Are you good? You could always cancel and tell them you're sick or something."

I straighten my shoulders before shaking my head. "No. They came all this way. I don't want to do that to them. Especially today."

Concern flickers in her eyes as she reaches out and wraps her fingers around mine. "I love you, Fall."

I force a smile and some of the anxiety that has been ever present since I woke up this morning fades. "I love you, too. And I'm glad you transferred here this year. Living with you has been the best."

"It has been." She squeezes my hand one last time before I slip from the vehicle. "Tell Aunt Eleanor and Uncle Hugo that I miss them and will see them soon."

"I'll be sure to do that. They'll appreciate it."

With that, I slam the car door and force myself to walk into the restaurant on wooden legs. I spot my parents seated at a table and let the hostess know I can find my own way.

As soon as Dad catches sight of me, he rises to his feet and opens his arms for a hug. I step into his warm embrace as his lips brush against my cheek. "It's good to see you, sweetheart. How's everything going?"

I hug my mother before settling on a chair between them. "It's good."

"I'm sure it's a huge relief that the situation with financial aid has been settled and you were able to stay at Western."

"Yeah." My father would blow a gasket if he knew that Wolf was the one who covered the tuition payment this semester. Even if I didn't mention the part where I put my virginity up for sale, he'd still be furious. Any time the company or partnership with the Westervilles is brought up, Dad froths at the mouth.

Wolf is right. There's no way they'll accept his presence in my life.

Even if I make every attempt to ease them into it. A year from now, their reaction will be the same.

It doesn't give me a lot of hope for the future.

It's only when Mom reaches out and lays her hand over mine that I blink back to the present. "It's almost difficult to believe that he's been gone for five years, isn't it?"

Her soft words only make me feel worse because I wasn't dwelling on my brother, I was thinking about Wolf and if they'll ever accept that I'm in love with the person they consider our enemy.

The waiter stops by and takes our drink order along with our meal selections.

"How's your job at the diner going?" A small smile lifts the corners of Dad's lips. "I can only imagine that you have a newfound respect for the profession. I'm proud of you for going out and finding a job to cover some of your expenses. You were never afraid of a little hard work."

Guilt suffuses me as I shift on my chair. Even though it's not a huge lie in the grand scheme of things, it's still not the truth. It feels like I'm keeping so many secrets from them. That's not something I ever did before. And I hate it.

Hate that I've resorted to being so deceptive.

I gnaw my lower lip and contemplate the situation.

If I can't come clean about Wolf, the least I can do is tell them where I'm really working. It's always possible they won't have an issue with it, and I've made a bigger deal out of it than necessary. And if that's the case…

Maybe I'm wrong about how they'll react to me dating Wolf.

I clear my throat, deciding to take a chance and come clean. "Actually, it's not a diner. It's a bar near campus."

"A bar?" Mom frowns as her brows pinch together. "Did you quit the diner and get a new job?"

With a shake of my head, I force myself to continue. "No, I've always worked at the bar."

"So…you lied?" Surprise and hurt weave their way through her voice.

"I did and I'm really sorry for hiding the truth. I should have been honest from the very beginning."

"I don't understand. Why on earth would you do that?"

"Sweetheart," Dad cuts in, trying to stay calm. "Just tell us what's going on. Why would you deceive us?"

The words burst free in a torrent. "Because I knew that you wouldn't want me working in a place like that. You guys are so overprotective."

Smothering.

A myriad of emotions flash across Dad's face as he lifts the tumbler of brandy to his lips and takes a sip. An uncomfortable silence stretches between us before he murmurs, "Considering what happened, I think we have every right to be protective. You're our little girl. And no matter what, that will never change."

I stare down at the thick white cloth that covers the table and realize this was a mistake. But it's much too late to backtrack now.

And part of me doesn't want to.

"I'm almost twenty-one years old. Not so little anymore."

"It doesn't matter how old you are, Fallyn. We'll always worry." The tears that gather in Mom's eyes turn them shiny. "After Miles, I don't think my heart could withstand another loss."

"Mom…" It's hard to hear her talk like that.

"I'm serious," she says in a shaky voice.

"I know. But nothing is going to happen to me."

She reaches out and lays her hand over mine before squeezing until it becomes borderline painful. "Unfortunately, no one can make such promises."

Before Mom can get any more emotional, Dad says, "All right, so you're working at a bar. I assume you aren't getting off until two or three in the morning. How are you getting home at night?"

It would probably be best to tell them that Viola picks me up, but the last thing I want to do is drag her into this mess. Plus, I'm trying to be honest with them. I don't want to add more lies to it.

"A friend gives me a ride. I'm not walking home if that's what you're worried about."

My anxious gaze bounces between them as I hold my breath, waiting to see if they'll pepper me with more questions.

"I don't like it," Mom says with a watery sniff. "You should quit and find a different job. Maybe something on campus with hours during the day." She perks up. "Like at the library."

My father nods in agreement. "That's an excellent idea, Ellie."

I shake my head. "I don't want to look for another job. I like this one. Sully, the owner, is really nice and flexible with hours. And the people I work with are great. Gerry, the bouncer, always keeps an eye on things so that situations don't get out of hand."

I don't mention that Wolf is always there as well. He shows up after practice or games and would never let anything happen to me.

"What's the name of this bar?" Dad asks. "Maybe we'd feel better about it if we stopped by and checked the place out for ourselves." He glances at his wife. "Don't you think that might put your mind at ease?"

Mom scrunches her face. "I don't know. I hate the idea of you working around a bunch of drunk men."

"The place is called Slap Shotz," I mumble.

With a tilt of his head, Dad narrows his eyes. "What is that? Like a sports bar or something?"

I wince. I can almost see the wheels in his brain turning.

As tempting as it is to lie, I refuse to do it anymore. "Yes."

He straightens in his chair. "Who exactly makes up the clientele?"

"Um, well, a lot of people. Mostly college students."

Mom blinks as if trying to play mental catchup. "Hugo?"

He doesn't bother to glance at her. Instead, his steely gaze remains pinned to mine. "Have you run into him there?" he asks softly, voice shaking as if he's trying to keep a firm handle on his temper.

"Please tell me that we're not talking about that boy. Not today of all days."

"I'm sorry, Mom. I'm not trying to upset either one of you. I just wanted to be honest about where I'm working. I didn't want to keep lying."

Even though this has gone just as bad as I suspected, it's still a relief to get it out in the open.

"Well, it's settled then," my father says with a growl. "You'll quit immediately. I don't give a damn if you can't pay rent or tuition. It's better than being around Wolf Westerville."

"I knew allowing you to come here for school was a mistake," Mom says with a small cry.

With a glance in her direction, I shake my head. "No, it wasn't. I'm happy at Western."

I jump almost a foot when my father bangs his fist on the table, rattling the silverware. "I don't give a damn! That family has not only stolen our son but bankrupted us! Over my dead body will you socialize with that little prick!"

My eyes flare wide as the customers seated around us swivel in our direction and stare at Dad with wide eyes. Heat scalds my cheeks as people whisper to one another with bent heads and hushed tones.

"Dad," I mumble, embarrassed by the way he's losing it. He's normally so calm and controlled. It just shows how enraged he is. "Please."

He sticks two fingers in the collar of the pressed button down, yanking it away from his throat as if it's strangling him. "I'd murder every single Westerville in their sleep if I could get away with it."

"Dad!" I gasp. "You can't say things like that!"

Just as he opens his mouth, his eyes shift to something over my shoulder. They widen as he slams it shut again before jerking to his feet and nearly toppling the chair over in the process.

"What the hell are you doing here?" he growls.

Unease skitters down my spine as I spin around and find Wolf standing a dozen feet away. He's wearing a light blue dress shirt and pressed tan khakis. The colorful tattoos that decorate his neck peak out from his buttoned collar before disappearing beneath the smooth cotton fabric. My heart clenches painfully at the sight of him. It's so tempting to leap to my feet and throw myself into his arms.

Instead, I remain seated.

Paralyzed.

Color drains from my mother's face as she stares at him. It's like she's seeing a ghost. Tears spring to her eyes as she shakes her head and sucks in an unsteady breath.

Wolf takes a few awkward steps, closing the distance between us before grounding to a halt at the table.

His gaze stays locked on my father as he says quietly, "Hello, Mr. DiMarco. I was hoping that maybe we could sit down and talk. Miles was such a massive part of my life. Actually, your entire family was, and the loss has been devastating."

Before Dad can even open his mouth, Mom snaps, *"The loss has been devastating?* How dare you even say that! We lost our *son!* Our family was shattered. And you're the cause. So don't you dare waltz in here and tell us that you're devastated. You have no idea what true devastation is."

The anguish that twists Wolf's features are enough to break my heart.

Yes, my parents lost their son, and I lost my big brother. But Wolf lost his best friend. And me. All of us. A safe place to grow up.

My parents are steeped so deeply in their own grief that they're unable to see that. Sometimes I don't know if they'll ever find their way out of it and that breaks my heart more than anything. They didn't die the day Miles did, but they might as well have.

Hot tears sting my eyes. "Mom, that's not fair. Wolf was a kid, and it wasn't his fault. It was an accident."

"Don't you dare defend him," she snaps, barely taking her eyes off Wolf. "He was always leading Miles into mischief. I should have put an end to their friendship when they were children. Then my poor baby would still be here."

Wolf sucks in a harsh breath before straightening his shoulders. "I'm really sorry, Mrs. DiMarco. You have to know how much I loved Miles. Every happy childhood memory I have is filled with you guys. I hate that I caused so much pain for your family. If there were a way to go back in time and make a different decision, I'd do it in a heartbeat. I'd do anything to have Miles back with us."

"Your apology means nothing," My mother seethes, her voice

turning shrill. "If you had any decency whatsoever, you'd leave us in peace."

His gaze shifts to mine. The misery brimming from his green eyes tears me to pieces. Even though I should tell them the truth about our relationship, the words stick uncomfortably in my throat, refusing to budge.

"You heard my wife," Dad growls. "Leave now before I have the management throw you out."

Wolf jerks his head into a nod and breaks eye contact. "If that's what you want."

"It is." Tears streak down Mom's cheeks before she buries her face in her hands and weeps, her shoulders shaking uncontrollably.

Shock holds me paralyzed as he spins around and walks toward the entrance of the restaurant.

"Good riddance," Dad says, watching his retreating form. "If I never see that boy again, it'll be all too soon."

With each step that takes Wolf further from me, my heart shatters into even more jagged pieces until there's no way for it to be whole again.

CHAPTER 37

WOLF

This was a mistake.

I shouldn't have come here.

What the fuck had I been thinking?

That I was actually going to fix anything with these people?

Desperate laughter bubbles up from deep in my throat.

Yeah, that was never going to happen.

Have I ever seen so much hatred on anyone's faces before?

And Fallyn...

She'd just sat there, frozen in place, like a deer in headlights. That's the moment I realized that no matter how much I love her, no matter how much I'd bleed for her, I'll be damned if I put her through any more pain.

What kind of shitty human would I be to force her to choose between me and her parents?

Who the fuck does that after they've already caused so much heartache?

No...I just can't.

My steps quicken with the need to get the fuck out of here. I need time to figure out how I'm going to move forward. How I'll wipe her from both my mind and heart.

As if that's possible.

"Wolf! Wait!"

I spin around only to find Fallyn bursting through the glass doors and rushing toward me. The wetness that streaks her pale cheeks breaks my fucking heart because I know I'm the cause of it.

I never should have forced my way back into her life. All I've done is cause chaos and grief.

My tongue darts out to moisten my lips. Before I can blurt out the words, she hurtles herself at me like a small projectile and wraps her arms around my neck.

"I'm so sorry about that," she whispers fiercely, clinging as if she'll never let go.

Even though it's the last thing I want to do, I grip her wrists and carefully untangle her arms before holding her at a distance. It hurts too damn much to have her this close.

"There's no way for us to be together if you can't tell your parents that I'm part of your life. I love you, Fallyn." I search her shiny eyes for understanding. "I've always loved you, but I won't hide our relationship. The last thing I want is to come between you and your family." My voice dips, sounding as if it's been roughed up and scraped raw. Just like my heart. I jerk my head toward the restaurant. "You saw what happened in there. They'll never be okay with us together."

More crystal-like tears flood her eyes, turning them luminous in the bright winter sunlight.

Before she's able to respond, a deep voice growls, "What the hell is going on here?"

My gaze slices from Fallyn to her father as he stalks across the parking lot, eating up the pavement with long-legged strides. His hands are clenched as color gathers in his cheeks, giving them a mottled appearance.

His wife is hot on his heels, attempting to keep up with him. Her blue eyes are flared wide with shock as she stares at us.

Fallyn searches my face for a long heartbeat before a look of determination flashes across her features and she swings toward her parents.

"I love him," she says simply.

Her mother's mouth falls open before she slams it shut and shakes her head. "No. Don't you dare say that! You can't possibly be in love with him. Not after what he did!" More tears trek down her cheeks as she blurts, "He stole Miles from us!"

Fallyn's gaze shifts to mine, and I steel myself, unsure if she'll agree with the accusation. It would break my fucking heart if she did.

"I've loved Wolf since I was a kid and in all these years, that's never changed. And it never will." The edges of her lips quirk before she turns her attention back to her parents and straightens her shoulders as if preparing for battle. "What happened to Miles was an accident. *A tragic accident.* You've spent all these years blaming Wolf even though it wasn't his fault. All three of us made the decision to sneak out of the house that night. We all bear culpability for it." There's a pause before she adds in a softer voice, "Even Miles."

More wetness streams down Eleanor's face.

Hugo moves closer to his wife before slipping an arm around her waist. "You'll break your mother's heart if you do this."

Fallyn's soft gaze returns to mine, and she searches it for a long, painful moment before stepping closer and pressing a chaste kiss against my lips. When her warmth disappears, it takes every ounce of strength I have not to reach out and yank her to me.

Her attention returns to her parents as she closes the distance between them and embraces her mother before meeting her father's eyes.

"It's been five years since we lost Miles and neither of you have healed. Your pain is as fresh as it was the night it happened. Don't you think it's time to change that?" Fallyn's gaze shifts to me. "The first step in the process is to stop blaming Wolf. No matter what you want to believe, Miles loved him, and he wouldn't want you to blame his best friend for something that was a tragic accident. And he wouldn't want you to live like this either. Both of you need to find a way to heal and move on. This isn't healthy for any of us. And I can't do it anymore. I won't."

Tears prick Hugo's eyes as he attempts to blink them away. In this moment, he looks every day of his fifty years.

"You need to accept that I'm with Wolf because that isn't going to change." Fallyn reaches out and wraps her fingers around Hugo's hand before giving it a squeeze. "I don't want to lose either one of you. Please don't make me choose."

Eleanor's shoulders continue to quake with emotion.

Only then does Fallyn untangle herself from her mother and step back toward me until she's able to slip an arm around my waist and lean against my chest. I can't resist dropping a kiss against the crown of her head. No matter what I was expecting to happen, this wasn't it.

I couldn't be more humbled by what she's willing to sacrifice for me.

And our love.

My other hand settles beneath her chin before tipping it upward until our gazes can lock and hold.

I search her eyes carefully, looking for any shred of doubt. "Are you sure about this?"

Her lips lift into a radiant smile as she nods. "I am. I love you."

Emotion fills my heart, making it feel as if it'll burst from the intense pressure. Never in my life have I felt anything like it before.

And I know without a shadow of a doubt that I'll never experience anything like it again.

"I love you too, angel."

CHAPTER 38

FALLYN

olf pulls the Mustang to the curb in front of the house before cutting the engine. For a moment, I stare at the white sign that dots the front yard. A pang of sadness fills me to see my childhood home up for sale. But ultimately, the change is needed and will be good for everyone. It's something my parents should have done a long time ago.

All three of us need a clean break from the past.

With one squeeze of my fingers, Wolf draws my attention back to him. "You still doing all right over there?"

I smile, surprised that it doesn't feel forced. "Actually, I am. I'd thought seeing the house would be more upsetting. Instead, I'm relieved. It's time for everyone to move on. Instead of living in the past, we need to look forward to the future and everything that lies ahead."

He nods as his gaze shifts to the brick mansion that looms in front of us.

"Ready to head inside?"

When I slide the brand-new license from the pocket of my jeans, a smile flashes across his face as he slips his hand around the nape of my neck and tugs me closer. The warmth of his lips glide over mine before he pulls away just enough to say, "I'm so proud of you, angel."

I'm proud of myself for conquering my fears and learning to drive. I passed my test last week with flying colors.

After one last lingering kiss, we exit the vehicle before meeting on the curb and walking up the concrete pathway that cuts through the snow-covered lawn. Not bothering to knock on the front door, I throw open the thick wood and step inside the grand foyer. There's an ocean of brown packing boxes stacked everywhere. For a second time, I steel myself for the inevitable wave of sorrow to crash over me but there's nothing except relief.

We find Mom and Dad in the living room, wrapping up old, framed family photos.

I take a minute to glance around the empty space. "Wow. It really looks different in here."

Bigger.

Not only that but it feels lighter. As if all the sadness has been stripped away.

Mom straightens before looking around. A small puff of air escapes from her as she agrees with the sentiment. "We held a sale last week and sold a lot of furniture we won't need for the new house. Did Dad mention that the new owners are paying us extra to be out by the end of the week?"

I shake my head before glancing at my father. He's dressed in faded jeans and an old T-shirt from his alma mater.

"Twenty grand," he adds.

"That's great."

"With the sale of the house and furniture, we were able to pay off all the debt that's been accumulating over this past year. There was even enough left over for a small downpayment for the new house your mother fell in love with."

Mom's blue eyes light up. "It has the most perfect yard that backs up to a stream with lots of wildlife."

I haven't seen her this excited in a long time, and it's almost enough to bring tears of joy to my eyes. Instead, I keep the emotion locked down tight, not wanting to spoil this moment. It shouldn't surprise me when Wolf slips an arm around my waist. He's always been attuned to both my thoughts and feelings.

"That sounds great, Mom. I can't wait to see it."

Her face fills with emotion as she takes in the spacious living room. Only this time, it lacks the grief and heartache that has been her constant companion throughout the years.

"As much as I hate to sell the place, it's time. You were right about needing a fresh start. The family that bought the house has three small children and I just know they'll enjoy it."

I nod. "It was a great place to grow up. Miles and I were happy here."

"We all were," Mom adds softly.

A heavy silence falls over the four of us before Dad clears his throat. "We packed up some boxes of Miles' stuff for you to take."

"Thank you," I murmur. It couldn't have been easy for them to sift through the past and make their peace with it.

Dad's gaze flickers from me to the man at my side. "I, ah, was talking to Wolf."

Wolf's eyes widen in surprise. It's only been a couple weeks since the outburst at the restaurant. After the shock of my new relationship wore off, they called to tell me that I was right and that they were going to work on leaving the past where it belonged.

In the past.

"It's a lot of hockey and school memorabilia." Dad shifts and glances away as his voice deepens with emotion. "He'd want you to have it."

Wolf offers his hand for Dad to shake. My breath catches at the back of my throat as we all wait to see how my father will react. Tension ratchets up in the sun-filled room before Dad reaches out and meets him midway.

"Thank you, sir. I really appreciate it."

Dad jerks his chin into a tight nod before his lips lift into a reluctant smile. "You're welcome."

Heavy emotion hangs in the air before my father turns to me, blinking away the wetness that shines in his eyes. "So, are you ready to do this?"

That question is enough to have nerves leaping to life inside me before scuddling across my arms. When I nod, he slips his hand into the pocket of his jeans and pulls out a key ring with a hockey puck. A thick lump gathers in my throat, making it impossible to breathe, as he sets it in the palm of my hand.

After all these years, I never imagined this day would come.

With Wolf's arm wrapped around my waist, we trail after my parents to the garage out back where Miles' Porche has been sitting idle. The closer we get, the harder my heart slams against my ribcage.

"You still doing okay?" Wolf asks, his lips pressed against my ear.

I tilt my head just enough to meet his probing gaze. "Better than okay."

It's not a lie. This feels like a new beginning, and I love that we're all moving forward together.

As a family.

The way it should be.

"Good."

Dad unlocks the three-stall garage and steps inside the dark space. We trail after him as he hits the opener on the side of the wall and the large door creaks before rising, allowing enough bright sunlight to pour inside and chase away the shadows. The last time I was here, there was a large cloth covering the Porsche. That's no longer the case. The little sports car is bright and shiny as if raring to go.

Dad shifts, stuffing his hands into his pockets. "I took it out for a spin last week and then dropped it off at the mechanic to make sure everything was running smoothly. They changed the oil and checked all the fluids. They said it was in great shape and shouldn't give you any trouble."

I blink away the hot sting of tears that fill my eyes as I step closer and trail my fingers over the red paint. Miles loved this car so much. It was his baby. Dad bought it for him when he was fifteen years old, and my brother spent all his spare time working on it.

There were so many hours I sat in here with Miles and Wolf while they joked around with each other. Once Miles turned sixteen and passed his driver's exam, it unlocked a whole new level of freedom for the three of us.

"You want me to drive the Porsche back to school, angel?" Wolf asks, thumbing away a tear and drawing my attention back to the present.

"No. I'd like to do it myself."

More like I *need* to do it myself.

He doesn't argue. "Okay. I'll grab the boxes from inside and be right behind you."

"Thank you."

My hands tremble as I slide behind the wheel and turn the key in the ignition. The engine purrs to life and I glance at my parents to find that, like me, they're trying to hold their emotions in check.

But it's hard.

Even though it's time we all move on with our lives, that doesn't mean it's easily accomplished.

Wolf kisses me one last time before I wave to my parents. It's gently that I press the clutch and shift into first gear. As soon as I accelerate, the engine revs and the vehicle shoots out of the garage. I draw in a deep breath, attempting to calm the nerves that skitter across my skin, leaving a trail of goose bumps in their wake.

At the end of the long drive, I pause and glance one way, then the other before shifting again into first and turning toward Western's campus. As I pick up speed and my nerves begin to settle, I turn on the radio. 'Best Day of My Life' by American Authors fills the small cabin. Memories of Miles cranking up the volume and us sing-shouting the lyrics at each other swamp me.

For years afterward, I couldn't bear to hear the song. But this time, I turn it up and belt out the lyrics. Instead of bringing me sadness the way it used to, my heart fills with joy because I feel my brother sitting beside me, smiling that the people he loved most have finally found peace.

CHAPTER 39

WOLF

"It's already been a couple of days. When are you going to show me the new tattoo? I'm dying to see the artwork you decided on." Fallyn sticks her lower lip out in a pout. "I don't understand why you're being so secretive about it."

I roll my eyes and suppress the grin attempting to break loose. I don't think I've smiled so much as I have in the past couple weeks. It's taken some getting used to. More than that, I feel a million pounds lighter. And that has everything to do with the girl at my side.

The one I love more than anything.

"I wanted it to heal up a bit before I showed you. It's not really that big of a deal." I yank the T-shirt over my head and toss it onto the bed. "Why don't you do the honors?"

Her face lights up with a smile. "Really?"

Her exuberance is infectious, and a chuckle tumbles from my lips. "Yeah. Have at it."

She steps closer before her fingers flutter to the edges of the bandage. Her gaze flickers to mine in question. "Are you sure it's healed?"

"Yup." A large pit settles at the bottom of my belly as air stalls in my lungs.

At the time, this had seemed like a good idea.

Now, however?

I'm not so sure.

Maybe it's too early to think along these lines and I'm jumping the gun. All I know is that I want this.

Just like I want her.

I need to know Fallyn feels the same way.

Because if she doesn't…

It would probably crush my soul.

The tip of her tongue peeks out between her lips as she concentrates on the task at hand and peels away the edges, lifting the bandage from my skin until it's fully removed, and the newest tattoo is on display.

When her movements still and she stares silently at it, my heart lurches painfully, becoming lodged in the middle of my throat.

It takes every bit of self-control to remain calm and force out the question. "Well, angel? What's it going to be?"

She rips her attention away from the two words in swirling black cursive and lifts her chin enough for our gazes to collide.

The blue of her eyes burn even brighter. Any moment, they'll swallow me whole. It wouldn't be such a bad way to go.

Especially if she turns me down.

"Are you serious?" she whispers, sounding as if she's being strangled.

I huff out a nervous breath as my fingers slip under her chin to hold her in place. I need to touch her. "Baby, I couldn't be more serious about spending the rest of my life with you. Haven't you figured it out by now that you're it for me?" I search her gaze, sifting through all the emotion within her eyes. "There could never be anyone other than you."

She swallows thickly and the delicate column of her throat works. "Yes."

Unable to believe my ears, my brows rise. "Did you just agree to marry me?"

A smile spreads across her face. "I did!"

Air leaks from my lungs as a relieved chuckle slips free. "Thank fuck. For a minute there, I started to doubt myself."

A burst of laughter escapes from her. "Is that why you've been acting so weird the past couple of days?"

I lift her into my arms and hold her close. "Come on. Was I really acting that strange?"

"Umm, yeah. You kept staring at me."

"I love staring at you." I smack a kiss against her lips. "Nothing strange about that."

"You looked constipated. I was thinking about buying you some laxatives."

A snort slips free from me. "It was more like—if this girl says no, where do we go from here? And it was a little too late to hold off since I'd already inked the question onto my skin."

She winds her arms around my neck and pulls me close enough for her lips to drift over mine. It's only when I sink into the caress that she pulls away.

Seriousness brims in her eyes. "I love you, Wolf. And I can't wait to spend the rest of my life with you."

All of the tension filling my muscles drains away. "I love you, too. More than anything."

I set her on the bed before following her down onto the mattress and caging her in with my arms so that all my hard muscles align with her softer curves. As soon as I settle on top of her, she spreads her legs. My cock grows unbearably hard as I nestle against the V between her thighs. I can't resist flexing my hips.

The need to get her naked pounds through me, and I roll to the side, gripping the hem of her pale blue sweater before shoving it past her breasts. When my hand slips around her ribcage, she arches so that I can unlatch the elastic band and pull the silky material free before tossing it to the floor. My fingers trail over her naked breasts, tweaking and teasing the rosy nipples until they stiffen. Leaning closer, I kiss each tip as my fingers drift to the waistband of her jeans. I flick open the button before dragging down the zipper and shoving the dark wash denim down her hips and thighs. Her panties come away with them, leaving her gloriously naked.

For just a moment, I sit back and soak in the sight of her. Fallyn is flawless. It wouldn't matter if her breasts were larger or smaller. Her waist nipped in or thicker. None of that matters because this girl is the only one who has ever owned my heart. She's perfect just the way she is, and I wouldn't change one damn thing about her.

When I can't hold back another second, my fingers trail down to her pussy, stroking her delicate flesh just the way she likes it. The feel of her silky softness is all it takes for my dick to stand at attention.

There's no better feeling in this world than being buried balls deep inside her welcoming heat. It's when I feel the closest to her, like we're truly one person instead of two. Everything outside the four walls of our bedroom fades to the background.

Her pupils dilate as she widens her thighs, giving me more room to maneuver. I fucking love when she opens herself up to me. She spreads herself impossibly wide as my fingers slip inside her tight heat and I press my mouth against hers in order to swallow down every delicious moan.

A few pumps later and she's writhing beneath me.

"Please."

My tongue slides inside her mouth to tangle with her own before I pull away just enough to ask, "What do you need, angel?"

"You," she whispers. "Just you."

My heart contracts because her sentiments echo my own.

I just need this woman.

I press another kiss against her lips before sliding down her naked body until I reach her pussy. When she flexes her hips in an attempt to close the distance between us, I give her clit a little slap with the tips of my fingers.

A garbled sound of pleasure escapes from her as her core floods with moisture.

We might have both been virgins not too long ago, but I've made sure to learn all I can about what turns her on. We've spent a lot of time exploring in order to figure out what the other person likes.

What I've discovered is that Fallyn really enjoys having her pussy licked.

And since I love her more than anything in this world, I aim to please.

And then please some more.

When I slap her clit for a second time, her body bows.

"Oh god, Wolf…"

I slip my tongue deep inside her shuddering softness before dragging it out and circling that tiny bundle of nerves. "That's right, baby. I'm your god. The only one you need to worship."

She groans before shifting beneath me. Her shuddering softness is completely drenched. I just want to lap up all her cream until there's not a single drop left. And then I want to make her pussy sob all over again.

It's a vicious cycle.

One I'll never grow tired of.

Unable to get enough, I lap at her delicate flesh until her muscles tighten and her breathing picks up its tempo. Just when she's on the cusp of falling apart, I pull back.

With a gasp, she cries out. "Wolf!"

I can't help but grin as I swipe her wetness from the corners of my lips before crawling up her body until the head of my cock is perfectly aligned with her soaked entrance.

"You know I love when we come together."

As soon as the growled-out comment escapes, I slide deep inside her tight heat. The way her inner muscles clench around my dick is almost enough to make me lose it.

I grit my teeth and hang on to my self-control for as long as possible.

Which, in case you're wondering, is no more than a dozen strokes.

When she tightens around me and screams out my name, chanting it over and over again, I do the only thing I can and follow her over the precipice and into oblivion.

Watching her fall apart is a beautiful thing.

And I'll be the only one who gets to do it for the rest of my life.

CHAPTER 40

FALLYN

The bar is packed as I slip through the crowd with a tray full of drinks. Tonight's game ended in a tie. None of the players are particularly happy about it but it's better than a loss.

As soon as I reach the table of rowdy hockey players, I pass out the bottles of cold beer and the shots that were ordered. Once all the drinks have been distributed, Wolf pulls me onto his lap and nuzzles my neck.

"I can't wait to get you alone tonight, angel."

Thoughts of exactly what that entails drift through my head.

"Mmm, me neither."

He nips my ear, tugging on the lobe. When I giggle and attempt to escape, he sets me free. The man loves to rile me up at work so that I'm begging for it by the time we walk through the apartment door.

I twist on his lap and press my lips to his, inhaling his woodsy scent. Then I pull away just enough to slip my fingers beneath his sweatshirt and trail them over the newest tattoo added to his collection.

I still can't believe he asked me to marry him.

We haven't told anyone yet. Not even Viola, who I share almost everything with. For now, I just want it to be our little secret. If Wolf had his way, we'd get hitched immediately. I'm not sure how long I want to wait. Maybe we'll tie the knot after graduation this spring.

For now, I'm just enjoying the beginning of our relationship.

Even though I'd much rather stay with him, I joke, "I should get moving. Those drinks aren't going to deliver themselves."

With a groan, Wolf tugs me closer before burying his nose against the delicate curve of my neck. "I've already told you that you don't have to work here. Whatever you need, I'm happy to give you."

This isn't the first time we've had this conversation. And it probably won't be the last. "I know and appreciate the offer, but I like working at Slap Shotz." Even though I haven't had the job for long, all the employees feel like family. And we take care of each other.

Plus, it's nice to have my own money that I don't have to ask anyone for.

Not my parents.

Or Wolf.

I know he'd give me the shirt off his own back if I needed it, but I want to pay my own way. At least as much as I can. Now that I've had a little taste of independence, I like it.

Want more of it.

My lips drift over his as I whisper, "I'm also going to pay you back."

"That's not necessary."

"Still happening. Even if it takes years."

"Fine," he grumbles. "Whatever you want, angel."

I rise to my feet in one swift movement before leaning down and pressing one last kiss against his lips. "I'll be back in a bit to check on you."

"Better be. Otherwise, I'll have to hunt your ass down." His eyes glow with green fire. "And you know what will happen then."

His gruff promise has a shiver racing down my spine. It settles somewhere in the vicinity of my core.

On more than one occasion, he's dragged me off to Sully's office before locking us away and reminding me exactly who I belonged to.

And yeah…I loved every single minute of it.

With a smile, I take off, stopping by the tables in my section and filling orders. As I wait at the bar, Juliette, Carina, Viola, Stella, and Britt stop by. There are hugs all the way around. We had a girls' night out last weekend and danced the night away at Blue Vibe. It was so much fun. Then I went home to Wolf, and he made love to me.

Slowly.

Twice.

"Hey, Fallyn."

I turn at the sound of my name and find Colby McNichols. He's a talented left winger who gets lots of love from the ladies on campus.

He flashes a dazzling grin before jerking his head toward the group of rowdy hockey players. "Would you mind bringing a round of shots to our table when you get a chance?"

His smile almost has the power to turn my insides to mush. I blink away the sensation before shaking it off.

They don't call him the baby-faced assassin for nothing.

Especially when his dimples pop.

The man is completely dangerous.

And he knows it.

That's all it takes for me to narrow my eyes. "Put those damn things away before you get yourself killed." I glance toward Wolf and find him watching the interaction with interest.

Colby grins before glancing at my boyfriend, who also happens to be one of his good friends.

"What's wrong? A little harmless flirting never hurt anyone."

I snort. "Wanna bet? I'd hate to see you miss the rest of the season because all your bones have been broken."

He mulls over my answer before shrugging. "You're probably right about that."

His blue eyes dance with mischief as they shift to the girls. All except Britt are with hockey players.

If I'm being completely honest, Colby isn't the kind of guy I'd want dating one of my girlfriends. From all the gossip that floats around campus—and trust me, there's a lot of it—he's the piped piper of pussy. He sleeps with girls but doesn't get involved in relationships.

His attention gets snagged by Britt. It's slowly that his gaze slides down her body before rising to her face and sparking with more interest.

"I don't think we've had the pleasure of meeting." He turns up the wattage of his smile and the dimples wink and flash. "What's your name, beautiful?"

I steel myself, fully expecting Britt to melt into a puddle of goo at his feet. I've witnessed it happen on more than one occasion.

It's almost a surprise when she flicks a glance at him and then turns away before giving him a snappy response. "I'm not interested. So, feel free to move it along."

Colby blinks in confusion as his brows slant together. "Excuse me?"

She stops her conversation with Carina and turns toward him again before enunciating with more care. "I said that I wasn't interested. Hockey players aren't my thing. Now, if you'll—"

He flashes another dazzling smile that's even more high wattage than the first one before giving her an *are you crazy look*. "Sweetheart, I'm everybody's thing."

Her eyes widen as a burst of laughter escapes from her. I almost fall over when she pats his cheek as if he's an errant child. "I'm sure you are, pretty boy. But not mine."

Instead of walking away and moving on to greener pastures, Colby's eyes spark with challenge as he steps closer. "Hey, I have an idea. How about you let me buy you a shot, and we'll see just how wrong you are when I roll out of your bed in the morning?"

My mouth falls open as my gaze bounces to Britt. This is like a Wimbledon match. And yeah, I'm totally here for it. It's not often you see Colby McNichols get shot down.

I rack my brain.

Or like, ever.

Britt shakes her head and holds her ground. "No thanks." She points toward the crowded table in the back that's buzzing with puck bunnies. "You seem to have your hands full already. My advice is to stick with the groupies. You wouldn't know what to do with a girl like me."

A roguish grin slides across his face. "Is that so?"

She lifts her chin a notch. "Yup. Accept defeat gracefully while you still have the chance."

"Oh, I think we're way past that now. Don't you, firecracker?"

"*Firecracker?*" Laughter escapes from her before she cocks a hip. "Do the cutesy names actually work for you? My guess is that it's so you don't have to remember someone's name in the morning, right?"

His eyes darken.

Needing to defuse the situation before it can escalate, I pick up my tray now loaded with drinks and turn to Colby. "Hey, look—I have your shots. Why don't you follow me to your table?"

For a long moment, he stares at Britt. My gaze bounces to her only to find my new friend glaring in return.

When I tap him on the shoulder to get his attention, he glances at me. "Here's the shots you ordered. Ready to head back?"

His gaze flickers back to Britt. "Yup. Let's go."

I blow out a relieved breath that a potential disaster has been averted before sliding through the thick press of bodies.

Colby raises his voice to be heard over the music and chatter. "This isn't over, sweetheart."

Britt shakes her head and rolls her eyes. "Actually, it is. You've just been hit in the head with a hockey puck too many times to realize it," she says sweetly before tipping her bottle of beer at him and taking a sip.

It's almost a surprise when he swings around and follows me instead of continuing their conversation.

When we're about halfway to the table, he asks, "Who is that girl?"

"Her name is Britt." My brows draw together. "She transferred to Western last semester."

He throws a considering glance over his shoulder. "Hmmm. I don't think I've seen her around. Pretty sure I'd remember if I had."

Even though I don't know Colby well, I twist around and poke him in the chest. "Do me a favor and stay away from her. She's not one of your puck bunnies."

He flashes his signature grin before taking one of the glasses off my tray and lifting it to his lips. "Unfortunately, I can't make any promises."

He sends a little wink my way before belting back the shot.

Argh.

The last thing I need is Colby McNichols, manwhore extraordinaire, messing with one of my friends.

Just as that thought rolls through my head, strong arms wrap around me from behind, and a deep voice whispers near my ear, "You look tense, angel. Need my special brand of stress relief?"

That's all it takes for my muscles to loosen as Wolf presses his hard body against mine.

I turn my head just enough to meet his eyes. "Always."

"Good. Because I plan to give it to you for the rest of your life."

A sigh escapes from me as I think about all the years stretched out ahead of us. It's amazing how much everything can change in a matter of weeks. "I can't wait."

"Me neither, angel. Me neither."

EPILOGUE

FALLYN

wo weeks later...

WOLF PRESSES me to his chest as he uses the key card to open the door. With one arm wrapped around me, he yanks on the handle before bursting into the beautifully decorated hotel suite. As soon as we're over the threshold, he pauses. His green eyes search mine as his lips stretch into a wide grin that overtakes his handsome face.

It's one that has the power to make my heart thump harder.

Faster.

"It's official, Mrs. Westerville. You now belong to me."

Before I can say anything in response, his mouth crashes onto mine. As soon as the velvety softness of his tongue sweeps across the seam of my lips, I open so they can tangle. That's all it takes to lose track of how long we stand in the middle of the entryway and kiss. My fingers dig into the fine fabric of the tuxedo he's wearing as I tug him closer.

Even though we just got hitched in Vegas, we still dressed the part.

The black tux and stark white shirt somehow make him look even more handsome than usual.

All I can say is that my new husband is seriously hot.

And I'm wearing a simple white dress that's embroidered with tiny seed pearls. A possessive light flashed in his eyes the moment he caught sight of Dad escorting me down the aisle. The full force of it was enough to weaken my knees.

In a room filled with friends and family, it made me feel as if I was the only person he saw.

Or would ever see.

It's the exact same way I feel about him.

I'm sad that Wolf's parents refused to join us. They were invited and declined the invitation. There's a lot of hurt and pain between our families. At some point, in the not-so-distant future, it'll have to be addressed.

By the time Wolf draws away, my pulse is racing. "And you belong to me."

"Angel, I've belonged to you since I was thirteen years old."

My palm drifts to his face, rubbing the shadowed jaw as everything within me softens. "I know."

And I do.

This man has done everything to prove that I was always in his heart.

The only one who would ever be in his heart.

Once I finally let him in, there was no turning back. The only thing we could do is move forward with our lives forever entwined.

He sets me gently on my feet before taking a step in retreat. His hot gaze licks over me, setting everything in its path ablaze. "As beautiful as you look in that dress—and you do, angel—I can't wait to get you out of it. I haven't been inside your pussy since this morning, and that's entirely too long. I'm dying for a taste of you."

The way he growls out the words has my core flooding with heat and clenching with arousal.

His need is insatiable.

But then again, so is mine.

In every way, we're a perfect match.

"Turn around. I want you naked so I can finally show you exactly how much I love having you as my wife."

Shivers dance down my spine as I spin and give him my back. Unable to help myself, I glance over my shoulder to meet his smoldering gaze. The grind of metal teeth is all that can be heard in the silence of the room. Once he reaches my lower back, the cool air caresses my bare flesh. His fingers ghost over my shoulders before pushing the delicate fabric down my arms. It slides in a silky waterfall along the length of my body before puddling around my ivory heels.

My eyelids feather shut as he presses his lips against my shoulder before taking a step away.

"You look good enough to eat," he growls in a raspy tone that arrows straight to my core before exploding on impact.

"I certainly hope that'll be the case," I tease, tossing another peek over my shoulder to meet his hot gaze.

A devilish grin tugs at the corners of his lips. "Count on it. I don't plan on leaving this suite until they kick us out at the end of the weekend."

As the green fire of his eyes lick over me, his fingers rise to the elegant bowtie, and he pulls at the shiny black material until it loosens. Tugging it off, he tosses it on the desk before removing the jacket. His eyes never deviate from mine as they make quick work of the pearly buttons that run down the middle of the snowy white fabric. The shirt is peeled away along with the T-shirt beneath until he's naked from the waist up. My gaze slides over his bare chest as need pools like warmed honey in my core.

He's so gorgeous.

All that hard, sun-kissed flesh decorated with ink.

"See something you like, angel?"

My gaze lifts to his smirking one. Maybe in the beginning, I would have been embarrassed to be caught ogling him but that's no longer the case. I want Wolf to know just how hungry I am for him.

"Always."

With a groan, he eats up the distance that separates us. His hands settle on my shoulders as he aligns himself against my back. My heart-beat thrums a mad rhythm as his fingertips glide down my arms and goosebumps rise in their wake.

He presses his lips against the long column of my neck. For the ceremony, my hair was styled in an intricate updo. His teeth scrape across my flesh as he removes the pins from the thick mass. There must be a hundred of them. One by one, they clatter onto the wood beneath our feet. It's slowly that my tresses tumble around my shoulders and down my back. My eyelids drift closed as he finds the last one. His spread fingers settle against my scalp before massaging it.

A throaty moan of pleasure escapes from me as I press into his hands. Somehow, he always knows exactly what I need. My head tilts backward, resting against the solid strength of his chest as he continues to rub my scalp. Long minutes pass before he presses his lips to the curve of my cheek as his hands slide around my ribcage to cup my breasts through the lacy undergarment I'm wearing.

The sheer material leaves little to the imagination.

He toys with my nipples until they're hard points that poke through the delicate fabric. Another whimper escapes from me as I arch into his touch.

His hands drift along my ribcage as his lips and teeth graze my spine until he reaches the small of my back before dipping to the elastic band of my thong.

"Fuck, you're so damn sexy in this," he growls, nipping at my cheeks. He fills his palms with the firm flesh and squeezes. "I almost don't want to take it off."

Standing erect takes effort.

All I want to do is melt into a puddle at his feet.

I love the way Wolf touches and teases me.

Stoking the flames until I want to self-combust before giving me exactly what I need.

His teeth sink into one bare cheek before doing the same to the other side.

"Maybe I won't," he growls before rising to his feet and pressing against my back. His hot breath feathers over the outer shell of my ear. "I want you kneeling on the mattress with your ass in the air. Understand, angel?"

My mouth turns cottony at the growled-out command.

When I fail to respond, he reaches around and tweaks my nipples. "Did you hear me?"

"I did."

"Good. Now, are you ready to get fucked by your husband?"

"God, yes."

"Then get on the bed."

That's all the prodding it takes for me to scramble to do his bidding. My elbows and knees sink into the pillow-top mattress.

"Look at that pretty ass in the air. You know exactly how I like it."

Another shiver zips down my spine because he's right. I know exactly how he likes it because I enjoy it too.

I arch my back so that my ass sticks farther out. When he groans, I peek over my shoulder and find him with his black slacks unzipped and his fingers wrapped around his thick erection. Heat floods my core as I watch him stroke the length of his shaft.

"Please, Wolf. Don't make me wait any longer."

I'm so horny for my husband.

The only man I'll ever love.

"Don't worry, angel. I'm going to give you exactly what you want and everything you need. Just like I always do."

He closes the distance between us before sliding one palm over the rounded curve of my ass. I squeeze my eyes tightly closed, only wanting to enjoy the sensation of his strong hands. A gasp escapes when the blunt tip of his cock presses against my rosebud through the thin fabric of my thong. His hands settle on my cheeks before he pulls them apart so that the head of his erection is nestled between the globes. One shift of his hips and he'd sink inside that untouched hole.

"One day, I'm going to take you here."

It's a dark promise. My breath hitches as a potent concoction of fear and anticipation spirals through me. He's slipped his fingers inside my rosebud, and I've enjoyed it, gotten off to it, but having his thick cock penetrate me there is a different story.

"But not today."

As soon as the words escape from him, his thick length disappears. His fingers yank the delicate fabric aside and his hot tongue slides deep inside my pussy. He grips a palmful of ass in each hand, pulling it so that I'm completely exposed to him.

"Fuck, angel. I've never seen a more beautiful sight. It's enough to bring me to my knees every single time."

He laps at my shuddering softness until I have no other choice but to explode around his tongue. My orgasm seems to go on forever. He licks me the entire time until I melt into the king-sized mattress. Only then does he rise to his feet and position himself behind me. In one smooth stroke, he slides inside my shuddering heat. He holds my hips steady as he pumps into me until finding his release. I love the feeling of his cock buried deep, connecting us in the most intimate way possible, making us one. It's only after the last shudder racks his body that he collapses with a contented sigh, caging me in with his strength.

"I love you, Mrs. Westerville," he whispers against my ear.

"I love you too, Mr. Westerville."

"Good." There's a pause before he whispers, "How about we order some room service and then check out the bathroom? I hear there's a waterfall shower and giant tub."

"That," I say with a chuckle, "sounds pretty amazing."

"Which part? Room service or fucking in the bathroom?"

"Room service, of course."

"You're a girl after my own heart, Fallyn Westerville."

"As long as I'm the only girl in your heart, that's all that matters."

"You are, angel. And that will never change."

BONUS EPILOGUE

WOLF

Two years later...

A sigh of relief escapes from me as I slam the apartment door closed and drop my duffle in the entryway.

Damn but it's good to be home.

We had some mandatory team building bullshit this weekend at a resort outside the city. Now that it's finally over with, all I can think about is my wife. Although, there's nothing new about that.

If Fallyn weren't in a graduate program for psychology here in Boston, I would have made her come with me. But she stayed and worked on a paper that's due at the end of the week. She's also been applying for Ph. D programs for next fall. Her dream is to open up her own practice down the road. And she'll be awesome at it too. Both her fieldwork and practicum were spent working with people who have suffered the loss of loved ones. It's something she's intimately acquainted with. She understands the stages of grief and how to navigate through them in order to reach the other side and find happiness again.

I saunter through the sprawling apartment, searching each room. It's only when I end up in the living area with its wall of windows that showcase amazing views of the city that I spot Fallyn sitting on the balcony with a textbook splayed open in front of her.

As soon as she glances up, a smile lights up her face. I pull open the slider and step outside into the warm sunshine that pours down on us.

"Hey, angel," I say before leaning down to take her lips with my own.

Fuck, but I missed her.

More than usual, and that's really saying something.

When she opens, allowing me entrance, I deepen the kiss until our tongues can mingle. It's been two years, and I still can't get enough of this girl.

The reality is that I'll probably never get enough.

And I wouldn't have it any other way.

I pull away just enough to growl, "Missed you."

"Missed you too, boo." A sexy gleam fills her eyes. "I've been waiting patiently for you all day."

A groan slides from my lips as I wrap my arms around her waist and haul her from the chair until her long legs can tangle around my waist. Already I'm hard for her. I can't resist flexing my hips against her softness, wanting her to understand exactly how she affects me.

Her arms twine around my neck as my hand settles on her ass, and the other closes the slider. Then I walk us into the living room before swinging into the hallway that leads to our bedroom.

Our mouths are crushed together as she grinds her needy core against me.

"Fuck, baby. You make me so damn hot."

It's gently that I set her on the bed. Her inky black hair is in a messy bun at the top of her head, and she's wearing a bright pink T-shirt with my name and number stamped across it. Seeing her wear my gear always makes me hard as stone. Black leggings hug her lower half—they're the first thing that she needs to lose.

My fingers settle at the elastic waistband before dragging the stretchy material down her hips and thighs. I'm delighted to find her totally bare beneath.

No panties in sight, which means easier access for me.

Before I can force her thighs apart, she spreads them wide, giving me a tantalizing view of heaven. My mouth waters for a taste of her sweetness. I've been dying for it all weekend. I'm not ashamed to admit that I whacked off twice to thoughts of her.

Unable to stand another moment, I kneel on the bed and delve straight in. She groans as my tongue slides across her slit, dipping inside her entrance before circling her clit with the tip. That's all it takes for her to arch into my mouth, silently pleading for more.

Damn right I'll give it to her.

I'll give this woman everything she could possibly need.

And then some.

It doesn't take long before her muscles tighten and her fingers are tunneling through my hair, clasping me to her. I continue to eat at her flesh until her pussy spasms, soaking my face. I make sure to lick up every last drop of cream until her body is as limp as a noodle and her eyelids are barely able to stay open. Only then do I press a kiss against her shuddering softness before shoving the T-shirt up her torso.

I want her buck-ass naked. That's when I catch sight of a small square bandage on side of her belly. With a frown, I pause and carefully run my finger over it before meeting her gaze.

"What happened here?"

Seems like a strange place to cut yourself.

Her eyelids snap open, and she clears her throat. "Oh. I, um, decided to get a tattoo while you were away."

Shock slides through me as my brows rise. "Really?"

Not once has Fallyn ever mentioned marking her body with something permanent. Even when she comes to help pick out the design for my yearly tattoo. I'd never say it, but I like that her skin is creamy and unblemished. I like the contrast between us when we're naked. The way my flesh is full of color and hers isn't.

Although...

Maybe seeing her skin inked will be more of a turn-on than I've always assumed.

Interest piqued, my fingertips hover at the edges of the bandage.

"Can I take a look?" My brows furrow as another thought slams into me. "You'd better have gone to Max. He's the best."

The last thing I want is for her to get an infection. That shit is no joke and happens more often than you'd think.

"No need to worry. It should be fine now."

Her teeth sink into the plumpness of her lower lip as anxiety flickers in her eyes.

Almost like she's nervous.

Now I really want to see this tattoo.

I peel back the edge only to find letters.

Not a design like I was expecting.

Hmmm. That's interesting.

"Does it hurt?" I ask, still trying to figure out what it says.

It's only when the bandage has been completely removed that I realize it's a temporary one. I stare at the three little words. Their meaning doesn't immediately sink in.

Baby on board.

I blink.

Baby on board.

My eyes widen as they slice to Fallyn's face.

"You're...*pregnant?*"

With a nod, she presses her lips together.

"You're pregnant," I repeat, louder this time.

"Yes," she whispers.

"We're having a baby?" I ask, just to clarify matters, because my brain doesn't seem to be working properly at the moment.

"Yes! Oh my god, are you upset?" Her voice escalates with each word. "This is good news, isn't it?"

I give my head a little shake to clear it. "Are you kidding me? Of course, it is!" I suck in a deep, cleansing breath and continue staring in amazement. "How did this happen?"

She quirks a brow. "Really? I need to explain it?"

A chuckle escapes from me. "That's not what I meant. I know how it happened. I just thought...you know, that we were being careful."

She shrugs. "No method of birth control is totally foolproof."

I press a kiss against her toned belly and whisper, "I can't believe we're having a baby."

"You're going to be a dad," she murmurs.

Holy shit. She's right. I'm going to be someone's father. I glance at Fallyn. Fuck but she looks so damn beautiful.

"And you're going to be a mom."

"That's generally how it works."

My concerned gaze resettles on her pussy. "I didn't hurt you, did I?"

She shakes her head. "Hardly."

"It's still safe to have sex, right?"

"One hundred percent safe." She waggles her dark brows. "In fact, I'm hoping that we're going to have it right now. That orgasm was good, but I need more."

I press my lips against her again before crawling up her body and kissing her mouth. Then I roll us both over so that she's sprawled out on top of me. Her hand drifts across my shadowed jaw before sliding over my chest and belly and delving inside my joggers to cup my thick length.

I groan as her fingers tighten around me.

Yup, I've definitely missed this.

"It would be a real shame to waste a perfectly good boner," she whispers before straddling my waist.

The woman does make a fair point.

Fallyn tugs off her T-shirt so that she's completely naked. Then she rises to her knees and shoves down my joggers and boxers until my cock can spring free. With her fingers wrapped around my dick, she guides it to her entrance.

A sigh of contentment escapes from her as she slides down the thick length until she's able to take me fully inside the warmth of her body. As much as I want to squeeze my eyes tightly closed and enjoy her soft heat, I keep them pinned to my wife.

The one who's now carrying our baby.

My hands settle around her hips, only wanting to hold her in place as she moves against me. With each shift, pleasure reverberates throughout my entire being until the world shrinks down enough to only encompass the two of us.

Actually, it shrinks down enough to encompass the three of us.

The way it was always meant to be.

The End

Thank you so much for reading Wolf and Fallyn's story! I hope you enjoyed reading it as much as I loved writing it!

The Western Wildcats Hockey series continues with Britt & Colby! One-click Never Say Never now!

Colby McNichols, otherwise known as the baby-faced assassin, is the left wing for the Western Wildcats hockey team. All he has to do is sign his name on the dotted line and he'll play for the pros after his senior season. What I've heard from the girls on campus, who aren't shy about spilling the tea, is that he's totally earned his reputation.

And then some.

It's just one of the reasons I choose to steer clear.

Trust me when I say that my life is complicated enough without getting tangled up with a player.

For reasons I can't fathom, Colby has decided to insert himself in my life. Everywhere I go, there he is. Which makes holding him at a distance nearly impossible. He might be smoking hot but there's zero point in starting something with this guy. Especially since I can't be honest about who I am.

Unfortunately, a weekend spent in Vegas changes everything.

Turns out that our friends weren't the only ones who tied the knot in Sin City.

I can only hope that what they say is true—what happens in Vegas stays there.

Because if it doesn't…

I'm screwed.

And not in a good way.

One-click Never Say Never now!

HATE YOU ALWAYS

JULIETTE

"*I* had a really good time tonight," Aaron says, gaze pinned to mine with an intensity that has me wanting to take a quick step in retreat.

Instead, I force a smile. "Yeah. Me, too."

It's not a total lie. I did have a good time. But that's all it was—*good*. Kind of like when we study together at the library or grab coffee at the Roasted Bean before class.

He glances away and shoves both hands into the pockets of his perfectly pressed khakis. "I hope we can do this again." There's a pause before he tacks on, "Soon."

I'm treated to a long, soulful stare that leaves me feeling borderline uncomfortable.

Yeah...I'm pretty sure that's not in the cards for us.

Aaron is nice.

Really nice.

Super-duper nice.

There's just no spark between us.

I'm searching for that elusive little tingle you get at the bottom of your tummy whenever you're near that person or even catch a glimpse of them from across a crowded room. It's the kind of irrepressible energy that sizzles in the air, charging it until drawing a full breath into your lungs feels impossible.

No matter how much I might wish otherwise, Aaron and I just don't generate that kind of chemistry.

There's only one person—

No.

I take a deep breath, slamming the door closed on those thoughts.

What I feel for that guy isn't attraction.

It's irritation.

Annoyance.

Aggravation.

Trust me, if you gave me enough time, I could come up with a laundry list of descriptive words that start with a vowel.

I blink back to awareness, only to realize that Aaron is patiently awaiting a response.

Oh, right. He wants to do this again.

As I open my mouth to let him down gently, the words stick in my throat. The last thing I want to do is lead him on, but at the same time, I don't want to hurt him either. What I need to do is strike the perfect balance. We have several pre-med classes together this semester. If I'm sick and can't attend class, Aaron is the one who catches me up to speed and makes sure I have all the notes.

They're usually color coded and placed in order of importance.

If there's been one lesson learned this evening, it's that I should avoid dating guys I see on a daily basis.

As Carina, my roommate, would say—don't shit where you eat.

She's right about that.

He inches closer. "If you're in agreement, I'd like to move this relationship forward. I like you, Juliette." He glances away briefly before his muddy-colored eyes refocus on me with a mixture of heat and intensity. "I'm probably getting a little ahead of myself here, but I think we could be a real power couple. We share similar aspirations—both of us have set our sights on furthering our studies in medicine and becoming physicians. I've never found someone who fits so perfectly into my five- and ten-year plan. It's almost like we were made for one another."

My eyes widen as a garbled sound escapes from me.

A little ahead of himself?

Five- and ten-year plan?

We've been out precisely three times, and the chances of there being a fourth have dwindled to the single digits.

I need to tell him that this—whatever he thinks *this* is—isn't going to happen. "Aaron..."

He perks up and sways closer. "Yeah?"

There's so much hope and expectation packed into that one word. Argh.

Why does this have to be so difficult?

The problem is that he really *is* a nice guy. And what he said is absolutely true, we *do* have a lot in common. It's the reason I talked myself into giving him another chance.

And then a third.

There are a lot of douchey guys at this school who are only inter-ested in sleeping with a chick before moving onto the next warm body. Sometimes within the span of the same evening. They don't have five- or ten-year plans that involve one specific girl. They don't even have twenty-four-hour plans that involve the same female.

So, when you happen to find a guy who has the opposite mindset, you need to take the time to delve deep and really get to know him before tossing him back into the wild for someone else to snap up.

"I had a nice time, too," I say carefully.

"Good." The tension filling his narrow shoulders drains as he beams in relief.

Aaron has a wiry build. His limbs are long and lean, much like a runner. Unlike some of the football or hockey players that strut around campus with their muscles on display as if they're god's gift to the female species.

Ugh. They seem to be everywhere.

As I stare into his earnest eyes, I make a last ditch effort to convince myself that he's exactly the type of guy I'm attracted to.

Deep down, in a place I'm loath to acknowledge, I know it's a lie.

Carina, damn her, would also tell me that the worst lies are the ones we tell ourselves.

That girl really needs to stay out of my head.

His hands reemerge from the depths of his pockets before rising to my face. It would be difficult not to notice their slight tremble. I force myself to stand perfectly still and not evade his touch at the last moment. And if that doesn't tell you everything you need to know about this situation, I'm not sure what will.

His eyelids droop to half-mast. "I'm going to kiss you now, Juliette," he mutters thickly. "I hope that's all right."

And with that, the mood has officially been killed.

Not that there was much of one to begin with, but still...

Unlike him, my eyes stay wide open as he moves toward me in slow motion. I steel myself for impact instead of flinching away.

Maybe I'm wrong.

Maybe Aaron will surprise the hell out of me and will end up being a phenomenal kisser. I'll magically lose myself in the caress as time and space cease to exist.

It's tentatively that his lips settle over mine. They're dry and papery to the touch. It's kind of like being pecked by a distant aunt or uncle.

Everything inside me deflates with the knowledge that this isn't going to end any other way than me carefully letting him down, because there's no way in hell I can do this again.

In fact, I'd pay good money to never do *this* again.

I press my palms against Aaron's chest to push him away when someone clears their throat. Aaron jumps back as if he just stuck his finger in an electrical outlet.

My gaze slices to the tall, muscular blond guy who has ground to a halt beside us.

Ryder McAdams.

My belly does a strange little flip before I swiftly stomp out the sensation.

Dark blue eyes pin me in place for a drawn-out heartbeat, making it impossible to breathe before shifting to Aaron. It's only when I'm released from his penetrating stare that the air trapped in my lungs rushes from me and I realize there are five more oversized hockey players crowded in the hallway outside my apartment door.

Ford Hamilton, Wolf Westerville, Colby McNichols, Riggs Stranton, and Hayes Van Doren are seniors on the Western Wildcats hockey team. Wherever they go, fangirls are sure to follow. I glance around only to realize they're all by themselves. It's weird not to see their entourage trailing after them.

Is it possible that hell has officially frozen over?

Colby flashes an easy-going grin as he snags my gaze. "Hey, McKinnon. Looks like someone has a hot date tonight." Like Ryder, he's blond and entirely too handsome for his own good.

His dimples are lethal to any female with a beating pulse in the vicinity.

Present company excluded.

Heat scalds my cheeks until it feels like they've caught on fire. The last thing I need is for the pretty hockey player to open his big yap to my brother.

Like I need the fifth degree from him.

Hard pass, thank you very much.

I might be the older sibling by fifteen months, but that, apparently, doesn't matter. Maverick takes his protective brother duties seriously. Dad drilled that into his head when he arrived at Western the year after I did.

Before I can snap out a response, they jostle and joke their way down the hall to the apartment next door. Ford lives there with Wolf and Madden while Ryder and five other teammates have a place located a couple blocks off campus known around school as the hockey house. For the last three decades, the residence has been exclusively occupied by Western hockey players. The current group of guys who rent the property will select the teammates who live there the following year.

It's a whole thing.

Eyeroll.

Thankfully, my brother lives off campus at the house. He's the only junior who was invited to do so and that has everything to do with Ryder. They've been tight since elementary school. I seriously don't think I could handle having him in the same building. He's all up in my business enough the way it is.

My skin prickles with awareness when I realize that Ryder hasn't followed his friends down the hallway. His gaze is still locked on Aaron, who looks seconds away from pissing himself.

And I get it.

Ryder McAdams can be intimidating.

Especially when he glares.

Which is exactly what he's doing at the moment.

Poor Aaron. In comparison, he looks like a scrawny, underdeveloped high schooler.

Awkwardness descends.

My date clears his throat before mumbling, "I, ah, should probably go."

There's a pause before he hesitantly sways toward me again. He only gets a few inches before Ryder crosses his thickly corded arms over his brawny chest. Aaron's movements stall as his face turns ashen.

"Umm..." He releases a high-pitched laugh that's strained around the edges. "How about a hug instead?"

When Ryder's eyes narrow, Aaron gulps, his throat muscles convulsing with the movement. In the silence of the hallway, the sound is deafening.

He finally reaches out, wrapping his sweaty palm around my hand before giving it three hearty pumps and promptly releasing it. I don't even get a chance to say goodbye as he swings around and races to the elevator like the hounds of hell are nipping at his heels.

He stabs the button a bunch of times and glances over his shoulder at us warily. When the bell chimes, announcing the car's arrival, he shoves his way inside before the doors have a chance to fully open, disappearing from sight.

Once the metal contraption closes, I scowl at Ryder. "Why'd you do that?"

One thick brow slinks upward. It's enough to have me gritting my teeth.

"Do what? I never said a word."

True enough. But still...

I'm aggravated with him for messing with my date. There was absolutely no reason for it.

"You purposefully stood there and made him feel uncomfortable."

Why am I picking a fight?

It's not like I wanted to kiss Aaron. If anything, I should be thanking Ryder for his timely interruption.

I almost snort, because there's no way in hell *that's* going to happen.

"How'd I do that? By standing here and patiently waiting for an introduction?" His gaze stays locked on mine as he tilts his head and scratches his shadowed jaw. "Seems kind of odd."

I bare my teeth before swinging away to dig through my purse for the apartment key. As soon as my fingers wrap around cool metal, I yank it out and jamb it in the lock with more force than necessary. The door reverberates on its hinges as I step inside and swivel to face Ryder once more before promptly closing it with a loud bang.

One-click Hate You Always now!

CAMPUS PLAYER

DEMI

"Morning, Demi!" Gary, one of the stadium custodians, calls out with an easy smile and wave as he saunters toward me. "Up and at 'em bright and early this morning, I see."

My heart jackhammers beneath my ribcage from the twenty-minute run as I flash him a grin. "Always!"

"You have a good one! I'll see you tomorrow!"

Since I've already moved past him, I holler over my shoulder, "Same place, same time!"

Even with *The Killers* pumping through my earbuds, I almost hear the deep chuckle that slides from his lips. Our morning greetings are a ritual three years in the making. I've been running through the wide corridor that leads to the stadium football field since I stepped foot on campus freshman year. This will be something I miss when I graduate in the spring. Five days a week, I'm up at six, logging in a four-mile run before returning home, jumping in the shower, and heading off to class.

At this time of the day, the stadium is still relatively quiet, with only a few people wandering the hallways. There's something both serene and eerie about it. I've been here on game days when there are thirty thousand fans packed shoulder to shoulder, rooting on the

Western Wildcats football team. Three-fourths of the stadium filled with black and orange is an amazing sight to behold. Football is a religion at Western. Unfortunately, the same can't be said for the women's soccer team. We're lucky if there are a couple of hundred spectators in the stands.

I've come to terms with it.

Sort of.

I keep my gaze trained on the light at the end of the tunnel and push myself faster. As soon as I burst out of the darkness, bright sunlight pours down on me, stroking over the bare skin of my arms and shoulders. It's late August, and summer is still in full swing. A whistle cuts through the silence of the stadium, and my gaze slices to the field. Nick Richards has been head coach of the Wildcats for the last decade. He also happens to be my father.

Two days a week, the guys are up at six in the morning for yoga. Dad is a big believer in flexibility. Even though I'm winded, a smirk lifts the corners of my lips. Watching two-hundred-and-eighty-pound linebackers contort their bodies into Downward-Facing Dog, the Warrior II Pose, and the Cobra is enough to bring a chuckle to my lips. Some of the guys actually like it, but most grumble when they think Dad isn't paying attention. Little do they know that he sees and hears everything.

My father catches sight of me and flashes a quick smile along with a wave in my direction. He has a black ball cap pulled low and aviators covering his eyes. There's a clipboard in one hand as he paces behind the instructor.

When I point to the field, he shakes his head. He might make the guys do yoga, but he refuses to participate. Something about old dogs and new tricks. Every once in a while, I'll tell him that he needs to get out there and set a good example for the team. He usually shoots me a glare in return.

Every Wednesday night, Dad and I get together. Our weekly dinners became a thing when I moved out of the house and into the dorms freshman year. He's busy coaching football, and my schedule is packed tight with school and soccer. Getting together once a week is the best way for us to stay connected. It doesn't matter if we're in the middle of our seasons; we always make time for each other. Especially since Mom lives in sunny California. After eighteen years of marriage, she got fed up with being a distant second to the Western University football program. She packed up her bags and walked out. I hate to say it, but Dad didn't notice her absence for a couple of days. Which only proved her point. Now she's remarried, learning to surf, and is a vegan. I visit for a couple of weeks during the summer before soccer training camp starts up at the end of June.

Even though it's only the two of us, our weekly dinners are set for three people.

I tell myself to stare straight ahead and not glance in his direction.

Don't do it!

Don't you dare do it!

Damn.

My gaze reluctantly zeros in on him like a heat-seeking missile. Long blond hair, bright blue eyes, sun-kissed skin, and muscles for miles. And he's tall, somewhere around six foot three.

I'm describing none other than Rowan Michaels.

Otherwise known as the bane of my existence.

My dad discovered the talented quarterback the summer before we entered high school and took him under his wing. Which has been...aggravating. In the seven years since, Rowan has become an irritatingly permanent fixture in my life. He's the brother I never wanted or asked for. He's the gift I wish I could give back. He's the son my father never had but secretly longed for.

On a campus with over thirty thousand students, one would think that avoidance would be easy to accomplish. That hasn't turned out to be the case. Somehow, we ended up in the same major—Exercise Science. I get stuck in at least one class with the guy each semester. This time it's statistics, which is a requirement. Three times a week, I'm forced to see him. And then there are the weekly dinners at Dad's house.

Every Wednesday, Rowan shows up without fail.

It's so annoying.

No, *he's* annoying!

Our gazes collide, and electricity sizzles through my veins before I immediately snuff it out and pretend it never happened.

I am not attracted to Rowan Michaels.

I am not attracted to Rowan Michaels.

I am not attracted to Rowan Michaels.

Maybe if I repeat the mantra enough times, it'll be true. That's the hope I cling to. I've made it through the last seven years trying to convince myself of this. I only have to get through our final year together, and then we'll go our separate ways—me to graduate school or maybe to the Women's National Soccer League, and Rowan to the NFL. He's one of the most talented quarterbacks in the conference. Hell, probably the country. There is little doubt in my mind that he'll be a first-round draft pick come next spring.

Trust me when I say that Rowan Michaels fever is alive and well at Western University. His fanbase is legendary. The guy is a major player.

Both on and off the field.

Girls fall all over themselves to be with him. They fill the stands at football practice, show up at parties he's rumored to be at, and basically stalk him around campus.

It's a little nauseating. Don't these girls have any self-respect when it comes to a hot guy?

I wince at that unchecked thought.

Fine...I'll begrudgingly admit it; he's good-looking.

I shake my head as if that will banish the insidious thoughts currently invading my brain. Enough about Rowan. It's time to focus on the reason I'm at the stadium at this ungodly hour. I rip my gaze from him as I hit the cement staircase. After half a flight, all thoughts of the blond quarterback vanish from my mind. How could they not when my quads, glutes, and calves are on fire, screaming for mercy as I force myself to the nosebleed section. By the time I finish, my legs are Jell-O, and I still have a two-mile run back to the apartment I share with my best friend off-campus.

I give Dad a half-hearted wave before leaving. It's the most I can muster. His lips quirk at the corners as he shakes his head. He thinks I'm crazy. At the moment, I can't argue with his assessment of the situation. Although, it's the extra training I put in that helps me run circles around the other team in the second half of the game.

The jog home feels like it will last forever. By the time I unlock the apartment door, I'm ready to collapse. I beeline for the shower and jump in before it's fully warm. My skin prickles with goose flesh, but it feels so damn good. Twenty minutes later, I'm dressed and ready to take on the day. My hair has been thrown up in a messy bun, and I'm making a protein smoothie that will fuel me for my morning classes.

Just before taking off, I poke my head into Sydney's room. I know exactly how I'll find her, and that's buried beneath a small mountain of blankets. She doesn't disappoint. We met the summer before freshman year in training camp and have been besties ever since. She's the yin to my yang. The peanut butter to my jelly. The Thelma to my Louise. Where I'm more introverted and cautious, she's loud and boisterous. She's been known to leap without necessarily looking at what she's jumping into. Every so often, it gets us into trouble. Sydney and I have lived together since sophomore year. I gave up trying to cajole her ass out of bed for a six o'clock run after the first week of us cohabitating when she nearly took my head off with an alarm clock.

"It's that time again," I sing-song obnoxiously, "rise and shine."

There's a grunt and then some shifting from under the blankets that tells me she's alive.

When I chant her name repeatedly, each time escalating in volume, she growls, "Get the fuck out!"

"Awww," I mock, "that's so sweet. I love you, too."

Sydney snorts before a hand snakes out from beneath the blankets to give me a one-fingered salute. Then she grabs a pillow and tosses it in my general vicinity. It falls about five feet short of its mark.

I stare at the dismal attempt. "If you're trying to cause bodily harm, you'll have to do better than that."

"Piss off."

"All right then." I shrug. "See you after class." With that, I close the door behind me.

My farewell is met with another indecipherable mouthful. If this weren't something we went through on the daily, I'd worry she was in the midst of a stroke. Sydney is definitely not a morning person. She's more of an early afternoon person. Another thing I've learned over the years? The action of waking up to a brand-new day is a gradual process. She's like a bear rousing prematurely from hibernation. It's not a pretty sight. She's lucky I don't take her insults personally.

I grab my backpack from the small table crammed into the breakfast nook area along with a coffee before heading out the door. The apartment I share with Sydney is located three blocks from campus, which is highly sought out real estate. We're fortunate Dad is friends with the guy who manages the building. It's probably one of the only perks of having a father who is a head coach of a college football team.

You'd think there would be more, but you'd be wrong. Honestly, being Nick Richard's daughter is more of a hindrance than anything else. People assume you receive special treatment on campus, from professors, or that you have an in with all the football players.

Or worse...

Much worse.

After a bunch of ugly—not to mention untrue—rumors circulated freshman year, I've done my best to distance myself from the Wildcats football team. They're a great bunch of guys, but I don't need all the ugly gossip and speculation that comes along with being friends with them.

As I reach Corbin Hall, the mathematics building for my stats class, my gaze is drawn to a clump of students standing around outside the three-story, red-brick building. In the center of that crowd is Rowan. I don't have to see him physically to know that he's close. The muscles in my belly contract with awareness. It's like a sixth sense. One I wish would go away. He's the last person I want to be cognizant of.

As I jog up the wide stone stairs to the entrance, my gaze fastens on him. A smirk twists the edges of his lips, and my eyes narrow before I drag them away and yank open the door to the building.

Relief rushes through me as I step inside the air conditioning and disappear from sight.

"Hey, Demi, wait up!"

I turn at the sound of my name before slowing my step. The dark-haired guy jogging to catch up smiles before falling in line with me.

Justin Fischer.

He's a baseball player and teammates with Sydney's boyfriend, Ethan. We've been seeing each other for about a month. It's still casual at this point. With school and soccer, I don't have a ton of time to invest in a relationship. He seems to understand that and isn't pushing to be more serious.

When he leans in for a kiss, I angle my head. At the last moment, he tilts in the opposite direction, and we end up bumping teeth instead of locking lips. With a grunt, I pull away and chuckle. My fingers fly to my mouth to make sure I haven't chipped a tooth.

Maybe I've been reluctant to admit it to myself, but that kiss sums up our relationship perfectly.

Awkward and a step out of sync with each other.

"Sorry," he murmurs with a slight smile. I search his face and wait for any telltale sign of sexual chemistry to ping inside me. Unfortunately, my insides remain completely unfazed, which is disappointing but not altogether unexpected. I had a sneaking suspicion when we first got together that it might turn out this way.

"No problem," I say, hoisting my smile and brushing aside those thoughts.

"I haven't seen you for a couple of days," he remarks as we turn a corner and continue walking.

"It's been busy." Which isn't a lie. School might have recently started, but the academics at Western are rigorous. And being a Division I athlete is more like a job. If you're not ready to put in the work, don't bother showing up. There's no half-assing it around this place.

"When's your next game?" he asks.

"Tomorrow at six." My gaze flickers in his direction. Not that I expect him to come, but...

Fine, so maybe I do. If he wants to be my boyfriend, then he needs to show a little support.

His dark brows draw together. "That sucks. I've got a mandatory study hour I have to attend."

I shrug off the disappointment. It's another nail in the coffin of this relationship as far as I'm concerned. "That's cool. It's not a big deal."

"But I'll see you tonight?"

Oh. Right.

Tonight.

Well, damn. In a moment of weakness, I threw out an invitation to join our Wednesday evening dinner. It's one I now regret. If only there were a gracious way to rescind the offer.

"If you're busy, I totally understand—"

"Are you kidding? No way." With a grin, he shakes his head. "I wouldn't miss it for the world. I'm looking forward to meeting Coach Richards."

Great. So this is more about my father than me? Exactly what every girl wants to hear.

I force a brittle smile. "Awesome. He's excited, too."

That might be something of an overstatement.

Justin nods toward the end of the corridor. "I better get moving. Professor Andrews is a real stickler for punctuality."

"Yup. See you later."

This time, when he leans in, our lips align perfectly. The kiss is nothing more than a fleeting caress. There and gone before I can sink into it.

And I'm left feeling...absolutely nothing.

I bury the disappointment where I can't inspect it too closely before giving him a wave as he takes off. For a moment, I stand rooted in the hallway and watch as he disappears through the crowd. There's nothing to distinguish Justin from the thousands of guys who look exactly like him on campus. He's of average height and build with dark hair and espresso-colored eyes. He's nice enough. Although, if I'm completely honest, he's a little self-absorbed. He talks about baseball all the time. If Ethan hadn't introduced us, he's not someone I would have looked twice at. We don't have a ton in common.

As much as I hate to admit it, this relationship has probably reached its expiration date.

Now it's a matter of pulling the plug.

Ugh. I hate breakups. Although, it's doubtful this will end up destroying him. I'll have to make it through tonight and figure out the rest.

With a sigh of resignation, I head to the classroom and find a seat tucked away in the far corner of the small lecture hall. A lanky guy I recognize from a few of my other classes settles beside me. He flashes a dimpled smile as we empty our backpacks.

The tiny hair at the nape of my neck rises seconds before Rowan enters the room. It's like my body knows when he's within a thirty-foot radius. I glance at him from beneath the thick fringe of my lashes before shifting away. Air becomes wedged in my lungs as I wait for him to take a seat. And it won't be next to me because I'm—

"Hey man, would you mind moving?"

Surrounded on both sides.

Damnit. I'm hoping the cutie next to me will tell Rowan to go take a flying leap.

What? It could happen. Not everyone at this university is enamored of the football-playing god. Although I realize the odds aren't stacked in my favor. Rowan is the most recognized athlete on campus. People fall all over themselves to accommodate him.

It's a little sickening.

Okay, maybe more than a little.

"Sure, no problem, Michaels." The guy next to me hastily packs up his books before vacating the desk. Unable to ignore him any longer, I glare as Rowan slides onto the seat next to me.

"Did you really think you could evade me that easily?" Laughter brims in his deep voice. A voice, I might add, that does funny things to my insides.

"One can always hope, right?"

"Oh, answering a question with a question." He leans closer, eating up some of the much-needed distance between us. "I like it."

I roll my eyes as his lips stretch into a satisfied grin. Irritation bubbles up inside me when sexual tension blooms at the bottom of my belly. Or maybe that tension has settled a little lower.

It's definitely lower.

I'm tempted to swear like a sailor. How is it possible that I feel nothing for the guy I'm actually dating, and yet my pulse skitters out of control for someone I don't even like? It's so freaking ironic. It's been this way since we met, and nothing I do stomps it out. I can try to fool myself into believing it's not there, but that doesn't make it any less true.

It's a relief when Professor Peters takes his place at the podium and clears his throat. Once he's captured everyone's attention, he delves headfirst into the probability of dependent and independent events.

Grateful for the excuse to ignore Rowan for the next fifty minutes, I open my textbook and concentrate on the lesson. Just as the blond boy fades into the background, his bare knee bumps into mine. Electricity ricochets through my entire being. I glance at him to see if he's noticed the strange energy we always seem to generate and find his ocean-colored gaze fastened to mine.

My guess is that he does.

Damnation.

One-click Campus Player now!

MORE BOOKS BY JENNIFER SUCEVIC

<u>The Campus Series </u>(football)

Campus Player

Campus Heartthrob

Campus Flirt

Campus Hottie

Campus God

Campus Legend

<u>Western Wildcats Hockey</u>

Hate You Always

Love You Never

Always My Girl

Dare You to Love Me

Never Mine to Hold

Never Say Never

<u>The Barnett Bulldogs </u>(football)

King of Campus

Friend Zoned

One Night Stand

If You Were Mine

<u>The Claremont Cougars </u>(football)

Heartless Summer

Heartless

Shameless

<u>Hawthorne Prep Series</u> (bully/football)

King of Hawthorne Prep

Queen of Hawthorne Prep

Prince of Hawthorne Prep

Princess of Hawthorne Prep

<u>The Next Door Duet</u> (football)

The Girl Next Door

The Boy Next Door

<u>What's Mine Duet</u> (Suspense)

Protecting What's Mine

Claiming What's Mine

<u>Stay Duet</u> (hockey)

Stay

Don't Leave

<u>Stand-alone</u>

Confessions of a Heartbreaker (football)

Hate to Love You (Hockey)

Just Friends (hockey)

Love to Hate You (football)

The Breakup Plan (hockey)

<u>Collections</u>

The Barnett Bulldogs

The Football Hotties Collection

The Hockey Hotties Collection

The Next Door Duet

ABOUT THE AUTHOR

Jennifer Sucevic is a USA Today bestselling author who has published twenty-four new adult novels. Her work has been translated into German, Dutch, Italian, and French. She has a bachelor's degree in History and a master's in Educational Psychology from the University of Wisconsin-Milwaukee. Jen started out her career as a high school counselor before relocating with her family and focusing on her passion for writing. When she's not tapping away on the keyboard and dreaming up swoonworthy heroes to fall in love with, you can find her bike riding or at the beach. She lives in Michigan with her family.

If you would like to receive regular updates regarding new releases, please subscribe to her newsletter here-
Jennifer Sucevic Newsletter (subscribepage.com)

Or contact Jen through email, at her website, or on Facebook.
sucevicjennifer@gmail.com

Want to join her reader group? Do it here -)
J Sucevic's Book Boyfriends | Facebook

Social media links-
https://www.tiktok.com/@jennifersucevicauthor
www.jennifersucevic.com
https://www.instagram.com/jennifersucevicauthor
https://www.facebook.com/jennifer.sucevic